D0948591

Eden

Eden

STANISLAW LEM

Translated by Marc E. Heine

A Helen and Kurt Wolff Book

Harcourt Brace Jovanovich, Publishers

SAN DIEGO   NEW YORK   LONDON

HBJ

English translation copyright © 1989 by
Harcourt Brace Jovanovich, Inc.

Requests for permission to make copies of any
part of the work should be mailed to:
Copyrights and Permissions Department,
Harcourt Brace Jovanovich, Publishers,
Orlando, Florida 32887.

Library of Congress Cataloging-in-Publication Data

Lem, Stanisław.
[Eden, English]
Eden/Stanislaw Lem; translated by Marc E. Heine.—1st ed.
p. cm.
Translation of: Eden.
"A Helen and Kurt Wolff book."
ISBN 0-15-127580-7
I. Title.
PG7158.L39E313   1989
891.8′537—dc19   89-1963

Designed by Michael Farmer
Printed in the United States of America
First edition
A B C D E

Eden

I

Because of a miscalculation, the craft dipped too low and hit the atmosphere with an earsplitting scream. Lying flat in their bunks, the men could hear the dampers being crushed. The front screens showed flame and went black; the cushion of incandescent gas at the bow was too much for the outside cameras. The control room filled with the stench of hot rubber. Under the force of the deceleration, the men temporarily lost their vision, their hearing. This was the end.

No one could think. No one had the strength, even, to inhale. Breathing was done for them by the oxypulsators, forcing air into them as into straining balloons. Then the roar abated. The emergency lights went on, six on either side. The crew stirred. Above the cracked instrument panel, the warning signal showed red. Pieces of insulation and Plexiglas rustled across the floor. There was no roar now, only a dull whistle.

"What—" croaked the Doctor after spitting out his rubber mouthpiece.

"Stay down!" warned the Captain, who was watching the one undamaged screen.

The ship somersaulted, as if hit by a battering ram. The nylon netting that enfolded them twanged like the string of a musical instrument. For a moment everything was poised upside down, and then the engine began to rumble.

Muscles that had tensed in anticipation of the final blow relaxed. The ship, atop a vertical column of exhaust flame, slowly descended; the nozzles throbbed reassuringly. This lasted several minutes. Then the walls throbbed; the vibration increased—the turbine bearings must have worked loose. The men looked at one another. They knew that everything depended now on whether or not the vanes would hold.

The control room suddenly shook, as though a steel hammer were striking it furiously from the outside. The last screen became covered with a cluster of circles; the convex phosphorescent shield darkened. The faint light of the emergency lamps cast enlarged shadows of the men on the sloping walls. Now the engine howled. Beneath them there was a grating, a breaking; then something split with a shrill sound. Jolted repeatedly, the hull was like a blind and lifeless thing. They held their breath in the darkness. Their bodies suddenly were flung against the nylon cords, but did not strike the shattered panels, which would have torn the mesh. The men swayed like pendulums. . . .

The ship seemed to move in an avalanche. There were distant, dull reverberations. Lumps of earth that had been thrown up slid along the outer hull with a feeble sound.

All motion stopped. Beneath the men, something gurgled. The gurgling became louder, more rapid—the sound of water leaking—and there was a repeated, penetrating hiss, as though drops were falling, one by one, on heated metal.

"We're alive," said the Chemist. In total darkness, he could not see a thing. He was hanging in his nylon bag fastened on four sides by cords. The ship had to be lying on its side: otherwise the berth would have been horizontal. There was a crackle, and the pale glimmer of the Doctor's old lighter.

"Roll call," said the Captain. A cord on his bag snapped, causing him to rotate slowly, helplessly. He reached out through the nylon netting and tried unsuccessfully to grab a knob on the wall.

"Here," said the Engineer.

"Here," said the Physicist.

"Here," said the Chemist.

"I'm here," said the Cyberneticist, holding his head.

"And here, that's six," said the Doctor.

"All present and accounted for. Congratulations." The Captain's voice was calm. "And the robots?" There was no reply.

"Robots!!"

Silence. The lighter burned the Doctor's fingers; he put it out. "I always said we were made of better stuff."

"Anyone have a knife?"

"I do. Should I cut the cords?"

"It would be better if someone could crawl out without cutting them. I can't."

"I'll try."

Struggling, heavy breathing, then a pounding, and a grinding of glass.

"I'm at the bottom. On the wall, that is," said the Chemist. "Doctor, throw a little light here, so I can help you."

"Hurry up. The thing's almost out of fluid." The lighter

brightened again. The Chemist went to the Captain's cocoon but could reach no farther than the legs. At last he managed to open a side zipper, and the Captain dropped to his feet with a thud. The two of them together could work faster. Soon everyone was standing on the slanted wall of the control room, which had a semielastic covering.

"Where do we begin?" asked the Doctor, applying a band-aid to the cut on the Cyberneticist's forehead. The Doctor always carried odds and ends in his pockets.

"We see if we can get out," replied the Captain. "First we need light. Doctor, shine it over here—there may still be current in the panel, or at least in the alarm system."

This time, the lighter produced only a spark. The Doctor thumbed the flint over and over again above the Captain and the Engineer as they rummaged through fragments of metal on their knees.

"Found anything yet?" asked the Chemist, behind them.

"Nothing yet. Anyone have a match?"

"The last time I saw matches was three years ago. In a museum," the Engineer muttered indistinctly. He was attempting to strip the end of a wire with his teeth. Suddenly a small blue glow filled the Captain's cupped hands.

"Here's current," he said. "Now for a bulb."

They found an undamaged bulb in an emergency display above a side panel. A sharp electric light illuminated the control room, giving it the look of a tunnel with curved walls. High above them was the door.

"More than twenty feet," said the Chemist gloomily. "How are we going to get up there?"

"I once saw, in a circus, five men standing on top of one another," said the Doctor.

"We're not acrobats. We can climb up the floor," the Captain said. He took the Chemist's knife and began making cuts in the spongy floor covering.

4

"Steps?"

"Yes."

"Why is the Cyberneticist so quiet?" asked the Engineer. He was sitting on the shattered instrument panel, applying a voltmeter to some protruding cables.

"The man feels orphaned," replied the Doctor with a smile. "What's a cyberneticist without his robots?"

"I'll fix them," said the Cyberneticist. He was looking at the screens. Their yellow glow grew dimmer.

"The accumulator, too," muttered the Physicist. The Engineer got to his feet.

"So it would appear."

A quarter of an hour later, the six-man expedition was working its way toward the front of the ship. First they entered the corridor; from there they went to their separate quarters. In the Doctor's cabin they found an old flashlight. (The Doctor liked to collect things.) They took it with them. There was devastation everywhere. The furniture, bolted to the floor, had not been damaged, but the instruments, tools, vehicles, and supplies made a sea of junk through which they waded.

"Now let's try to get out," said the Captain when they were back in the corridor.

"What about suits?"

"They're in the air lock. They should be all right. But we won't need suits. Eden has a breathable atmosphere."

"Has anyone ever been here before?"

"There was a cosmic probe twelve years ago, when Altain disappeared with his ship. Remember?"

"But no men landed?"

"No, none."

The inner hatch was overhead, at an angle. Their feeling of unfamiliarity—because the walls were floors and the ceilings walls—gradually passed.

"Here we *will* need a living ladder," declared the

Captain. He began a careful inspection of the inner hatch with the Doctor's flashlight. The hermetic seal was intact.

"Looks good," said the Cyberneticist, craning his neck.

"Yes," agreed the Engineer. He had feared that the terrific force that bent the girders and crushed the main instrument panel between them might also have jammed the inner hatch—but he had kept the thought to himself. The Captain asked the Chemist to stand by the wall and bend over.

"Legs apart, hands on your knees—it'll be more comfortable for you that way."

"I always wanted to be in the circus!" the Chemist said, crouching. The Captain placed a foot on his shoulder, climbed up, and, pressing against the wall, caught hold of the nickel-plated lever with his fingertips.

He tugged at it, then hung from it. With a grating sound, as though the lock mechanism were full of crushed glass, it made a quarter-turn and stopped.

"Are you pulling in the right direction?" asked the Doctor, who was shining the flashlight from below. "The ship is on its side."

"I've taken that into account."

"You can't pull it a little harder?"

The Captain said nothing. Hanging from the lever with one hand, he tried bringing the other hand up as well. This was difficult because of his position, but he finally managed it. He drew up his knees to avoid kicking the Chemist beneath him and gave the lever several jerks—by pulling himself up and then dropping with the full weight of his body. He grunted when his torso hit the wall.

On the third or fourth drop, the lever moved a little more. There were still about two inches to go. The Captain braced himself and did one more drop. The lever engaged the catch with an awful squeak: the bolt had been pulled.

"Perfect, perfect," said the Physicist, delighted.

The Engineer said nothing, his mind elsewhere.

Now they worked at opening the inner hatch—a more difficult task. The Engineer tried the handle of the chamber door, but knew it was hopeless: the pipes had burst in a number of places and all the fluid had leaked out. In the light of the Doctor's flashlight, the wheel gleamed above them like a halo, too high for their gymnastic abilities: more than twelve feet.

They gathered broken equipment, cushions, books. The library proved particularly useful, with its thick celestial atlases. Under the Engineer's direction, after a few false starts, the men built a pyramid of these, like bricks. It took them almost an hour to make a six-foot pile.

"I hate physical work," wheezed the Doctor. The flashlight, wedged into an aperture in an air-conditioning unit, lit their way as they hurried to the library and returned, their arms filled with books. "I would never have believed that such makeshift measures could be taken—on stellar voyages." He was the only one talking now. At last the Captain, helped by his colleagues, gingerly climbed the pyramid and touched the wheel with his fingers.

"Not quite," he said. "Two inches short. If I jump, the whole thing will come down."

"I happen to have here *The Theory of Tachyons*," said the Doctor, hefting a volume in his hand. "That should do the trick."

The Captain clung to the wheel; as the flashlight moved, his shadow leaped across the white plastic that covered what was now the ceiling. Suddenly the mountain of books shifted.

"Careful," said the Physicist.

7

"There's nothing to push against," complained the Captain in a muffled voice. "Damn!" The wheel slipped from his hands. He swayed for a moment, then regained his balance. No one looked up now; the men linked arms and pressed the unstable structure from all sides to keep it from separating. The Captain caught hold of the wheel again. Suddenly there was a scraping sound, and the books tumbled. He hung in midair—but the wheel had made a complete turn.

"Eleven more times," he said, dropping onto the pile of books.

Two hours later, the problem of the inner hatch had been solved. When it began to open, the entire crew cheered.

Suspended halfway up the corridor, the open hatch formed a kind of platform from which the chamber could be entered without much difficulty. The suits turned out to be undamaged. The lockers that contained them were now horizontal. The men walked across the locker doors.

"Do we all leave?" asked the Chemist.

"First let's see if we can open the outer hatch. . . ."

But the thing would not budge, as if the levers had fused with the main body. All six pushed together with their shoulders; then they tried turning the screws in different ways, but the screws would not turn.

"Arriving is easy—the hard thing is to disembark," concluded the Doctor.

"Very clever," muttered the Engineer. The sweat was burning his eyes. They sat down on the locker doors.

"I'm starved," the Cyberneticist said in the general silence.

"We'd better get something to eat," said the Physicist. He offered to go to the storeroom.

"The kitchen would be better. There's food in the freezer. . . ."

"I can't do it by myself. There's a ton of junk in the way. Any volunteers?"

The Doctor agreed to go; then the Chemist reluctantly stood up. When their heads disappeared over the edge of the half-open inner hatch, and the last gleam of the flashlight, which they took with them, was gone, the Captain said in a hushed voice:

"I didn't want to say anything. You understand the situation?"

"Yes," said the Engineer. In the darkness, he touched the Captain's shoe and kept his hand on it. He needed the contact.

"You think we can cut through the outer hatch?"

"With what?" asked the Engineer.

"We have a blowtorch."

"Did you ever hear of a blowtorch that could cut through a foot and a half of ceramite?"

They fell silent. From the depths of the ship came a hollow noise, as if from a vault.

"What's that?" asked the Cyberneticist nervously. He got up.

"Sit down," said the Captain gently but firmly.

"Do you think the door . . . fused with the hull?"

"I don't know," the Engineer replied.

"Do you have any idea what happened?"

"We ran into atmosphere at cosmic velocity, where atmosphere should not have been. Yet the autopilot could not have made an error."

"The autopilot didn't make the error, we did," said the Captain. "We forgot to correct for the tail."

"What tail?"

"The gas that extends behind every planet with an

9

atmosphere, in the direction opposite to its motion. You didn't know that?"

"Yes, of course. So we fell into such a tail? But it must be extremely attenuated."

"Ten to the minus six," said the Captain. "Or on that order. But we were traveling at more than forty-five miles a second, my friend. It stopped us like a wall. That was the first impact, remember?"

"Yes," said the Engineer, "and when we entered the stratosphere, we were still doing six or seven. We really ought to have smashed to pieces. It's strange that the ship withstood it."

"Strange?"

"She's designed for a load factor of twenty, and before the screen blew, I saw with my own eyes how the arrow jumped off the scale. The scale goes up to thirty."

"And how about us?"

"What do you mean?"

"How were we able to withstand a constant deceleration of thirty g's?"

"Not constant. At the maximum, yes. After all, the retarders gave their all. That's what started the pulsation."

"But the autopilot equalized. It was the air compressors . . ." said the Cyberneticist with annoyance in his voice. In the depths of the ship something began rolling. It sounded like iron wheels on sheet metal. Then it stopped.

"Don't blame the air compressors," said the Engineer. "If we went to the engine room, I could show you that they did five times more than they were supposed to do. Remember, they're only auxiliary units. First of all, their bearings were loosened, and when the pulsation began—"

"You think there was resonance?"

"Resonance is a different matter. The fact is, we should have been smeared across several miles of space, like that freighter on Neptune—remember? You'll believe me when you see the engine room. I can tell you now what's there."

"I'm in no hurry to see the engine room. What's taking them so long? I can't see a thing."

"We'll have light, don't worry," said the Engineer, unaware that he still had his fingertips on the shoe of the Captain, who remained silent and did not move.

"Let's go to the engine room, then. It'll kill time. What else can we do?"

"You really think we won't get out of here?"

"I was just joking. I always joke."

"Enough of that," said the Captain, coming alive. "Anyway, in a pinch, there's the emergency hatch."

"Which happens to be underneath us. The ship must have cut one hell of a trench, and I'm not even sure the outer hatch is above ground."

"We have tools. We can dig a tunnel."

"And the loading bay?" asked the Cyberneticist.

"Submerged," the Engineer said. "I looked into the shaft. One of the main tanks must have burst. There's at least six feet of water there. And probably radioactive."

"How do you know?"

"The reactor cooling system always gives out first—you didn't know that? Forget the loading bay. We'll have to get out this way, unless—"

"Unless we dig a tunnel," the Captain said softly.

"Yes, that is possible," the Engineer agreed, and fell silent. There was the sound of footsteps; sudden light in the corridor beneath them made them blink.

"Ham, crackers, tongue, whatever you like. Everything in cans! There's chocolate, too, and we have thermoses," the Doctor shouted, clambering up first. He shined the flashlight for the others as they entered the chamber and passed out cans and aluminum plates.

"The thermoses are intact," the Cyberneticist observed, pouring coffee into his mug.

"Yes, and the cans held up well, too. But the refrigeration units, the ovens, the small molecular synthesizer, the water filters—they're all smashed."

"And the purifier?"

"That, too. We could repair it if we had the tools. But it's a vicious circle—to get a repair robot going you need current, but you can't get current unless you fix the generator, and to fix the generator you need a repair robot."

"So you've been deliberating, my scientific colleagues? What ray of hope have you to offer us?" asked the Doctor, spreading crackers with butter and laying slices of ham on top. Not waiting for a reply, he continued:

"The science-fiction books I read as a kid must outweigh this poor wreck of ours, yet not once did I come across a story anything like what has happened to us."

"Because it's so prosaic," the Cyberneticist said, grimacing.

"Yes, this is something original—a kind of interplanetary *Robinson Crusoe*," said the Doctor. He sealed the thermos. "When I get back, I must try to write it, to the best of my ability."

They began gathering the cans. The Physicist suggested throwing them into the lockers with the suits. The men had to press against the wall so the doors—on the floor—could be shut.

"You know, we heard a strange noise while we were rummaging in the storeroom," said the Chemist.

"What kind of noise?"

"As though something were crushing the ship."

"A rock?" asked the Cyberneticist.

"It's something quite different," the Engineer said. "When we hit the atmosphere, the external shield reached a very high temperature. The prow may have begun to melt. And now parts of the frame are cooling and shifting, and internal pressures will develop. Hence the noise. You can hear it even now. Listen. . . ."

They heard a groan in the interior of the craft—then a series of short, diminishing cracks—then silence.

"One of the robots, do you think?" said the Cyberneticist, hope in his voice.

"You saw how it was with the robots."

"But we didn't look into the reserve hold." The Cyberneticist leaned out over the edge of the platform and shouted into the dark corridor, "Reserve robots!"

His voice echoed. Silence was the only reply.

"Come, let's take a good look at this hatch," said the Engineer. He knelt at the slightly concave plate, shone the light along its rim, inch by inch. In the same way he checked the seals, which were covered with a network of tiny cracks.

"Nothing melted from the inside, which isn't surprising, since ceramite conducts heat poorly."

"Maybe we should try once more?" suggested the Doctor, touching the wheel of the outer hatch.

"There's no point," said the Chemist.

The Engineer placed his hand on the hatch, then jumped to his feet.

"We need water! Lots of cold water!"

"Why?"

"Touch the hatch!"

Several outstretched hands felt it simultaneously.

"Very hot," said someone.

"Fortunately for us!"

"How's that?"

"The hull, heated, has expanded, and the hatch, too. If

we cool the hatch, it will contract, and we might be able to open it."

"Water won't do it. There might still be some ice—in the refrigeration units," said the Captain.

One after another, they dropped into the corridor, which began to echo with their steps. The Captain remained in the chamber with the Engineer.

"It will open," he said softly, as if to himself.

"If it hasn't fused," the Engineer murmured. He ran a finger along the rim to check its temperature. "Ceramite starts melting over three thousand seven hundred degrees. You didn't notice what the shield registered at the end?"

"At the end the dials were useless. When we threw on the brakes, it was over two and a half, if I'm not mistaken."

"Two and a half thousand degrees is still not much."

"Yes, but later on!"

The Chemist's flushed face appeared over the edge of the platform. He had tied the flashlight around his neck. In its swaying light the pieces of ice in his bucket gleamed. He handed the bucket to the Captain.

"Just a minute. How are we supposed to—" The Engineer broke off. "I'll be back." And he disappeared into the darkness.

More steps could be heard. The Doctor arrived with two buckets of water, ice floating on the top. The Chemist held the light while the Doctor and the Physicist poured water on the hatch. The water flowed across the floor and into the corridor. After dousing the hatch for the tenth time, they heard a faint sound coming from it—a squeaking. They cheered. The Engineer appeared, wearing a reflector (from a suit) taped to his chest. Its glare made everything brighter. He threw an armful of plastic pieces taken from the control room onto the floor. The men began packing the hatch with chunks of ice, keeping them in place with the plastic, with air cushions, and with books that the Physicist kept bringing in. Finally, when their backs ached and little remained of the ice—the hot metal melted it very quickly—the Cyberneticist grabbed the wheel with both hands.

"Not yet!" shouted the Engineer. But the wheel turned with astonishing ease. Everyone jumped up. The wheel rotated more and more rapidly. The Engineer grabbed the center handle of the triple bolt securing the hatch and pulled. There was a sound like thick glass cracking, and the door fell inward, gradually at first, then suddenly striking those who stood closest. A black avalanche rushed in, covering them up to the knees. The Chemist was thrown; the hatch pinned him to the side wall but left him unharmed. The Captain, barely managing to jump free at the last moment, practically knocked the Doctor over. They all froze. The Doctor's flashlight had been hit and went out; the only light came from the reflector on the Engineer's chest.

"What is it?" asked the Cyberneticist in an unsteady voice. He stood behind the others, near the edge of the platform.

"A sample of planet Eden," the Captain replied. He was helping to extricate the Chemist from behind the door that had been pushed open.

"Yes," said the Engineer. "The whole hatchway is underground!"

"Then this must be the first landing *beneath* the surface of an unknown planet," observed the Doctor.

Everyone began to laugh. The Cyberneticist laughed so hard, tears came to his eyes.

"Enough!" said the Captain. "We can't carry on like this until morning. Get your tools, men, we have digging to do."

The Chemist bent down and picked up a heavy, compact lump from the mound on the floor. Earth protruded through the oval opening. Now and then blackish bits trickled down the surface of the heap as far as the corridor. The men withdrew to the corridor; there was no longer room enough on the platform. The Captain and the Engineer were the last to jump down.

"How deep are we, do you think?" the Captain asked the Engineer in a whisper. In the corridor, a patch of light moved far ahead of them. The Engineer had given the reflector to the Chemist.

"It depends on many things. Tagerssen penetrated two hundred and fifty feet."

"Yes, but what remained of him and his ship!"

"Or take the Moon probe. They had to tunnel into rock to get it out. Into rock!"

"On the Moon you have pumice. . . ."

"But who knows what we have here?"

"It looks like marl."

"At the hatchway, yes—but beyond?"

The instruments were a problem. Like all long-range craft, the ship carried a duplicate set of robots and remote-controlled semiautomata for every sort of task, including ground-surface tasks under various planetary conditions. But the machines were dead, and without current there was no chance of repairing them. The only large-scale unit they had, an excavator powered by a micro-reactor, also required electricity to be started. So they would have to make do with primitive tools: shovels and pickaxes. This, too, presented problems. After several hours of toil, the crew went back and got three hoes, flattened and curved at the end, two steel poles, and large sheets of metal—to reinforce the walls of the tunnel. They carried the earth in buckets as well as in large plastic boxes supported litter-fashion by short aluminum tubing.

Approximately eighteen hours had passed since the crash, and the men were exhausted. The Doctor felt that they should have at least a few hours' sleep. But first they needed to improvise beds of some sort, since the bunks in their sleeping quarters, bolted to the floor, were now vertical. It would have taken too much effort to detach them, so the men lugged air mattresses to the library (now almost half empty) and lay down side by side.

But, except for the Chemist and the Engineer, no one could sleep. So the Doctor got up again, took his flashlight, and went in search of sleeping pills. For almost an hour he cleared a path to the first-aid room through a hallway filled with broken equipment and instruments that had tumbled from the wall compartments. At last—his watch showed four in the morning, ship time—the pills were dispensed, the light was extinguished, and fitful breathing soon filled the dark room.

They awoke unexpectedly quickly—all except the Cyberneticist, who had taken too large a dose and was like one drunk. The Engineer complained of a sharp pain in the back of his neck. The Doctor discovered a swelling there: the Engineer had probably got a sprain when they were grappling with the hatch wheels.

Spirits were low. Even the Doctor was not talkative. The food supplies in the air lock were inaccessible now, buried beneath a heap of dirt, so once again the Physicist and the Chemist trudged off to the storeroom for cans of food. It was nine when work resumed on the tunnel.

They went at a snail's pace. There was little room to move about in the oval opening. The men in front broke the packed earth with their hoes, and those behind them removed it to the corridor. Then it was decided to pile the earth in the navigation room, which was closer and contained nothing that might be needed in the immediate future.

Four hours later, the soil in the cabin was knee-high but the tunnel was only six feet long. Though the marl, compact, was not that hard, the poles and hoe blades kept getting stuck in it, and the iron handles bent as the men labored frantically. The steel hoe that the Captain used worked the best. The Engineer, afraid that the ceiling might cave in on them, took care that it was always well propped. By nightfall, when, smeared with clay, they sat down to supper, the tunnel, which led up from the hatch at a steep, almost seventy-degree angle, extended no more than twenty feet.

The Engineer looked into the shaft that led to the lower level, where the loading-bay hatch, steel-plated, lay a hundred feet astern of the main hatch, but all he could see was black water. The level was higher than on the previous day; one of the tanks must still be leaking. The water was contaminated, radioactive. He verified this with his small Geiger counter, closed the shaft, and returned to his comrades without mentioning his discovery.

"If all goes well, we'll be out tomorrow. If not, it'll take us two days," the Cyberneticist declared, drinking his third mug of coffee from the thermos. They were all drinking coffee.

"How do you know?" the Engineer asked with surprise.

"Just a feeling."

"He has the intuition his robots lack," said the Doctor, laughing. As the day progressed, the Doctor was in increasingly good humor. When relieved of the digging, he would run back to the ship's quarters, scavenging. He added two magneto lanterns, a portable shaver, vitamin-enriched chocolate, and a stack of towels to their supplies. The men were filthy, their suits were covered with stains. No one had shaved, of course, given the lack of electricity.

The whole of the following day was spent digging the tunnel. The navigation room was now so full, it became difficult to dump the soil through the door. Next they used the library. The Doctor had misgivings here, but the Chemist, with whom he was carrying the improvised handbarrow, tipped a heap of marl onto the books without hesitation.

The tunnel opened up unexpectedly. The soil had been getting drier and less compact for a while now, and though the Physicist had noted this, the others did not agree: the soil they carried into the ship seemed to them no different. The Engineer and the Captain, beginning their shift, had just taken up the tools still warm from previous hands, and were hacking at the irregular wall, when a section suddenly disappeared and air poured in through the opening. They could feel the draft: the pressure of the atmosphere outside was a little higher than in the tunnel or the rocket. The hoes and steel poles worked feverishly. No one any longer carried away the soil. The rest of the crew, unable to help those in front because there was no room, formed a tight group at the rear. After a few final blows, the Engineer was about to crawl outside, but the Captain stopped him. The Captain wanted to widen the exit first. He also gave orders for the last chunks of soil to be carried into the ship, so that nothing would obstruct the tunnel. Another ten or twenty minutes passed, therefore, before the six men crawled out onto the planet's surface.

II

It was dusk. The tunnel opened near the base of a gently sloping knoll about forty feet high. Beyond, a vast plain stretched to the horizon, over which the first stars twinkled. There were vague, slender treelike forms in the distance, but the light of the setting sun was now so dim that everything merged into a uniform gray. The men stood silently. To their left, the huge hull of the ship jutted at an angle into the air. One hundred twenty of its two hundred feet, the Engineer estimated, were embedded in the knoll. But no one was interested any more in the silhouette of the tube ending in useless vanes and exhaust cones. The men inhaled the cool air, with its faint, unfamiliar odor that no one could give a name to, and a strong feeling of helplessness came over them. The hoes and pipes dropped from their hands. They stood gazing at the plain, its horizons in darkness, and at the stars shining overhead.

"The Pole Star?" the Chemist asked in a hushed voice, pointing to a low star flickering in the east.

"It wouldn't be visible from here. We're now . . . yes, we're directly under the Galactic South Pole. The Southern Cross ought to be over there somewhere. . . ."

They craned their necks. The black sky was bright with constellations. The men pointed them out to one another, naming them. This raised their spirits for a while. The stars were the only things familiar on the empty plain.

"It's getting colder, like the desert," said the Captain. "We'll accomplish nothing today. We'd better go back inside."

"What, back in that grave?" the Cyberneticist exclaimed, indignant.

"Without that grave we'd perish in two days here," the Captain said. "Don't be childish." He turned around, walked steadily to the opening, which was barely visible from several feet higher on the slope, lowered his legs, and pulled himself inside. For a moment his head was still visible; then it disappeared. The others looked at one another.

"Come on," muttered the Physicist. They followed him reluctantly.

As they began crawling into the narrow opening, the Engineer said to the Cyberneticist, who was last in line, "Did you notice the smell in the air?"

"Yes. Strange, pungent . . . Do you know its composition?"

"Like Earth's, with something added, I forget what. Nothing harmful. The data are in a small green volume on the second shelf in the—" Then he remembered that he himself had filled the library with soil. "Damn," he said, and squeezed himself through the hole.

The Cyberneticist, now alone, suddenly felt uneasy. It

wasn't fear but an overwhelming sense of being lost, of the strangeness of the landscape. And, too, there was something humiliating, he thought, about returning to the ground like worms. He ducked his head and crawled into the tunnel behind the Engineer.

The following day, some of the men wanted to carry their rations to the surface and have breakfast there, but the Captain was against this. It would cause, he maintained, unnecessary trouble. So they ate by the light of two lanterns, in the air lock, and drank coffee that had grown cold. Out of the blue, the Cyberneticist said, "Wait a minute. How did we have good air the whole time?"

The Captain smiled. There was gray stubble on his hollow cheeks.

"The oxygen cylinders are intact. But purification is a problem: only one of the automatic filters is functioning—the emergency one, on batteries. The electricals, of course, are worthless. In six or seven days we would have begun to suffocate."

"You knew that?" the Cyberneticist asked slowly. The Captain said nothing.

"Now what do we do?" asked the Physicist.

They washed their utensils in a bucket of water, and the Doctor dried them with one of his towels.

"The atmosphere has oxygen," said the Doctor, tossing his aluminum plate on top of the others. "That means there's life here. What information do we have?"

"Next to nothing. The space probe took a sample of the atmosphere, that's all."

"You mean it didn't land?"

"It didn't land."

"That's loads of information," said the Cyberneticist. He was trying to clean his face, using alcohol from a small bottle and a piece of cotton. With very little water fit for use, they had not washed for two days. The Physicist examined his face in the polished surface of an air-conditioning unit.

"It's something," the Captain replied softly. "Had the composition of the air been different—without oxygen—my mistake would have killed all of you."

"What?" The Cyberneticist almost dropped his cup.

"And myself as well. We wouldn't have had one chance in a billion. Now we have."

There was silence.

"Does the presence of oxygen mean plants and animals?" asked the Engineer.

"Not necessarily," said the Chemist. "On the Alpha planets of Canis Minor there is oxygen but no plants or animals."

"What is there, then?"

"Photoids."

"Luminescent bacteria?"

"No, they're not bacteria."

"It's not important," the Doctor said. He put the utensils and cans of food away. "We have other worries now. We can't activate the defenses—am I right?"

"We can't even get to them," the Cyberneticist acknowledged. "All the robots came loose from their moorings. We'd need the two-ton hoist to clear away all the scrap, and it's lying at the very bottom."

"But what do we do for weapons?" asked the Doctor.

"There are the jectors," said the Cyberneticist.

"And what are you going to charge them with?"

"There's no current in the control room? We had current before!"

"There must have been a short circuit in the accumulator," said the Engineer.

"Why aren't the jectors already charged?"

"Orders. We can't carry them charged," the Engineer muttered.

"Orders! Damn—"

"Cut it out!"

Hearing the Captain's voice, the Cyberneticist shrugged in exasperation. The Doctor walked out. The Engineer had taken a light nylon knapsack from his cabin, and was stuffing K rations into the pockets when the Doctor reappeared, holding a short oxidized cylinder that ended in a valve.

"And what is that?" the Engineer asked with interest.

"A weapon."

"What does it shoot?"

"Sleeping gas."

The Engineer burst out laughing.

"What makes you think that your gas can put to sleep anything living on this planet?"

"If you were attacked, you could always anesthetize yourself," said the Chemist. Everyone laughed, including the Doctor.

"This should knock out any oxygen-breathing creature," he said. "And if there's an attack—watch!"

He pulled a trigger at the base of the cylinder. A needle-thin stream of vapor shot into the darkness of the corridor.

"Well, for lack of anything better . . ." said the Engineer doubtfully.

"Shall we go?" asked the Doctor, slipping the cylinder into one of the pockets of his suit.

"Let's go."

The sun was high overhead—small and distant, yet hotter than the Earth's. But what struck them most was that the sun was not completely circular. They observed it through the cracks of their fingers and through the semitransparent red paper used for wrapping the individual antiradiation packs.

"It's flattened because of the velocity of its revolution

around its axis, is that right?" the Chemist asked the Captain.

"Yes. The flattening was more noticeable during the flight. You don't remember?"

"But, you see, I wasn't paying attention then. . . ."

They turned away from the sun and looked at their ship. The white cylindrical hull jutted obliquely from the low hill in which it was embedded, resembling a gigantic cannon. Its surface—milky white in shadow and silvery in sunlight—appeared undamaged. The Engineer approached the spot where the ship had entered the ground, stepped over the rim of upthrown soil that surrounded the hull like a collar, and ran his hand along the plating.

"Not bad material, this ceramite," he said, not turning around. "If I could just have a look at the funnels. . . ." He looked wistfully up at the jets suspended above the plain.

"We'll do that later," said the Physicist. "But now let's reconnoiter."

The Captain had reached the top of the elevation. The others hurried after him. Smooth and buff-colored, the sun-drenched plain stretched unvaryingly in all directions. The slender silhouettes that they had observed the day before rose in the distance, but in the bright sunlight it was clear that these were not trees. The sky, overhead as blue as Earth's, took on a distinctly greenish tinge at the horizon. To the north, faint cirrus clouds moved slowly. The Captain was checking directions on the small compass strapped to his wrist. The Doctor bent over and began poking at the soil with his foot.

"Why isn't anything growing here?" he asked, amazed.

They were all struck by that. The plain was bare as far as the eye could see.

"It seems to be a region subject to increasingly steppe-like conditions," said the Chemist uncertainly. "Farther on, there to the west—see those patches?—it gets yellower. That must be desert. And the wind blows the sand here. Because this knoll is clay."

"That we certainly know," said the Doctor.

"We need a plan of some sort for our expedition," the Captain began. "The supplies we're taking with us will last two days."

"Not even that—we don't have much water," the Cyberneticist said.

"We'll ration the water until we locate some here. Where there's oxygen, there's water. I suggest we proceed as follows: from the base we go in a straight line, and only so far that we can return safely and without haste."

"A maximum of fifteen miles in any direction," the Physicist said.

"Agreed. The only question is the kind of reconnaissance."

"Wait," said the Engineer, who had been standing apart as though mulling something over. "Don't you think this is a little crazy? We've crashed on an unknown planet, we've just managed to crawl out, and instead of doing the most important thing, instead of concentrating all our energies on repairing what can be repaired, on digging the ship out, and so on, we're going exploring—with no arms, no means of defense, and no idea at all of what we will find here."

The Captain heard him out in silence, looking around at the men. They were all unshaven, and their three-day's growth had begun to give them a wild look. The Engineer's words made an obvious impression, but no one spoke, as if they were all waiting to see what the Captain would say.

"Six men can't dig out a spaceship, Henry," he said, weighing his words carefully. "You know that perfectly well. As things now stand, we can't even tell how long it will take to get the smallest unit operating. The planet is inhabited. Yet we know nothing at all about it. We didn't even circle it before the crash. We approached from the nightside and by error fell into its tail. As we fell, we reached the terminator. I was lying near the last screen to go. I saw, or at least I thought I saw, what resembled . . . a city."

"Why didn't you tell us?" the Engineer asked slowly.

"Yes, why?" the Physicist also asked.

"Because I wasn't certain. I don't even know in which direction to look for it. The ship was spinning. But there is a chance, a small chance, that we will receive help. You all know how desperate our situation is. We need water. Most of it flooded the lower level and is contaminated. So I think we can allow ourselves to take risks."

"I agree," said the Doctor.

"So do I," said the Physicist.

The Cyberneticist moved off a few paces and faced south, as though not wanting to hear what the others said. The Chemist nodded. The Engineer walked down the knoll, put on his knapsack, and asked, "Which way?"

"North," said the Captain. The Engineer began walking, and the others joined him. When they looked back a few minutes later, the knoll was barely visible—only the ship's fuselage stood against the sky.

It was hot. Their shadows grew shorter the farther they walked. Their boots sank in the sand, and the only sounds were their footsteps and their breathing. As they approached one of the slender shapes that in the twilight had resembled trees, they slackened their pace. Out of the buff-colored soil rose a perpendicular trunk, as gray as an elephant's hide and with a faint metallic luster. The trunk, no thicker at the base than a man's arm, developed, at the top, into a flattened cup-shaped structure some seven feet above the ground. It was impossible to see whether or not the calyx was open at the top. It was completely motionless. The men stopped about twenty feet from this extraordinary growth, but the Engineer continued toward it and was lifting his hand to touch the "trunk" when the Doctor cried, "Stop!"

The Engineer drew back reflexively. The Doctor pulled him away by the arm, then picked up a small stone and tossed it high into the air. The stone described a steep arc and dropped straight into the flattened top of the calyx. They all gave a start, so sudden and unexpected was the reaction. The calyx began undulating and closed; there was a brief hissing sound, like gas escaping, and the whole grayish column, now trembling feverishly, sank into the earth as if sucked in. The hole that was created was instantly filled by a greasy, foaming brown substance. Then particles of sand began to float on the surface, the coating of sand became thicker, and in a few seconds no trace of the hole remained: the ground was smooth and unbroken. They were still standing there in amazement when the Chemist shouted, "Look!"

They lifted their heads. Before, they had been surrounded, at a distance of a few hundred feet, by three or four similar tall and slender growths—now there was not one.

"They all disappeared!" exclaimed the Cyberneticist.

They strained their eyes but could see no trace of the calyxes. The sun was growing stronger; the heat was hard to bear. They moved on.

After an hour they had spread out in a long file, like a caravan. First came the Doctor, now carrying his knapsack under his arm; behind him was the Captain; the Chemist brought up the rear. They had all opened their suits, rolled up their sleeves. Bathed in sweat, their mouths parched, they slowly dragged themselves across the plain.

A long horizontal strip loomed on the horizon. The Doctor halted and waited for the Captain.

"How far do you think we've gone?"

The Captain looked back into the sun, in the direction of the ship. It was no longer visible.

"The planet has a smaller radius than Earth's," he said, wiping his face with a handkerchief. "I'd say about five miles."

The Doctor squinted, his eyelids swollen. His black hair was covered with a cloth cap. Every now and then he dampened the cap with water from his canteen.

"This is madness, you know," he said, as they both looked at the spot on the horizon where, not long before, the ship had stood, a faint oblique line. All they could see there now were the slender silhouettes of the calyxes, pale gray in the distance. The calyxes had re-emerged behind them. The other men came up, and the Chemist threw his tent roll on the ground and sat on it.

"Strange, that there are no signs of civilization," said the Cyberneticist, rummaging in his pockets. He found some vitamin pills in a crumpled packet and offered them around.

"You wouldn't find such desolation on Earth," the Engineer agreed. "No roads, no aircraft of any kind."

"What, you expect to find a replica of Earth's civilization?" the Physicist snorted.

"This system is stable," the Doctor began, "so a civilization on Eden could be older than on Earth, and therefore . . ."

"Assuming it's a civilization of anthropoids," the Cyberneticist said.

"Let's get moving," said the Captain. "In half an hour we ought to reach that." And he pointed at a thin purple strip on the horizon.

"What is it?"

"I don't know. Water, maybe."

"Shade would be enough for me right now," the Engineer croaked. He rinsed his mouth and throat with a gulp of water.

There was a squeaking of straps as they hoisted their packs onto their shoulders, and the group spread out once more and resumed its trek across the sand. They passed a dozen more calyxes and several larger growths that appeared to be supported by lianas or creepers, but none of these was closer than six hundred feet, and they had no wish to deviate from their line of march.

The sun was at its zenith when the landscape changed. There was less sand. Red, sun-scorched earth began to show in long, low ridges overgrown here and there with clumps of gray moss. When the men nudged the moss with their boots, it crumbled like burned paper. The purple strip, they saw, was made of separate groups of squat shapes, and its color was now clearer—more a green sprinkled with faded blue. A northerly breeze brought a delicate fragrance, which the men drew into their nostrils with cautious curiosity. As they neared a bent wall of tangled shapes, the men in front slowed so that the others could catch up, and the whole group finally came to a halt before a motionless façade of bizarre forms.

From a hundred feet, the forms still looked like scrub, like a bluish thicket full of birds' nests—not so much because of any true resemblance as because of the eye's endeavor to find the familiar in the alien.

"Are they spiders?" the Physicist asked hesitantly, and everyone saw spiders with small spindle-shaped bodies covered with thick bristles, standing motionless on extraordinarily long legs tucked under them.

"They're plants!" exclaimed the Doctor, drawing nearer to one of the tall gray-green creatures. In fact, its "legs" turned out to be stalks, whose thickened, hair-covered nodes could easily be taken for the joints of an arthropod. These stalks, emerging from the mossy ground in groups of six, seven, or eight, converged, archlike, to form a "body" that, surrounded by thin gossamer threads glittering in the sun, resembled a flattened arachnid abdomen. The vegetable spiders grew fairly close together, but it was possible to pass between them. Here and there on the stalks were brighter offshoots, almost the color of Earth leaves, and they ended in closed buds. Once again the Doctor threw a pebble into the "abdomens" suspended twenty feet above the ground; when nothing happened, he examined one of the stalks and finally nicked it with his knife. Out came tiny drops, a bright-yellow sap that immediately began to foam, turning orange, red. In a few moments it coagulated to form a thick resin with an intense aromatic odor that they all liked at first but soon found sickening. Beneath this curious shrubbery it was a little cooler than on the plain.

The plant abdomens offered shade, and there was more shade the deeper they went. They tried not to touch the stalks, and particularly the whitish buds at the ends of the youngest shoots, which aroused an unaccountable repugnance.

The ground was soft, spongy, and gave off a vapor that made it difficult to breathe. The shadows of the abdomens passed across their faces and hands—now larger, now smaller. Some abdomens were slender with orange spikes; others were withered, faded, with long flaccid threads dangling from them. When a wind came up, the entire thicket emitted an unpleasant hollow rustling, not the sigh of an Earthly forest but a sound like that of sandpaper. At times individual plants blocked the way with intertwined branches, and the men had to go around. Thus they proceeded even more slowly than on the plain. After a while they stopped looking up at the thorny abdomens, stopped trying to see nests, cones, or cocoons in them.

Suddenly the Doctor, who headed the column, noticed a thick black hair hanging before his face—a shiny thread, a painted wire. He was about to brush it aside with his hand, but since this was something new, he raised his eyes—and froze.

A pearl-colored, bulbous thing hanging from the stalks that converged at the base of one of the "cocoons" was watching him. The Doctor felt its gaze even though he could not locate the monster's eyes. He saw no head, no limbs—only puffy skin filled with blebs, glistening, and a dark, funnel-shaped protuberance from which dangled a thick black hair six feet long.

"What is it?" asked the Engineer, behind him. When the Doctor did not answer, he looked up and also froze.

"What's it looking with?" whispered the Engineer, and instinctively backed away, such was the revulsion he felt for the creature, which seemed to be piercing him with a greedy, extraordinarily intense gaze—though no eyes were visible.

"Disgusting!" the Chemist hissed. They were now all standing beside the Doctor, who had been the first to retreat from under the monster—the others stood as far away as the stalks allowed. The Doctor produced the oxidized cylinder from his suit, aimed it slowly at the swollen body, which was lighter than the vegetation surrounding it, and pressed the trigger.

In the next second a great deal happened. First there was a flash that blinded them all except the Doctor, who blinked at that exact moment. A thin stream was still squirting upward when the stalks began sagging, collapsing. A puff of black vapor enveloped the men, and the creature fell with a heavy, wet smack. It lay helpless for perhaps a second, like a gray, rough balloon deflating. The black hair alone danced and whipped above it like a mad thing, cleaving the air in lightning-fast convulsions. Then the hair disappeared, and shapeless pieces of the creature began to crawl like snails in all directions on the spongy moss at their feet. Before any of the men could say or do anything, the creature's escape—or dispersal—was completed: its last pieces, as small as caterpillars, burrowed into the soil beneath the stalks and were gone. All that remained was a nasty acrid smell.

"A colony of some kind . . . ?" the Chemist asked uncertainly. He pressed his hand to his eyes, still seeing black spots.

"*E pluribus unum,*" the Doctor replied. "Or, rather, *e uno plures,* if my Latin's right. This must be the sort of multiple monster that divides in an emergency. . . ."

"It stinks to high heaven," said the Physicist. "Let's get out of here."

"Let's," agreed the Doctor. But when they had gone about fifty feet, he said, "I wonder what would have happened if I had touched that hair."

"To find out might have cost you a lot," the Chemist suggested.

"Or possibly nothing. Evolution often gives fearsome forms to completely harmless species."

"Look, it's getting brighter over there, to the side," cried the Cyberneticist. "Let's get out of this damned spider forest!"

The sound of a brook reached their ears, and they stopped. They continued, and the sound grew louder, then fainter, then disappeared altogether. They could not find its source. The forest thinned, and the ground grew softer, almost boggy. It was unpleasant walking. Sometimes something creaked underfoot, like soaked grass, but no water was visible anywhere.

They found themselves on the rim of a circular depression a few hundred feet in diameter. A number of eight-legged plants stood inside it, not that close to one another. They seemed very old, their stalks splayed, as though supporting with difficulty the central swellings. They resembled spiders—huge emaciated spiders—to a greater degree than anything the men had encountered so far. At the bottom of the depression, here and there, were rust-colored, pitted hunks of metal half-buried in the ground and partly wrapped by plant tendrils. The Engineer immediately slid down the steep though short slope. Curiously, once he was inside it, what had looked like a depression to the men now looked like a crater—a bomb crater.

"A war?" said the Physicist. He stood at the top of the ridge, watching the Engineer approach a large fragment at the base of the biggest "spider" and attempt to move it.

"Iron?!" the Captain called out.

"No!" the Engineer shouted back. He disappeared behind an object that resembled a shattered cone, then emerged from a clump of stalks, which snapped as he pushed through them. He returned frowning. Several hands reached out to help him as he clambered up. Seeing the expectant faces of the others, he shrugged. "I don't know what it is. Ruins of some kind. Erosion is far advanced. They're a hundred, maybe three hundred years old. . . ."

The men filed past the crater in silence and headed for where the vegetation was lowest. Then it ceased—or, rather, it parted to form a narrow trench, a kind of corridor, perfectly straight. The stalks here seemed to have been cut and trampled, the large abdomens pushed aside onto other plants. These other plants were flat, dry, with husks that cracked underfoot like sloughed-off tree bark. The men decided to take the path. Though they had to wade through the dead stalks, they made better progress than before. The path arced northward. They left the dead vegetation and found themselves on a plain on the other side of the copse.

An indistinct line met the path at the point where it emerged from the forest, a continuation of the path, though not paved. In the barren soil there was a rut or groove about six inches deep and six inches wide, covered with a green-gray growth silky to the touch. This curious "moss," as the Doctor called it, went straight as an arrow, terminating at a bright strip that went like a wall from one end of the horizon to the other.

Above this wall—it *was* a wall—glimmered peaks resembling Gothic spires covered with silvery metal. As the men walked quickly, more and more detail emerged. Above the wall was a surface that stretched for miles in both directions; it rose in regular arches, like the roofs of giant hangars. Between the arches were downward bulges, from which something grayish fell in a fine dust or mist. Drawing closer, the men smelled a strange, bitter, but pleasant odor, as of unfamiliar flowers. The arched roofs loomed higher as the men approached, like an enormous suspension bridge inverted. Against the clouds, at a point where two arches joined, something shone brightly, as if mirrors had been placed there to direct the sun's rays downward. The wall opposite them was in motion. Grayish brown, it moved like a peristalsis; convex waves ran across it from left to right, as if, behind a curtain, elephants—or animals larger than elephants—were passing at regular intervals, brushing the material with their sides.

Where the narrow, moss-covered groove came to an end, the bitter odor grew intense, unbearable. The Cyberneticist, coughing, said, "It may be poisonous." Despite the odor, fascinated by the rhythm of the waves, the men moved closer, until only a few steps separated them from the "curtain." It looked like a thick mat of interwoven fibers. The Doctor picked up a pebble from the ground and tossed it at the wall. The pebble vanished, as if it had dissolved or evaporated before touching the moving surface.

"Did it go inside?" the Cyberneticist asked hesitantly.

"Impossible!" said the Chemist. "It never reached that . . . that . . ."

The Doctor picked up a whole fistful of pebbles and threw them in quick succession; they all disappeared a few inches away from the wall. The Engineer removed a key from a small key ring and threw it at the surface, which just then happened to be swollen. The key clinked, as if striking metal, then disappeared.

"What now?" asked the Cyberneticist, looking at the Captain. The latter said nothing. The Doctor put his knapsack on the ground, took out a can of food, with his knife cut from it a cube of jellied meat, and threw it at the "curtain." The piece of food stuck to the surface, hung there for a while, then began to disappear, as if melting.

"It's a kind of filter," said the Doctor, his eyes sparkling. "A selective membrane . . . something like that . . ."

In the buckle of one of his knapsack straps the Chemist found a withered tendril of the "spider" plant; it must have got caught there while they were pushing their way through the thicket. Without thinking, he tossed the tendril at the undulating wall. It bounced and fell at his feet.

"A selector . . ." he said uncertainly.

The Doctor went up to the wall, so close that his shadow touched it, aimed his sleeping-gas weapon, and pulled the trigger. The needle-thin stream instantly produced a hole in the wall, revealing a large dark space with sparks scudding along high and low, and a multitude of tiny white and pink lights glimmering deep inside. The Doctor pulled back, choking; the bitter odor had burned his nostrils and throat.

The aperture contracted like an iris. The waves in the wall slowed as they approached it, went around it, above or below, then picked up speed again. The hole grew smaller. All of a sudden a black fingerlike thing emerged from it and quickly touched all around the rim. The hole closed, and once more the men found themselves in front of a rhythmically rising and falling surface.

The Engineer suggested they stop and deliberate. The Doctor disagreed, feeling that that would be a sign of indecision. Finally they decided to continue along the wall, picked up their knapsacks, and moved on. They went about two miles, crossing more than a dozen moss-grooves that led out to the plain. They discussed what the grooves might be. The hypothesis of irrigation was rejected as unlikely. The Doctor attempted to examine a few plants plucked from the dark-green ruts. They did resemble moss, but their rootlets had beadlike swellings that contained tiny, hard black grains.

It was long past noon. Hungry, they stopped to eat. There was no shade anywhere, but they preferred not to return to the copse, which lay three thousand feet to their right, because the spider plants had made them uneasy.

"According to the stories I read as a boy," said the Doctor, his mouth full, "a hole belching fire ought to open up in this damned wall now, and out come a being with three arms and one leg. Under his arm he has an interstellar telecommunicator, or he's telepathic and tells us that he represents a highly developed but deranged civilization that—"

"Stop that jabbering," said the Captain. He poured some water from his thermos into his mug, which was immediately covered with condensation. "We'd better decide what to do."

"I think we should go in there," said the Doctor, and he got up as if intending to do just that.

"Go in where?" the Physicist asked lazily.

"You must be crazy!" the Cyberneticist exclaimed in a high-pitched voice.

"Not at all. Of course, we could keep on walking like this, hoping the aliens will toss us something to eat."

"Let's be serious," said the Engineer.

"I am serious, and do you know why? Because, quite simply, I've had enough of this." The Doctor turned on his heel.

"Stop!" shouted the Captain.

The Doctor walked straight toward the wall and was only a few feet from it when they jumped up and ran after him. Hearing their pursuit, he stretched out his hand and touched the wall. His hand disappeared. The Doctor stood motionless for a second, then stepped forward and was gone. The other five stopped, gasping, and knelt at the spot where his left boot print was still visible. Suddenly the Doctor's head appeared above them, his neck disembodied, as if severed by a knife; tears streamed from his eyes, and he sneezed loudly, repeatedly.

"It's stifling in here," he said, "and it stings your nose like the devil, but for a few minutes it's bearable. It's a little like tear gas. Come on in. It doesn't hurt—you don't feel anything at all."

And at the level of his shoulder an arm appeared in midair. "Damn you!" muttered the Engineer with a mixture of fear and admiration, and he clutched the Doctor's hand, which pulled him in, so that the Engineer, too, disappeared from sight. One by one the others entered the undulating wall. The Cyberneticist was the last. He hesitated. Then, his heart pounding like a hammer, he closed his eyes and took a step forward.

After a moment of darkness, everything brightened. He

found himself with the others, inside a vast place full of puffing and throbbing. Diagonally, vertically, and from side to side, enormous tubes moved, crisscrossing. Of varying thicknesses, bulging here and thinning there, they turned and vibrated, and from the depths of this vast, ceaselessly moving forest of glistening bodies a splashing noise could be heard. It accelerated, stopped, was followed by gurgling; then the sequence was repeated.

From the bitter air they began sneezing, one after another, and their eyes ran. Holding handkerchiefs to their faces, they backed away from the wall, which from the inside looked like a cascade of black syrup.

"Well, we're home at last—this is a factory, an automated factory!" cried the Engineer between two sneezes.

Gradually they got used to the smell, and the sneezing ceased. Blinking and watery-eyed, they looked about.

A dozen or so paces ahead, in the ground, which was as springy as rubber, they came to black wells; glowing objects the size of a man's head shot up out of them so quickly it was impossible to see their shape. As they flew up, one of the tubes sucked them in while continuing to turn. The objects did not completely disappear, because their pinkish glow showed faintly through the tube's quivering walls, as through tinted glass, so that it was possible to watch them travel inside the tube to somewhere farther on.

"A conveyor belt," the Engineer said through his handkerchief. "Mass production."

He walked around the wells, stepping carefully. What was the source of the light here? The ceiling was semitransparent, but its monotonous gray was dissipated in the sea of objects that flowed nimbly by on invisible currents. All this movement appeared to be orchestrated, to have the same tempo. Fountains of hot material gushed into the air, and the same thing was happening high above, where just beneath the ceiling they could see red arms in the air.

"We must find where the finished product is stored," the Engineer concluded.

The Captain tapped him on the shoulder. "What kind of energy do you think this is?"

The Engineer shrugged. "I have no idea."

"It would take you a year to locate the finished product—this room is miles long," the Physicist said.

It was curious, but the deeper they went into the hall, the easier it was for them to breathe—as if the bitter smell came only from the wall.

"Are we lost?" the Cyberneticist asked anxiously.

The Captain checked his compass.

"No. The reading is good. . . . There's probably no iron here, and no electromagnetism."

For more than an hour they wandered through the pulsing forest of this unusual factory, until the area around them became more open. They felt a cool, almost refrigerated gust of air. The network of tubes parted, and they found themselves near the mouth of an enormous helical funnel. Boughs from above descended to it, flapping like whips, each ending in a nodule, and from the nodules came a sudden hail of somersaulting objects, black and shiny, that dropped into the funnel in a place the men could not see, since it was twenty feet above their heads.

The dark-gray wall of the funnel now began to expand: something was pushing it from within. They stepped back instinctively, so ominous was the appearance of the swelling bubble. Then, without a sound, it burst, and a stream of black things poured from the opening at the top. At the same moment, lower down, a trough with outward-turned edges emerged from a wide well, and the objects dropped into it with a drumming sound. The trough shook in such a way that in a few seconds the black objects were resting in a neat quadrangle on its shallow bottom.

"The finished product!" cried the Engineer. He rushed to the edge and without a moment's hesitation bent over and grabbed the nearest black object. The Captain caught him by the belt of his suit at the last moment, and this was all that kept the Engineer from falling headfirst into the trough, because he refused to let go of the heavy object but was unable to lift it himself. The Physicist and the Doctor had to give him a hand, and together they hauled the thing out.

It was as large as a man's torso and had semitransparent segments, inside which were rows of small crystals, metallic, sparkling, and there were apertures surrounded by earlike swellings, and, at the top, an uneven mosaic of projections made of an exceptionally hard substance that did not reflect the light. In a word, the object was extremely complex. The Engineer knelt in front of it, fingered and tapped it, examined the apertures from various angles in an attempt to discover any moving parts.

Meanwhile the Doctor was observing the trough. After forming a geometric quadrangle of the black objects, it rose a little, pivoted, and suddenly softened, but only on one side. Changing shape, it turned into an enormous spoon. Then a large snout protruded and opened, giving off a hot, bitter stench; the opening sucked in all the objects with a loud smack and closed again, whereupon the snout began to glow in the middle. The Doctor could see the objects melting inside, fusing to form a fiery orange slurry. Then the glow dimmed; the snout went dark.

Forgetting his colleagues, the Doctor walked around two great soaring columns, inside which lumps of the molten material now flowed, as through a monstrous esophagus. Craning his neck and wiping his teary eyes from time to time, he attempted to trace the path of the incandescent slurry through the labyrinth of tubes. At times it disappeared from view, but he would come upon its trail again as it glowed in the depths of the tortuous black conduits. Finally he stopped at a spot that seemed familiar, and saw red-hot objects, already partly formed, flying into a pit, while nearby others shot out of one of the open wells— only to be swallowed up by a row of thick tubes dangling overhead like elephant trunks. Cooling, now pink, the objects traveled up through the tubes. The Doctor walked on, head back, oblivious to everything, then suddenly almost fell and uttered a strangled cry.

He had returned to the open space; before him the helical funnel was larger than ever as the volley of black objects, which had cooled completely after their travels, fell into it. The Doctor examined the sides of the funnel, now knowing in which direction the "delivery" would take place—and found himself back among the others gathered around the Engineer, who was still examining the black object. Again a huge bubble burst and spurted out more "finished product," and again a trough emerged.

"I've figured the whole thing out! I can tell you!" he shouted.

"Where were you? I was beginning to worry," the Captain said. "Have you really discovered something? Because the Engineer has drawn a blank."

"A blank wouldn't be so bad!" growled the Engineer. He got to his feet, kicked the object furiously, and glared at the Doctor. "Well, what's the big discovery?"

The Doctor smiled. "These things are drawn in here"— he pointed to the snout, which just then happened to open. "Now it's warming up inside, see? And now they're melting, fusing, being carried to the top in portions, where they're treated. Then, still red-hot, they drop to the bottom, underground—there must be another level there—

and something else happens to them, and they come back up, by the same well, pale but still glowing. They journey up to the ceiling, fall into this"—he indicated the funnel—"and from there go into the trough, then the snout, melt, and so on and so on, forming, melting, forming."

"Have you gone mad?" whispered the Engineer. On his forehead were large drops of sweat.

"You don't believe it? See for yourself."

The Engineer did, twice, which took him a good hour. By the time they returned to the trough, which was filling up with a new quadrangle of the "finished product," it was growing dark; the light was turning gray.

The Engineer looked demented; his face twitched. The others, though astounded, were less shaken than he by this mystery.

"We'd better leave now," said the Captain. "It may be difficult once it's dark." He took the Engineer by the arm. The Engineer first let himself be pulled away, but then suddenly tore free, ran back to the black object which they had left behind, and lifted it with difficulty.

"You want to take that with you?" asked the Captain. "All right. Someone give him a hand."

The Physicist grasped the earlike swellings and helped the Engineer with his burden. In this way they reached the concave wall. The Doctor quietly moved through the glistening, syruplike "waterfall" and found himself back on the plain, in the cool evening air. With joy he took a deep breath, filling his lungs. The others emerged behind him; the Engineer and the Physicist lugged the black object to the spot where they had left their knapsacks and dropped it on the ground.

The portable stove was lit, some water was heated, and meat concentrate dissolved in it. The men ate in silence, ravenous. It was now completely dark. The stars had come out, and their brilliance increased minute by minute as the murky brushwood of the distant copse disappeared into the night. Only the stove's bluish flames swaying gently in the breeze provided light. The high wall of the "factory" behind them made no sound, and it was impossible to see, in the darkness, whether the horizontal waves were still rippling across it.

"It gets dark here as in the tropics back home," said the Chemist. "Is this the equatorial zone?"

"I guess," said the Captain. "Though I don't even know the planet's angle with respect to the ecliptic."

"But that must be known."

"Yes, but the data are on the ship."

Silence. The cold was beginning to bite, so they wrapped themselves in blankets, and the Physicist began to pitch their tent, inflating the canvas until it was a taut hemisphere with a small entrance at the ground. He walked around looking for rocks to hold down the edges of the tent—they had pegs, but nothing to drive them with. All he could find were small chips, so he returned empty-handed and rejoined the others sitting around the blue glimmer. Then his gaze fell on the heavy object that they had brought with them from the "factory." He anchored the tent with that.

"At least it's useful for something," said the Doctor, watching.

The Engineer sat hunched over, his head in his hands, a picture of dejection. He said nothing, and even when receiving his plate of food only grunted. Then, unexpectedly, he stood up and asked, "Well, and what now?"

"We go to sleep, of course." The Doctor solemnly took a cigarette from his pack, lit it, and inhaled with obvious pleasure.

"And tomorrow?" asked the Engineer.

"Henry, you're acting like a child," said the Captain, cleaning the saucepan with a handful of sandy earth. "Tomorrow we'll investigate more of the factory. Today we must have covered a quarter of a mile."

"And you think we'll find something different?"

"I don't know. We'll have the whole morning. In the afternoon we return to the ship."

"Wonderful," grumbled the Engineer. He stretched, groaned. "I feel as if I've been beaten."

"So do we," the Doctor assured him good-humoredly. "But listen, you really can't tell us anything about this?" He pointed the glowing tip of his cigarette at the barely visible shape holding down the tent.

"Of course. Isn't it obvious? It's a device to—"

"No, seriously. After all, the thing has so many parts. But this is not my line."

"And you think it's mine?!" the Engineer exploded. "It's the work of a lunatic, or, rather"—he pointed in the direction of the factory—"lunatics. A civilization of lunatics, that's what this damned Eden is!" Then he added calmly: "The object we hauled here was manufactured by a whole series of processes—compression, segmentation, thermal treatment, polishing. It's made of polymers, inorganic crystals. What it's for, I have no idea. It's a part, not a whole. But even as a part, taken out of this crackbrained mill, it looks crazy to me."

"What do you mean?" asked the Captain. The Chemist, having put away the utensils, was spreading out his blanket. The Doctor extinguished his cigarette and carefully put the unsmoked half back in his pocket.

"I have no proof. There are power cells, units of some kind, in there—not connected to anything. Like a closed circuit, but crisscrossed by a strange insulating substance. This thing . . . cannot function. That's how it looks to me. After a number of years a man develops a kind of professional intuition. I could be mistaken, but . . . no, I'd rather not talk about that."

The Captain got up. The others followed his example. When they extinguished the stove, they were plunged into total darkness. The stars above sparkled intensely in what seemed a peculiarly low sky.

"Deneb," said the Physicist softly. The men looked up.

"Where? There?" asked the Doctor. Unconsciously they lowered their voices.

"Yes. And the smaller star nearby is Gamma Cygni. Very bright!"

"About three times brighter than on Earth," said the Captain.

"We're a long way from home," muttered the Doctor. Nobody said anything more. One by one they crawled into the round tent. They were so tired that, when the Doctor said his customary "Good night," deep breathing was the only reply.

He lay awake, thinking. Were they being careless? What if something nasty crawled out of the neighboring scrub during the night? They should have posted a sentry. For a while the Doctor considered getting up and standing guard, but then he smiled his ironic smile in the darkness, turned over with a sigh, and fell sound asleep.

The morning greeted them with sunshine. There were more white cumulus clouds in the sky than before. The men ate little breakfast, saving the rest of their food for a final meal before returning to the ship.

"If only I could wash!" the Cyberneticist complained. "I stink. There must be water here somewhere!"

"Where there's water, there must be a barber," the Doctor added, peering into a small mirror and grimacing. "Only I'm afraid that on this planet a barber, after shaving you, would put all the hairs back."

"You'll joke on your deathbed," the Engineer said.

"Well," replied the Doctor, "that's not a bad way to go."

They gathered their things, deflated and packed the tent, and set off along the undulating screen, until they were almost a mile from their campsite.

"Maybe I'm mistaken, but the wall seems a bit higher here," said the Physicist, squinting at the ripples going in both directions. Higher up, they shimmered, like silver.

The men put their packs down in one pile and entered the factory without incident, as on the previous day. The Physicist and the Cyberneticist were the last to enter.

"How does that disappearing work?" asked the Cyberneticist. "So much happened yesterday, I forgot all about it."

"Something to do with refraction," the Physicist replied, without conviction.

"And what supports the roof? It can't be that." He pointed to the rippling curtain before them.

"I don't know. Maybe the supports are inside somewhere, or on the other side."

"*Alice in Wonderland,*" the Doctor's voice greeted them. "Shall we begin? I seem to be sneezing less today. Perhaps we're adapting. Which way do we go first?"

The place was similar to what they had seen the day before. They walked through it now with greater confidence and speed. At first it seemed that everything was the same: the columns, the wells, the forest of pulsing tubes, the incandescence, the whole flickering confusion of processes taking place at different tempos. But the "finished products," whose troughlike receptacle it took them a while to discover, were not the same; they were larger and shaped differently from those of yesterday. And that was not all.

These "products," which were also being reclaimed and recycled, were not identical. They all resembled half of an egg, each notched at the top and with various details

47

that indicated it was to be joined to other things. The half-egg also had protruding pipes, in the mouths of which were lens-shaped pieces that moved like valves. But some of the objects had two pipes, and others three or four. The additional pipes were smaller and often seemed unfinished, as though work on them had been interrupted. Sometimes a lens filled the entire bore of a pipe, sometimes only part of it, and sometimes there was no lens, or only the "bud" of one, a particle hardly bigger than a pea. The surface of the half-egg was smooth, polished.

And the pipes varied in other ways: in one half-egg the men found two pipes fused together and communicating through a small opening, their lenses forming something in the nature of a figure eight. The Doctor called this "Siamese Twins." And the mouths of some small pipes were closed.

"What do you say to this?" asked the Captain, kneeling as the Engineer worked his way through an entire collection fished out of the trough.

"For the time being, nothing. Let's move on," said the Engineer, getting up. But it was obvious that his spirits were improved.

They now saw that the hall was divided into sections, according to the process being performed in the cycle. The production mechanisms themselves—such as the forest of esophaguslike tubes—were everywhere the same. Half a mile farther on, the men came to a section that, while going through the same motions as the one before, carried nothing in its tubes, deposited nothing into its wells, and absorbed, treated, and melted nothing. Thinking at first that the product was so transparent as to be invisible, the Engineer leaned over to a chute and put out his hand to catch what should have been dropping out, but there was indeed nothing.

"This is crazy," said the Chemist.

But somehow the Engineer was not that surprised. "Interesting," he said, and they walked on.

They approached an area of increasing noise. It was a dull noise, but deafening—as of millions of heavy, wet pieces of leather dropping on a huge untightened drum. Then the noise became more distinct.

From dozens of club-shaped, quivering stalactites hanging from the ceiling overhead, a veritable hail of black objects fell, and were deflected, now on one side, now on the other, by inflated gray membranes, like bladders, then were snatched in midair by fast arms and arranged neatly at the bottom, side by side, in quadrangles and straight rows. Every so often a huge thing, the size of a whale's head, would emerge and with a long sigh suck in several rows of "finished product" at a time.

"The storehouse," the Engineer explained. "They arrive from above—that's a kind of conveyor—and are collected and returned to the cycle."

"How do you know they're returned?" asked the Physicist.

"Because the storehouse is full."

Nobody really understood this, but they said nothing and continued on.

It was almost four o'clock when the Captain gave the order to leave. They were in a section consisting of two parts. The first part produced rough disks equipped with handles; the second cut off the handles and attached elliptical rings in their place, whereupon the disks journeyed underground and returned smooth—"clean-shaven," as the Doctor said—in order to have ear-shaped handles affixed to them again.

When the men came out on the plain, the sun was strong, still high overhead. As they walked to the spot where they had left their tent and packs, the Engineer said, "Well, it's beginning to make sense."

"Really?" the Chemist sneered.

The Captain nodded and turned to the Doctor. "How would you describe it?" he asked.

"A corpse," the Doctor said.

"What do you mean, a corpse?" asked the Chemist, who was still in the dark.

"An animated corpse," the Doctor added. They went on a bit farther in silence.

"Is someone going to explain or not?" asked the Chemist, irritated.

"It's an automated complex for the production of miscellaneous parts, which eventually, in the course of time, went completely out of kilter, because it was left unsupervised," the Engineer said.

"Ah! And how long ago, do you think . . . ?"

"That I don't know."

"A rough guess . . . several decades," said the Cyberneticist.

"Or even longer. I wouldn't be surprised if the complex was abandoned two hundred years ago."

"Or a thousand years ago," the Captain said.

"Management computing systems fail at a rate corresponding to the coefficient—" the Cyberneticist began, but was interrupted by the Engineer:

"Their systems may operate on different lines from ours; they may not even be electronic. Personally, I don't think they are. The elements are nonmetallic, semifluid."

"Never mind that," said the Doctor. "What do you think the prospects are? Myself, I'd say they're poor."

"You mean the planet's inhabitants?" asked the Chemist.

"That's precisely what I mean."

III

It was late at night when they reached the knoll where their ship was. To travel faster, and also to avoid meeting any denizens of the copse, they went by way of an area where the vegetation parted to form a lane about sixty feet wide, as though an enormous plow had gone through. Nothing grew here but a velvety lichen and moss.

Hungry, tired, with only one flashlight, they decided to pitch their tent outside the ship. The Physicist had such a terrible thirst—their water supply had run out on the trek back—that he entered the tunnel and went into the ship. He was gone a long time. They were inflating the tent when they heard him shouting in the tunnel. They hurried over and helped him out. He was trembling, so upset that he couldn't speak.

"What happened? Calm down!" they shouted. The Captain grabbed him firmly by the shoulders.

The Physicist pointed to the hull looming above them. "There was something in there."

"What was it?"

"I have no idea."

"How do you know something was there?"

"I entered the navigation room by mistake. It was full of soil before, and now the soil is gone."

"Gone? Where is it?"

"I don't know."

"You looked into the other rooms?"

"Yes. I . . . wasn't sure that the navigation room had been full of soil, so at first I dismissed the thought, and went to the storeroom, where I found some drinking water, but I didn't have a cup, so I tried your cabin"—he glanced at the Cyberneticist—"and there . . ."

"What was it, damn it?!"

"Everything was covered with mucus."

"Mucus?"

"Sticky, transparent mucus—I must still have some of it on my boots!"

"But that could have been something leaking from the tanks, a chemical reaction. Remember, half our instruments in the laboratory were smashed."

"Ridiculous! Look at my boots!"

The Doctor's flashlight wandered down to the boots in question, which in places gleamed, as though coated with polyurethane.

"But that doesn't mean we had a visitor," said the Chemist lamely.

"It didn't sink in at first," the Physicist went on. "I took a cup and returned to the storeroom. I felt my soles sticking, but paid no attention. I had a drink of water, and on my way back suddenly decided to check the library—I don't know why. I was uneasy. I opened the door and— no soil, not a trace! But I had dumped that soil myself! And then I knew that the soil had disappeared in the navigation room, too."

"And then?" asked the Captain.

"I ran back here."

The flashlight illuminated the patch of ground where the men stood around the Physicist, who was still out of breath.

"Do we go in, or what?" asked the Chemist, though it was obvious that he was not volunteering.

"Let me see those boots again," said the Captain.

He almost banged his head against the Doctor's when the latter bent over simultaneously. They exchanged glances. Neither said a word.

"We have to do something," the Cyberneticist said desperately, as the Captain carefully examined the shiny layer that clung to the leather.

"All that happened was that a specimen of local fauna entered the ship and, finding nothing of interest, left," said the Captain at last.

"Some worm, perhaps, the size of a shark or two," the Cyberneticist babbled. "But what about the soil?"

"Yes, that is strange. . . ."

The Doctor began to pace, then walked away. The beam of his flashlight swept the ground, then went higher, into the darkness.

Suddenly he shouted, "Here, I've found it!"

They ran over to him. He was standing near a furrow about thirty feet long that in places was covered by bits of shiny membrane.

"It looks as if it really was a worm," said the Physicist in a low voice.

"In that case we'll have to spend the night in the ship," the Captain decided.

"But we'll have to search the ship thoroughly before we can close the hatch."

"That will take all night!" groaned the Chemist.

"It can't be helped."

They left the tent to the mercy of whatever might be out there and went into the tunnel.

Every nook and cranny of the ship was inspected. The Physicist thought that pieces of broken panel in the control room had been moved, but no one was sure. Then the Engineer began to wonder if the tools used to dig the tunnel were in the same position in which they had left them.

"Look," said the Doctor impatiently, "we can't start playing detective now—it's almost two!"

At three they lay down on mattresses removed from the bunks, and it would have been even later had the Engineer not decided to forgo checking both levels of the engine room and simply to bolt from inside the doors leading to it in the steel bulkhead. The air was close, with an unpleasant lingering odor, but they were dropping with fatigue, and no sooner did they take off their boots and suits and extinguish the light than they fell into a heavy sleep.

The Doctor woke in total darkness. He raised his watch to his eyes—and was confused for a moment, because the time did not correspond to the darkness, but then he remembered that he was underground in the ship. The green dial said it was almost eight. Why did he wake so early? He grumbled to himself and was about to turn over when he froze.

Something was happening in the depths of the ship. He could feel it more than hear it: the floor throbbed. There was a distant thrumming, barely audible. He sat up, his heart pounding.

"It's come back!" he thought, imagining the creature whose slimy trail the Physicist had discovered. "It's trying to force open the entrance hatch."

The ship suddenly shuddered, as though some huge hand were trying to push it still deeper into the ground. One member of the crew groaned in his sleep. For a moment the Doctor felt his hair stand on end: the ship weighed sixteen thousand tons! The floor started shaking in a rapid, irregular rhythm. Then he understood. It was one of the drive units! Someone had got it going!

"Everybody up!" he shouted, groping for the flashlight.

The crew sprang to their feet, stumbling into one another in the dark and shouting, until the Doctor finally found the flashlight and turned it on. In a few words he explained.

The Engineer, still groggy, listened to the sound. The ship began to shake, and a mounting groan filled the air. "The air compressors in the port nozzles!" he cried.

The Captain said nothing as he zipped up his suit, and the others dressed hurriedly, but the Engineer ran out into the corridor as he was, in an undershirt and shorts, snatching the flashlight from the Doctor's hand on the way.

"What are you going to do?"

They hurried after him as he ran to the navigation room. The floor shook more and more violently. "Any moment now it'll snap the blades," he muttered, bursting into the room that had been cleared by the intruder. He rushed over to the main terminals and threw the switch.

A light went on in the corner. The Engineer and the Captain, now together, took the jector from the locker, removed it from its case, and connected it to the terminals as quickly as they could. The dials were broken, but the tube on the barrel showed bright blue. There was current; the jector was charging!

The floor shook so much that the metal tools on the shelves rattled, and a glass object fell off and shattered. Then suddenly all was still, and the light went out.

"Is it charged?" asked the Physicist.

"For two rounds at most. We're lucky to have even

that," answered the Engineer, and tore the jector from the terminals, pointed its aluminum barrel toward the ground, and, clasping the handle, went out into the corridor and made for the engine room. They were halfway there, near the library, when there was an ungodly grating, and two or three convulsive jerks rocked the ship. Something in the engine room raised an ear-piercing din, and then another silence followed.

The Engineer and the Captain reached the armored door together. The Captain slid aside the peephole cover and looked in.

"Let me have the flashlight," he said.

The Doctor immediately put it in his hand, but it was difficult to direct light through the narrow aperture and see at the same time. The Engineer opened a second peephole, put his eye to it—and gasped.

"It's lying there," he said after a long pause.

"What?"

"Our visitor. Give me more light, lower, that's it! It's not moving." Then: "The thing's as big as an elephant."

"Has it touched the manifold track?" asked the Captain, who could see nothing.

"It appears to have got into the power lines instead. I can see . . . ends jutting out from under it."

"Ends of what?" The Physicist, behind them, was growing impatient.

"High-tension cables. It's still not moving. Shall we open the door?"

"We have to," the Doctor said, and shoved the main bolt aside.

"Maybe it's playing dead," suggested someone in back.

The other bolts slid smoothly in their mounts, and the door opened. No one crossed the threshold—the Physicist and the Cyberneticist looked over the shoulders of the men in front of them. Inside, on fragments of the shattered screen, squeezed between partition walls that had been forced aside, lay a naked humpbacked mass, glistening. Now and then a tremor ran across its surface.

"It's alive," whispered the Physicist.

There was a sharp, foul stench like that of burning horsehair, and wisps of bluish smoke curled in the beam of the flashlight.

"Just in case," said the Engineer, and raised the jector, pressing the stock to his hip and aiming at the shapeless mass. With a hiss the shot hit the steeply arched hulk right below its hump. The huge body stiffened, swelled, and seemed to cave in a little, to flatten. The partition walls shuddered, buckling on either side under the body's weight.

"Finis," declared the Engineer, crossing the steel threshold.

They went in. They tried—unsuccessfully—to locate the creature's legs and head. It lay on a detached part of the transformer, an inert, shapeless mass, its hump to one side, like a sack filled with jelly. The Doctor touched the side of the dead body, then brought his hand to his nose.

"Smell this," he said, holding out his hand to them; something like a white glue glistened on his fingertips. The Chemist was the first to sniff it. He cried out in surprise.

"You recognize it?" asked the Doctor.

They all smelled the glue—and recognized the acrid stink that had filled the "factory."

In a corner the Doctor found a bar he could use as a lever, slipped one end of it under the creature, and tried to turn the thing over. But the bar, instead, went almost halfway into the flesh.

"Wait," said the Engineer. "How could an animal like this have got the unit going?"

Everyone looked at him in dismay.

"You're right . . ." muttered the Physicist.

"We have to turn this thing over," the Doctor insisted. "Come on, everyone together, on the same side. That's it, don't be squeamish! Now what?"

"Hold on," said the Engineer. He went out, and returned a moment later with the steel poles they had used to dig the tunnel. These were slipped under the body and, at the Doctor's command, all lifted. The Cyberneticist shuddered when his hand slid down the slippery metal and touched the skin. With a dreadful smack the creature was rolled over on its side. Everyone jumped back. Someone shouted.

As from a gigantic, elongated oyster, a small two-armed trunk emerged between the thick, fleshy folds that closed winglike around it; dangling, its knotty fingers touched the floor. The thing, no bigger than a child's head, swayed back and forth, slower and slower, suspended from pale-yellow ligament membranes, until finally it came to rest. The Doctor was the first to pluck up the courage to approach it. He grasped the end of a limp, multijointed arm, and the small veined torso turned, revealing a flat, eyeless face with gaping nostrils and something jagged, like a tongue bitten in two, in the place where a man's mouth would be.

"An inhabitant of Eden . . ." whispered the Chemist.

The Engineer, too shaken to speak, sat down on the generator shaft and began wiping his hands unconsciously on his suit, over and over again.

"So is this one creature or two?" asked the Physicist, who was watching closely as the Doctor carefully touched the chest of the lifeless "man."

"Two in one or one in two—or maybe they're symbionts. It could even be that they separate at times."

"Like that horror with that single hanging black hair?"

suggested the Physicist. The Doctor nodded and continued his examination.

"But this monster has no legs, no eyes, not even a head!" said the Engineer. He lit a cigarette—something he never did.

"That remains to be seen," replied the Doctor. "I suppose you won't mind if I dissect it? We'll have to cut up the thing anyway to get it out of here. I'd be grateful for an assistant, though this might be . . . unpleasant. Any volunteers?"

The Captain and the Cyberneticist stepped forward.

The Doctor stood up. "Good. I'll look for instruments—which will take a while. I must say, if the plot keeps thickening like this, a man will need a week to polish his shoes. We can't seem to finish anything we start."

The Engineer and the Physicist went out into the corridor. The Captain, returning from the first-aid room in a rubber apron and with his sleeves rolled up, carrying a nickel-plated tray full of surgical instruments, stopped and frowned at them.

"You know about the purifier. If you want to smoke, go outside."

So they made for the tunnel, and the Chemist joined them. Just to be safe, he took along the jector, which the Engineer had left in the engine room.

"How could that weird animal have set the generator going?" wondered the Engineer. He rubbed his cheeks: the stubble was so long that it didn't feel prickly. Everyone was growing a beard. They didn't seem to have the time to shave.

"At least the generator produced some current. That means the windings are sound."

"What about the short circuit?"

"It blew a fuse, that's all. The mechanical components

are completely broken, but we'll get around that. As for the sockets, we have spares—it's only a matter of finding them. Theoretically we could repair the cylinder, too, but without the proper tools that would take forever. I think the reason I didn't make a thorough inspection at first was that I feared everything had been pulverized. You know what our position would have been."

"The reactor . . ." the Chemist began, but the Engineer grimaced.

"The reactor is another matter. We'll get to the reactor. First we need current. Without current we can do nothing. The leak in the cooling system can be fixed in five minutes, by spot-welding. But for that, too, I need current."

"You're going to work on the machinery . . . now?" asked the Physicist, hope in his voice.

"Yes. We'll decide on the sequence of repairs—I've already spoken to the Captain about that. First we need at least one working unit. Of course, we'll have to risk reactivating the unit without atomic energy. God knows how! With a capstan arrangement, perhaps . . . I have no idea how long the electronic controls were out, or what's going on in the pile."

"The neutron irises can function independently," said the Physicist. "The pile automatically went into idle. Of course, too high a temperature, if the cooling system went, may have . . ."

"Wonderful! The neutron irises are fine, but the pile may have melted!"

They argued, drawing diagrams in the sand with their fingers, until the Doctor stuck his head out of the tunnel entrance and called to them. They jumped to their feet.

"Well, what did you learn?"

"Not very much in one respect, but in another quite a lot," replied the Doctor, who looked peculiar, only his head showing above the ground as he spoke. "I'm still not sure whether it's one creature or two. In any case it's an animal. It possesses two circulatory systems, but they're not entirely separate. The big creature—the carrier—seems to have traveled by hopping or striding."

"There's a big difference," said the Engineer.

"True," the Doctor agreed. "As for the hump, it turned out to contain the digestive tract."

"A stomach on its back?"

"That wasn't its back. When the current hit it, it fell belly-up."

"Then the smaller creature was like a rider," the Engineer said.

"Yes, in a sense it rode the carrier piggyback. Or not piggyback," the Doctor corrected himself. "More likely, it sat inside the larger body—there's a pouchlike nest there. The only thing to which I can compare it is a kangaroo's pouch, but the similarity is very slight and nonfunctional."

"And you're assuming that this was an intelligent creature?" said the Physicist.

"It had to be intelligent to open and shut doors, not to mention starting the generator," said the Doctor, for some reason remaining in the tunnel. "The only problem is that it has no nervous system in our sense of the word."

"How's that?!" The Cyberneticist jumped up.

"There are organs there," the Doctor went on, "whose purpose I can't even begin to fathom. There's a spinal cord, but in the cranium—a tiny cranium—there's no brain. There *is* something there, but any anatomist would laugh at me if I told him it was a brain. . . . A few glands, but they appear to be lymphatic—while near the lungs, and the creature has three lungs, I discovered the damnedest thing. Something I didn't like at all. I put it in alcohol—you can see it later.

"But now we have more urgent work. The engine room looks like a slaughterhouse. Everything will have to be taken out and buried, and since it's warm in the ship, haste is definitely advisable. You can cover your faces; the smell is not that bad, but with so much raw flesh . . ."

"You're joking?" the Physicist said.

"No."

Only now did the Doctor step out of the tunnel. His rubber apron and white smock were completely soaked in red.

"I'm sorry, the job might make you sick, but it has to be done. Come."

The gravedigging, as the Chemist referred to it, took them until the late afternoon. Working half naked to avoid staining their suits, they carried the dreadful stuff with whatever was at hand—buckets, litters—and buried the remains two hundred paces from the ship, at the top of the knoll; notwithstanding the Captain's plea to conserve water, they used five pails of it to wash themselves afterward. The creature's blood, before it coagulated, resembled that of humans, but then it turned orange and became powdery.

The weary crew stretched themselves out beside the ship in the setting sun. No one had an appetite, so they only drank a little coffee or water, then dozed off, one by one, without discussing how to begin the repair work. When they awoke, it was already dark. Again they had to go down to the storeroom for provisions, open cans, light a stove, cook, eat, and wash dishes. At midnight they decided, since everyone felt sufficiently rested, not to sleep but to begin tackling the repairs.

Their hearts beat faster as they removed the plastic and metal debris from the generator cover, using crowbars when necessary. They spent hours digging through rubble in search of missing parts, until finally the auxiliary generator was put in working order; they replaced the shattered socket with a new one, and the Engineer fixed the air compressor, resorting to a trick as simple as it was primitive: since there were not enough spare blades, he simply removed every other blade. The motor would operate with reduced efficiency, but it would operate. At three in the morning the Captain told them to stop.

"We'll have to go on more expeditions," he said, "to replenish our water supply, and for other reasons as well. So we should maintain our normal sleeping pattern. Let's sleep until dawn and then get to work again."

The rest of the night passed uneventfully. In the morning nobody expressed any desire to go up outside; everyone was anxious to get on with the repairs. The Engineer had by now put together a basic tool set, so there was no need to go running off to all the cabins in search of a wrench.

First they checked the distributor, which was so full of short circuits that they practically had to rebuild it from scratch, cannibalizing other broken units for parts. Then they set about getting the generator to start properly. The plan that the Engineer had decided on was risky: to turn the dynamos using as a turbine an air compressor driven by an oxygen cylinder. Under normal conditions the emergency unit would have been activated by high-pressure water vapor from the reactor, since the reactor, as the heart of the ship, was the most protected part. But that, with the total destruction of the circuits, was now entirely out of the question. So they would have to use their reserve oxygen. But this was not the desperate measure it might seem to be, because they were counting on being able to fill the tanks with atmospheric oxygen once the engine room was working. There was no other way: to activate the atomic pile without electricity would have been madness. But the Engineer, though he mentioned it to no one, was prepared to take even this step, if the oxygen plan failed—because it was possible that the compressed gas would run out before the pile was activated.

The Doctor, standing in a tiny gallery directly beneath the engine-room platform, called out the falling pressure readings on the oxygen manometers, while the other five men worked above him feverishly. The Physicist was stationed at a control board so makeshift that any Earth-based technician would have gasped in horror. The Engineer hung upside down beneath the generator ring, black with grease, fastening the contact brushes. And the Captain and the Cyberneticist watched the dial of the neutron counter, while the Chemist rushed back and forth like a messenger boy, delivering tools.

The oxygen hissed, and the air compressor made angry noises, rattling, because the rotor the Engineer had jury-rigged was poorly balanced. The RPM of the generator increased, and its wail went up in pitch. The lights suspended by cables from the ceiling now emitted a powerful white glare.

"Two hundred and eighteen, two hundred and two, one hundred and ninety-five," came the muffled voice of the invisible Doctor.

The Engineer crawled out from under the dynamo, wiping the grease and sweat from his unshaven face. "Ready," he panted. His hands trembled from exertion.

"I'm switching on the first one," the Physicist said.

"One hundred and seventy, one hundred and sixty-three, one hundred and sixty," the Doctor continued, raising his voice to be heard over the whine. The dynamo was now producing current for the reactor and with each second required more oxygen to maintain its RPM.

"Full load!" groaned the Engineer, watching the dials.

"All right!" said the Physicist in a strangled voice, and,

crouching as if in anticipation of a blow, he pressed the black handles with both hands.

The Captain was gripping his arm harder, without realizing it. They stared as all the pointers rapidly rose toward the vertical: the one indicating neutron flux, the one indicating isotope contamination, and the thermopile. The dynamo howled, sparks flew from under the rings, but inside the pile, behind the thick walls of steel, there was silence. Those indicators did not move. Suddenly the Physicist saw them blur. He squeezed his eyes shut, and when he opened them saw that they were in working position.

"We did it!" he shouted, and began to sob, still clutching both handles. Suddenly he felt very weak. He had been expecting an explosion the whole time.

"The indicators must have jammed," the Captain said calmly, apparently unaware of the Physicist's emotion. But he spoke with difficulty—his jaws were still tightly clenched.

"Ninety, eighty-one, seventy-two . . ." the Doctor intoned.

"Now!" cried the Engineer, and with a gloved hand pulled the main switch. The generator groaned, slowed. The Engineer rushed to the air compressor and closed both intake valves.

"Forty-six, forty-six, forty-six," the Doctor repeated.

The turbine was no longer taking oxygen from the tank. The lights dimmed; it grew darker in the room.

"Forty-six, forty-six . . ." the Doctor intoned from under the platform. Suddenly the lights blazed. The dynamo now barely turned, but there was current; all the dials showed current.

"Forty-six . . . forty six . . ." repeated the Doctor, who, in the steel well of the gallery, knew nothing of what was going on. The Physicist sat down on the floor and covered his face with his hands. There was now almost total silence. The generator rumbled slightly as it ground slowly to a halt; that was all.

"The leakage?" asked the Captain.

"Normal," replied the Cyberneticist. "The robot must have managed to seal the pile before it shorted." He spoke dryly, but everyone knew how proud he was of the robot. He clasped his hands to keep them from trembling.

"Forty-six . . ." intoned the Doctor.

"Enough!" the Captain shouted into the steel well. "It's no longer necessary. The pile is producing current!"

After a moment the Doctor's pale face and dark beard appeared below them. "Really?" he asked, then broke into a noiseless laugh. As the men stared at the dials, he clambered up from the gallery and sat down next to the Physicist. Like the others, he watched the pointers all in working position. "Do you know what?" he said finally, in a youthful voice. Everybody looked at him, as if waking up. "I've never been so happy," he whispered and turned away.

I V

Just before nightfall the Captain went out on top with the Engineer to get a breath of fresh air. They sat down on a bank of upturned earth and fixed their eyes on the last visible sliver of the ruby-red solar disk.

"I wouldn't have believed it," murmured the Engineer.

"Nor I."

"That pile—they built it well."

"Solid Earth workmanship."

They said nothing for a while.

"It's a good start," said the Captain.

"Yes, but we've only done about a hundredth of what has to be done in order for the . . ."

"I know," the Captain replied calmly.

"And we still don't know if . . ."

"Yes, the steering nozzles, the whole lower deck."

"But we'll do it."

"Yes."

The Engineer's eyes stopped on a long mound at the

top of the knoll: the place where they had buried the creature. "I completely forgot . . ." he said in amazement. "It's as if it happened a year ago."

"I haven't. I've been thinking about it—about the creature—the whole time. Because of what the Doctor found in its lungs."

"What did he find?"

"A needle."

"A needle?!"

"Or not a needle—you can see for yourself. It's in a jar in the library. A piece of thin tubing, broken, with a sharp end, almost like something used to give injections."

The Engineer stood up. "It's curious, but somehow I don't find that interesting. I feel now like someone at a foreign airport, at a stopover of a few minutes, who mixes with the local crowd and sees strange, incomprehensible things but knows that he doesn't belong to the place and that soon he will be flying away. So to him it's all distant, indifferent."

"It won't be that soon. . . ."

"I know, but that's how I feel."

"Let's go back. We have to replace the stopgaps before we turn in. And install proper fuses. Then the pile can be put on idle."

"All right, let's go."

They spent the night in the ship, leaving the small lights on. Every so often one of the men would wake up, check with sleepy eyes to see if the bulbs were glowing, and fall asleep again, reassured.

In the morning, the first piece of equipment to be mobilized was the cleaning robot. Every quarter of an hour or so, it became helplessly stuck in the wreckage that obstructed everything. The Cyberneticist, armed with tools, would run after it, extricate it from the rubbish, removing pieces that had proved too large for the neck of the

68

grasper, then start the thing up again. The robot shuffled forward, took on the next heap of wreckage, and soon got stuck again. After breakfast the Doctor tried out his shaver. The result was a man in a bronze mask: the forehead and skin around the eyes were tanned, but the lower part of the face was white. Everyone followed his example.

"We should feed ourselves better," concluded the Chemist, surprised by his gaunt reflection in the mirror.

"What do you say to fresh game?" proposed the Cyberneticist.

The Chemist shuddered.

"No, thank you. Don't even mention it. I had nightmares about that . . . that . . ."

"That animal?"

"Animal or . . ."

"What else could it have been?"

"Can an animal start a generator?"

Everyone was listening to the conversation.

"All things at a higher level of development wear clothing of one form or another," said the Engineer, "and that doubler was naked."

"Interesting. You said 'naked,'" observed the Doctor. "So?"

"You wouldn't say that a cow or an ape was naked, would you?"

"That's because they have hair."

"A hippopotamus or a crocodile has no hair, yet you don't call them naked."

"So? It just seemed the right thing to say."

"Precisely."

They fell silent for a while.

"It's almost ten," said the Captain. "We've had a rest, so I think we should make another excursion now. In a different direction this time. The Engineer was supposed to prepare the jectors—how is that coming along?"

"We have five, and all are charged."

"Good. We went north before, let's try east now. And don't use the jectors unless you have to. Especially if we come across those . . . doublers, as the Engineer called them."

"Doublers," the Doctor muttered to himself, as if trying out the name and not liking it.

"Shall we go?" asked the Physicist.

"All right. But let's secure the hatch first, to avoid new surprises."

"Shouldn't we take the jeep?" asked the Cyberneticist.

"I'll need at least five hours to get it working," said the Engineer. "Unless we postpone the excursion until tomorrow?"

But no one wanted to postpone it, so they set off around eleven, after preparing their equipment. As if by arrangement—though no one had suggested it—they went in pairs and kept close together; the only man without a weapon, the Doctor, was in the middle pair. Whether the terrain was more walkable or they simply walked faster, they lost sight of the rocket in less than an hour. The landscape changed. There were more and more slender gray "calyxes," which they avoided, and in the distance, in the north, they saw hills that appeared domed and met the plain in steep crags. But the hills ahead of them, as they marched, were covered with patches of vegetation darker than the soil.

The vegetation rustled underfoot and was the color of ashes. The young shoots, however, were whitish veinlike tubes with small beads growing out of them.

"Do you know what I miss the most here?" said the Physicist. "Grass, ordinary grass. I would never have thought that grass would be so . . ." He groped for the word. ". . . necessary. . . ."

The sun was brutal. As they approached the hills, they could hear a soughing sound.

"Strange. There's no wind, but there's the sound of a wind," remarked the Chemist, who was in the first pair.

"It's coming from higher up," the Captain said, behind him. "Look, those are Earth trees!"

"They're a different color. . . ."

"They're two colors," said the Doctor, who had sharp eyes. "They alternate—now they're violet, now blue with yellow highlights."

The men left the plain and entered a broad canyon with clay walls that were covered with a delicate mist. On closer inspection the mist turned out to be a kind of lichen that resembled loose fiberglass insulation.

They looked up as they passed the first clump of trees, growing at the edge of a precipice about forty feet above their heads.

"But those aren't trees at all!" cried the Cyberneticist with disappointment, at the end of the line.

The "trees" had thick, extremely shiny trunks, as though they had been greased, and multilayered crowns that pulsed rhythmically, darkening, then expanding and paling, letting the sunlight through in a hundred tiny places. This was accompanied by a sound, as though a chorus were whispering, over and over again, "fsss . . . hhaaa . . . fsss . . . hhaaa. . . ." Then they noticed, on the nearest tree, growing out of its twisting branches, blisters as long as bananas and swollen with grapelike excrescences that puffed and darkened, collapsed and paled, puffed and darkened, collapsed and paled.

"It's breathing," the Engineer murmured. He listened raptly to the sounds that drifted down and filled the canyon.

"But observe that each has a rhythm of its own," the

71

Doctor cried, excited. "The shorter it is, the faster it breathes! They are . . . lung-trees!"

"Let's keep moving!" called the Captain, who was a dozen or so paces ahead of the standing group.

They followed him. The canyon narrowed, and its floor led gradually uphill, bringing them to a domed rise between two clumps of trees.

"When you shut your eyes, it's like being at the seashore. Try it!" the Physicist said to the Engineer.

"I'll keep my eyes open, thanks," muttered the Engineer in reply. He left their line of march and made for the highest point on the rise.

Before them now lay a rolling landscape with copses of breathing trees here and there, olive and russet. There were hillocks with clay slopes the color of honey and patches of moss that were silver in the sun and gray-green in the shade. The whole expanse was crisscrossed by thin, narrow lines that went in different directions. They ran through the valleys but avoided the hills. Some were reddish, some white, as though strewn with sand, and some were black as coal.

"Roads!" exclaimed the Engineer, but corrected himself immediately. "No, they're too narrow for roads. . . . What could they be?"

"We found something similar beyond the spider grove," said the Chemist, raising binoculars to his eyes.

"No, that was different," the Cyberneticist began.

"Look! Look!" The Doctor's shouts made them all jump.

Something transparent was gliding along a yellow line that passed, descending, between two hillocks half a mile away. The thing shone pale in the sunlight; it was like a semitransparent wheel with spokes, rotating. When it appeared against the sky, it became almost invisible, but farther down, at the foot of a clay escarpment, it gleamed more clearly, a spinning cloud, and shot off in a straight line past a clump of breathing trees—and vanished into the mouth of a distant canyon.

The Doctor turned to his colleagues, his eyes bright, his teeth bared, as if smiling, but there was no gaiety in his face. "Interesting, no?"

"Damn, I forgot my binoculars. Give me yours," said the Engineer, turning to the Cyberneticist. "Never mind," he added, because it was too late.

The Cyberneticist hefted his jector. "We're not well armed," he mumbled.

"Why, do you think we're going to be attacked?" asked the Chemist, glaring at him.

They said nothing for a while, staring at the scene around them.

"Well, let's move on," the Cyberneticist suggested.

"Yes," said the Captain. "Wait! There's another!"

A second cloud, moving much faster than the first, snaked in and out of the hills. It kept low to the ground. When it came straight in their direction, they lost sight of it altogether; it was only when it turned that the blurred, revolving disk again became visible.

"Some kind of vehicle . . ." muttered the Physicist, putting his hand on the Engineer's shoulder but not taking his eyes off the gleaming cloud, which grew smaller and smaller as it retreated among the copses.

"I have a Ph.D.," said the Engineer, as if to himself, "but this . . . Anyway, there is something inside there, convex, like the hub of a propeller."

"Yes, and it's brighter than the rest," said the Captain. "How big do you think the craft is?"

"If the trees down there are the same height as the ones above the canyon, then I would say at least thirty feet in diameter."

The Doctor pointed to a line of hills. "Both of them disappeared there. So we should head in that direction, agreed?" And he began to descend the slope. The others hurried after him.

"We'd better prepare ourselves for contact," said the Cyberneticist, nervously licking his lips.

"We have no idea what form it will take. The best thing is to remain calm, to exercise self-control," said the Captain. "But we should change formation. One man in front, one in the rear, and let's spread out a bit more."

"Do we have to stay in the open?" asked the Physicist. "It might be better if we were less visible."

"We don't want to conceal ourselves too much. That will look suspicious. But, true, the more we observe without being observed, the better. . . ."

After descending a few hundred feet, they came to the first of the lines.

It resembled a furrow made by an old-fashioned plow; the soil, crumbly, had been thrown up on both sides of a groove no more than two hands wide. The sunken, moss-covered strips that they had encountered on their first expedition had been of similar dimensions, but here there was no moss, only bare, broken ground that ran through a uniform cover of whitish overgrowth.

"Strange," grumbled the Engineer, rising from his haunches. He wiped his hands on his suit.

"The grooves to the north, I think, are older," said the Doctor, "and haven't been used for a long time. While these . . ."

"That's possible," agreed the Physicist. "But what made this? Not a wheel—the track of a wheel would be totally different."

"Some sort of agricultural machine?" the Cyberneticist suggested.

"Why would they plow to a depth of four inches?"

They stepped across the line and walked on. As they passed a wooded copse, whose noise made it difficult even to carry on a conversation, they heard a piercing whistle from behind and instinctively dived behind some trees. From their concealment they saw, high above the meadow, a luminous perpendicular vortex traveling at the velocity of an express train. Its rim was darker, and the bright center shone violet, orange, violet, orange. The diameter of the center was from six to eight feet.

The craft rushed past and was gone. They continued in the same direction. When the copse came to an end, they were obliged to cross open country, which made them uncomfortable. They kept looking over their shoulders. The chain of hills was already quite close when they heard another piercing whistle. There being no cover whatsoever, they dropped to the ground. A gyrating disk hurtled by, its center a deep blue.

"That one must have been more than fifty feet high!" the Engineer hissed excitedly. They got up and dusted themselves off. Between them and the hills lay a hollow that was exactly bisected by a strangely colored ribbon: a brook with a bright, sandy bottom visible through the water. The flowing water was bordered on both sides by a strip of iridescent blue vegetation, followed by another strip of pale rose and, after that, thin silver plants that were interspersed with fluffy spheres as big as a man's head; above each sphere rose the three-lobed chalice of an enormous flower white as snow.

The men approached this unusual collection of colors. When they reached the fluffy spheres, the nearest flowers suddenly started quivering and slowly lifted into the air. They floated overhead for a while in a flock, emitting a soft hum, then soared upward, whirling and gleaming in the sun, and alighted in a thicket of spheres on the other side of the brook. Where the brook intersected the furrow, its banks were lined by an arch of a glassy substance perforated at regular intervals by circular openings. The

Engineer tested the strength of this bridge with his foot and gingerly crossed to the other side. As soon as he got there, a host of white flowers flew up from under his feet and circled above him anxiously like startled pigeons.

At the brook the men stopped to fill their canteens with water. Not for drinking, obviously, but to run tests on it later. The Doctor plucked one of the small plants that formed the rose strip and put it in his buttonhole, like a flower. Its stem was covered with tiny translucent flesh-colored nodes whose fragrance was exquisite. No one said so, but they were sorry to leave such a beautiful spot.

The hillside they ascended was overgrown with mosses that rustled underfoot.

"There's something at the top!" the Captain said. Against the sky, a vague shape moved. There were blinding flashes of light. Several hundred feet from the summit, they saw the object, a low revolving dome. On its surface were mirrors that reflected now the sun, now fragments of the landscape.

Running their eyes along the ridge, they noticed another, similar dome—or, rather, guessed its presence by its regular flashing. And there were more and more such points, sparkling along the ridge as far as the horizon.

From the top of the hill, they were finally able to gaze into the interior of a region hitherto unseen. The gentle slopes became fields crisscrossed by rows of pointed masts. The farthest masts blurred at the foot of a blue edifice made indistinct by the intervening atmosphere. Above the nearest masts the air roiled in vertical columns, as if from intense heat. Between their rows went dozens of grooves, all leading in the same direction, to the east. There, on the horizon, in a hazy mosaic of irregular angles, towers, and gold and silver spires, lay a multitude of buildings which, because of the distance, merged into a glimmering bluish mass. The sky was not as bright there, and in some places milky vapor poured into it and spread mushroom-like into a thin layer of cloud, in which, when they strained their eyes to the limit, they could see tiny black points appearing and disappearing.

"A city . . ." whispered the Engineer.

"I saw it, before we crashed . . ." said the Captain, at his side.

They began the descent. The first row of masts or pylons lay across their path at the bottom of the slope. These were pitch-black cones at the base, which, about ten feet above the ground, continued as semitransparent poles each with a central pin of some kind of metal. The air shimmered overhead, and they could hear a hollow, steady droning.

"Vents?" the Physicist asked.

They touched the cone bases, cautiously at first, then more boldly. There was no vibration.

"I feel no air current," said the Engineer. "Perhaps these are emitters. . . ."

They proceeded across gently undulating fields. The city was no longer in view, but there was no way they could get lost: the masts and the grooves both indicated the direction. Occasionally a luminous, spinning vehicle flew by, but always so far away that they made no attempt to conceal themselves.

A copse appeared up ahead, an olive-yellow patch of trees. At first they thought to go around it, as the row of masts did, but since it extended so far on both sides, they decided to cut through it instead.

Breathing trees surrounded them. Dry leaves crunched underfoot at every step, and the soil beneath them was covered with little tube plants and white moss. Pale, spiked flowers protruded here and there from among thick roots. Droplets of aromatic resin trickled down rough trunks.

The Engineer, at the head of the column, slowed down and said, "Damn! We shouldn't have come this way."

A deep hollow opened up between the trees; on its loamy walls were festoons of long, snakelike vines. The men had gone too far to turn back now, so they climbed down, using the vines, to the bottom of the hollow, where a thread of water flowed. The opposite wall was too steep, so they followed the bottom, looking for a place to climb up. After about a hundred feet, the sides became lower, and the light improved.

"What's that?" the Engineer asked suddenly. A breeze brought a sweetish, unpleasant smell, as of something burning. They halted. Speckles of sunlight moved across them; then it grew darker again. The canopy of trees rustled high overhead.

"There's something nearby," whispered the Engineer.

By now they could climb the other side, but instead, keeping close together and crouching slightly, they continued toward the thicket at the end of the hollow, through which they saw, when occasionally the breeze moved stalks aside, a pale, elongated mass. The ground grew muddy and squished, but they paid no attention to that. When the stalks, covered with racemose gnarls, were parted, the men beheld a sunny clearing. Through the clearing ran a single groove, which terminated in a ditch at a right angle to it and lined with upturned clay. They stood stock-still at the edge of the thicket. The stalks rustled as they rubbed against the men's suits, touching them lazily with their gnarls and then withdrawing, as if repelled. The crew stared.

The waxy heap along the edge of the ditch at first appeared to be a homogeneous mass. The men could barely breathe, the stench was so bad. Then they began to distinguish separate figures. Some creatures lay with their humps upward, others on their side; frail torsos with small upturned faces were wedged in between huge muscles, and massive trunks lay intermingled with tiny hands, knotty fingers, that dangled limply. The swollen bodies were covered with damp yellow patches. The Doctor gripped the men on either side of him so tightly that they would have cried out, had they been aware of him.

Slowly the men stepped forward, arms linked, eyes fixed on what filled the ditch. The ditch was big. Thick drops of fluid, glistening in the sunlight, trickled down waxy backs and sides, and collected in the sunken, eyeless faces. The men thought they could hear the sound of dripping.

An approaching whistle made them jump, and in a second they had rushed back to the thicket and dived through the vegetation to the ground, clutching their jectors. The stalks were still swaying when the whirling column appeared shining in the air between the trees opposite the men and entered the clearing.

It slowed when it was about a dozen feet from the ditch, but its whistle grew louder, and a strong wind blew around it. The craft circled the ditch. Suddenly clay exploded into the air, and a reddish cloud covered the luminous disk halfway up. A shower of fragments rained down on the thicket and on the men hugging the ground. They heard a ghastly sound, as though a gigantic spur were ripping wet canvas, and then the disk had reached the other end of the clearing and was returning. For a moment it halted, the whirling column shifting slightly to the right, to the left, as if taking aim, then suddenly accelerated, and the other side of the ditch was hidden in a cloud of exploding clay. The disk hummed, shuddered, appeared to be expanding. The men glimpsed mirrorlike bubbles on either side of it, which reflected the trees and scrub on a reduced scale, and inside something moved, shaped like a bear. The sharp vibrating sound grew fainter, and the column sped away along the same groove by which it had come.

A bulging ridge of fresh clay now rose above the clearing, and alongside it was a trench three feet deep.

The men got up slowly, brushing bits of plant filaments off their suits. Then, as if by agreement, they backtracked, leaving the hollow, the trees, and the rows of masts. They were halfway up the slope, in sight of the revolving mirror-dome, when the Engineer said, "Maybe they were only animals."

"And what are we?" asked the Doctor, like an echo, in the same tone of voice.

"No, I meant . . ."

"Did you all see what was sitting inside that disk?"

"I didn't see anything," said the Physicist.

"It was in the middle, sitting in something like the gondola of a balloon. Did you see it?" the Captain asked the Doctor.

"I did. But I'm not sure . . ."

"You mean, you'd rather not be sure?"

"Yes."

They climbed higher, passing the ridge in silence, and then the brook. When some luminous disks approached from the next copse, the men hit the ground.

"It's odd they haven't noticed us so far," remarked the Engineer, when they got up and moved on.

The Captain suddenly stopped. "The lower RA channel is undamaged, am I right, Henry?"

"Yes, it's intact. Why?"

"There's a reserve in the pile. We could draw off some of it."

"As much as five gallons!" said the Engineer, and a wicked smile spread on his face.

"I don't understand," the Doctor said.

"They want to load the gun," explained the Physicist.

"With uranium?" The Doctor went pale. "You can't be thinking of . . ."

"We're not thinking," the Captain snapped. "From the moment I saw that thing, I stopped thinking. Later we can think. But now . . ."

"Look out!" shouted the Chemist.

A luminous disk flew past, but then slowed and circled back toward them. Five jector barrels rose from the ground, looking like children's rifles against the colossus that filled half the sky with its flickering.

The disk hovered; the noise intensified, then died away; and the whirling slowed. They saw a broad azure polygon, which began to tilt, as though about to tumble, but two arms extended to support it. From the central gondola, which had lost its mirrorlike sheen, a thing emerged, small, dark, hairy, and with rapid movements of its limbs, which were connected by a loose membrane, it clambered down the slanting perforated edge, sprang to the ground, and in a half-crouch made straight for the men.

At the same time, the gondola unfolded on all sides at once, like a flower opening, and a large gleaming body floated down on a thick oval surface that immediately shrank and disappeared. The big creature then slowly straightened to its full height. They recognized it, though it was strangely altered—wrapped in a lustrous, silvery material that spiraled from bottom to top, where a small flat face appeared in a black-rimmed opening.

The furry thing that had leaped from the now-motionless disk came nimbly and quickly toward them, not losing contact with the ground. They saw that it dragged behind it a very large, flat, spatulate tail.

"I'm shooting," the Engineer said in a low voice. He pressed his face to the stock of his jector.

"No," cried the Doctor.

The Captain was about to say "Wait" when the Engineer shot at the crawling creature and missed. The electric beam was invisible; they could only hear a feeble hiss. The Engineer still had his finger on the trigger. The huge silvery creature had not budged. Suddenly it moved — and whistled — and the crawling creature sprang, covering something like fifteen feet in one leap. As it landed, it rolled itself into a ball, bristling and strangely swollen. Its spatulate tail stiffened, stood vertical, and spread, and from its surface, which was cupped like a clamshell, something flickered and drifted in the crew's direction, as though carried by the wind.

"Shoot!" yelled the Captain.

A ball of flame, no larger than a walnut, floated gently on the air, moving a little to one side, to the other, but approaching steadily. And it hissed, a sound like drops of water dancing on a hot plate. They all shot at once.

Hit several times, the small creature dropped to the ground and curled up with its fanned tail completely covering it. Almost simultaneously, the ball of flame veered, as if suddenly losing its direction. It passed them at a distance of a dozen feet and disappeared from sight.

The large silver creature drew itself up still higher. Something gossamer appeared above it, and the creature began to climb up that web toward the open gondola. The men could hear the smack of the shots hitting its body; then it folded and fell to the ground with a thud.

They got up and ran to it.

"Overhead!" shouted the Chemist.

Two gleaming disks emerged from the forest and flew toward the hills. The men dived into the hollow, ready for anything, but, strangely, the disks went by without slowing down and disappeared.

Then came a muffled boom. The men turned around:

it was from the copse of breathing trees behind them. One of the trees had split in two and come crashing down, branches crackling, spewing a cloud of vapor.

"Hurry!" shouted the Captain. He rushed over to the small creature, whose paws protruded from under its hairless, fleshy tail; pointing his barrel at it, he fired continuously for fifteen seconds, then scattered its burned remains with his boot and stamped them into the ground. The Engineer touched its hump, which was bulging and appeared to be slowly expanding.

"Burn it!" shouted the Captain, running over to them. He was very pale.

"It's too big," muttered the Engineer.

"We'll see!" the Captain said through clenched teeth and fired from a distance of two feet. The air around his jector barrel shimmered. Suddenly in the silver carcass there were patches of black, soot began whirling, an awful stench filled the air as the creature's flesh began to bubble. The Chemist watched for a while, then turned away. The Cyberneticist also withdrew. When the Captain was finished discharging his weapon, he reached for the Engineer's without a word.

The carcass, black, collapsed and flattened. Smoke circled above it, and pieces of ash rose into the air. The bubbling turned into a crackling, as of logs in a fireplace, but the Captain went on squeezing the trigger with a numb finger, until there was nothing before him but a pile of glowing cinders. Holding his jector high, he jumped on them and began to kick them apart.

"Give me a hand!" he cried hoarsely.

"I can't," groaned the Chemist. He was standing with his eyes shut, his forehead beaded with sweat, and clutching his throat with both hands, as if prepared to strangle himself.

But the Doctor joined the Captain in kicking the

cinders apart. The two of them looked funny, jumping up and down. When they had stamped the burned lumps into the ground, they raked the soil over the spot, using the butts of their jectors, until no trace was left.

"How are we better than they?" asked the Doctor when they paused to rest, covered with sweat and panting.

"It attacked us first," snarled the Engineer, wiping the soot from his jector, both furious and revolted.

"All right, it's done!" the Captain called to the others. They approached slowly. There was a piercing smell in the air, and the plant cover was charred across a wide radius.

"And what about that?" asked the Cyberneticist, pointing to the azure craft, which towered over them at a height of four stories.

"Let's see if we can get it going," said the Captain.

The Engineer's eyes opened wide. "You think we can?"

"Watch out!" cried the Doctor.

Three disks appeared over the copse, one after another. The men ran and hit the ground. The Captain checked his battery charger and waited, elbows spread wide against coarse moss. The disks passed over and continued on.

"Are you coming with me?" the Captain asked the Engineer, nodding at the gondola that hung twelve feet above the ground.

Without a word, the Engineer ran to one of the arms supporting the craft and, putting his hands in the perforations, quickly climbed up. The Captain followed on his heels. Reaching the gondola ledge first, the Engineer moved something—whatever it was, the men could hear the sound of metal against metal. Then he pulled himself up and extended a hand to the Captain, who grabbed it; both men disappeared from view. For a long while nothing happened; then the five outspread sides of the gondola slowly closed without making the slightest sound. The men below shuddered and stepped back.

"What was that ball before?" the Doctor asked the Physicist as they looked up. Inside the gondola shadows were moving around.

"It looked like spherical lightning," said the Physicist after some hesitation.

"But it was the animal that emitted it!"

"Yes, I saw that. Maybe some local electrical effect—look!"

The azure polygon suddenly shook, clanged, and began revolving. It almost fell when the arms supporting it spread and twisted. At the last moment, as it teetered dangerously, there was another clang, and this time a high, piercing tone; the entire craft dissolved in a blur, and a breeze swept over the men below. The disk whirled, faster, slower, but stayed in place. It roared like the engine of a giant plane; the men moved back. One supporting arm, then the other, rose and disappeared into the luminous vortex. Like a shot, the disk sped along the groove, left the groove, and slowed down just as suddenly, kicking up soil. It made a dreadful noise, but little progress. When finally it returned to the groove, it flew off at a terrific speed, and in fifteen seconds diminished to a glimmer on the slope where the forest was.

On its way back, the disk left the groove again and slowed to a crawl, moving with apparent difficulty, and the cloud of dirt churned into the air enveloped it at its base.

There was a clang as the arms extended and the craft became visible. The gondola opened, and the Captain leaned out and shouted, "Everybody get in!"

"What!" cried the Chemist in amazement, but the Doctor grasped the situation.

"We're going for a ride."

"Will we all fit?" asked the Cyberneticist, clutching a metal support. But the Doctor was already on his way up.

Several disks flew past the copse, but none appeared to notice the men. In the gondola there was seating space for four, not six, so two had to lie on the concave floor. A familiar bitter smell assailed their nostrils, reminding them of everything that had happened, and their euphoria vanished.

The Doctor and the Chemist, on the floor, could see nothing. There were long panels under them, like the staves of a boat. Another shrill clang, and they could feel themselves moving. Almost immediately the panels on which they were lying became transparent, and they could see the plain below them, as though they were sailing over it in a balloon. There was a great noise around them. The Captain talked feverishly with the Engineer, both forced to assume unnatural and extremely tiring positions near the finlike object in the front of the gondola, which held the controls. Every few minutes one of them would spell the other, and that exchange required the Physicist and Cyberneticist to lie on top of the two men at the bottom.

"How does it work?" the Chemist asked the Engineer, who had inserted both hands into the deep openings in the fin and was keeping the craft on a straight course. They were moving rapidly, along a groove. In the gondola there was no sense of gyration—it was as if they were floating.

"I have no idea," groaned the Engineer. "A bad cramp—you take it now!" As he slid over and the Captain squeezed in, the disk shook, jumped off its groove, braked violently, and began making a sharp turn. The Captain put his hands into the control mechanism and a moment later steered the gigantic top out of its turn and back onto the groove. They sped along faster now.

"Why does it travel so slowly outside the groove?" asked the Chemist. He was propped against the Engineer's shoulders to keep his balance; between his outspread legs lay the Doctor.

"I told you, I have no idea," said the Engineer, massaging his wrists, which bore welts from the steering. "It may have something to do with a gyroscope. Who knows?"

They passed a second chain of hills. The terrain below appeared familiar—they had crossed it before, on foot. Around them was the barely visible outline of their disk. The groove suddenly changed direction: to return to the ship, they would have to leave it. Their speed fell to less than fifteen miles an hour.

"These craft are practically useless outside the grooves—we'll have to remember that!" the Engineer shouted over the noise.

"Take over!" cried the Captain.

This time the switch went smoothly. Then they were ascending a steep slope at little more than a walk. The Engineer found the canyon with the clay walls. When they reached the lung-trees, he got a cramp.

"Take it!"

As he pulled out his hands, the Captain rushed to replace him. The disk tilted and came dangerously close to the precipice. At that point there was a sharp crack; the rim of the whirring craft had hit a treetop. Broken branches flew, and the gondola crashed sideways with a hellish din. An uprooted tree swept the sky with its crown, and thousands of blister-leaves exploded with a hiss over the craft, as a landslide half-buried it. A cloud of white seeds filled the air; then there was silence. The gondola, dented, was embedded in the cliff.

"Crew?" said the Captain, shaking his head to clear it. His ears rang.

"One," groaned the Engineer, on the floor.

"Two," came the Physicist's weak voice.

"Three," said the Chemist, holding his bloody mouth.

"Four," said the Cyberneticist.

"Fi . . . ve." The Doctor was under everyone else, at the very bottom of the gondola.

They all laughed.

They were covered with a layer of fluffy, tickling seeds that had found their way inside through the apertures at the top of the gondola. The Engineer banged on the wall of the craft to make the door open. The others, whoever had the room to, pushed against the concave surface. The hull shuddered, a faint cracking could be heard, but the gondola would not open.

"Try again," said the Doctor in a muffled voice. He was unable to move. "I'm getting tired of this. Oof, hey, don't step on me!"

Although the situation was hardly amusing, they laughed, and together pulled a comb-shaped frame off the front and used it like a battering ram against the ceiling. The ceiling bent, became covered with pits, but would not open.

"Enough is enough," growled the Doctor, and tried to get up. At that moment the bottom gave way, and everyone spilled out, rolling down the steep twenty-foot slope to the floor of the canyon.

"Anyone hurt?" asked the Captain, the first to get to his feet. He was covered with clay.

"No, but you're bleeding! Let me have a look," said the Doctor.

Indeed, the Captain had a deep cut on his head. The Doctor bandaged it as best as he could. The others were only bruised, but the Chemist spit blood—he had bitten his lip. They set out for the ship, without even glancing at the shattered craft.

88

V

The sun was touching the horizon when they reached the knoll. The ship cast a long shadow across the sands of the plain. Before they entered, they searched the vicinity thoroughly, but found no traces of any visitor in their absence. The pile was working perfectly. The cleaning robot had managed to clear the halls and the library before becoming hopelessly stuck in the thick layer of broken plastic and glass that covered the laboratory.

After supper, which they wolfed down, the Doctor had to sew up the Captain's wound, because it wouldn't stop bleeding. Meanwhile the Chemist analyzed the water samples from the brook and pronounced it drinkable, though it contained a lot of iron, which spoiled the taste.

"It's time to have a council of war," said the Captain. They were sitting on air cushions in the library, the Captain in the middle, his white bandage like a hat.

"What do we know?" he began. "Well, we know that the planet is inhabited by intelligent beings, which the

Engineer calls 'doublers.' The name doesn't fit the thing that . . . But it doesn't matter. We've come across various artifacts of the doubler civilization. First, an automated factory that we concluded was abandoned and gone haywire—I'm not so sure of that now. Second, mirrorlike domes on the hilltops, of unknown function. Third, masts that emit some kind of energy—we don't know their function, either. Fourth, the flying disks, one of which we captured after an attack, operated, and crashed. Fifth, we saw their city, though from too great a distance to make out any detail. Sixth, the attack that I mentioned, in which a doubler set upon us an animal that was specially designed to throw a small fireball, which it seemed to operate or control until we killed it. Finally—seventh—we witnessed the covering of a burial ditch filled with dead inhabitants of the planet. That's all—as far as I can remember. Correct me if I've made a mistake or left anything out."

"That's pretty much it," said the Doctor. "Except for what happened the day before yesterday, in the ship . . ."

"True. And you were right—the creature *was* naked. Perhaps it was trying to escape, and in its panic crawled into the first opening at hand, which happened to be the tunnel leading to our ship."

"A tempting hypothesis, but risky," said the Doctor. "Being human, we make associations and interpretations that are human, we apply human laws, arrange facts into patterns brought from Earth. I am absolutely certain that we all thought the same thing this morning: that we had come upon the grave of victims of violence, of murder. But we don't really know. . . ."

"You don't believe that," objected the Engineer.

"It's not a question of what I believe. Eden is not the place for our beliefs. The hypothesis, for example, about the doubler 'siccing' its electric dog on us . . ."

"What do you mean, a hypothesis? That's what happened," the Chemist and the Engineer said, almost together.

"You're wrong. We have no idea why it attacked us. We might resemble some local cockroaches here, or game. . . . But we saw it as an act of aggression, associating it with what we had just found, a thing that made such an impact on us that we lost our ability to think calmly."

"And if we had kept calm and not fired immediately, it would have been *our* ashes stamped and scattered," muttered the Engineer angrily.

The Captain said nothing, moving his eyes from one man to the other.

"We did what we had to do," replied the Doctor, "but it is very likely that there was a misunderstanding. On both sides . . . You think we've fitted in all the pieces of this jigsaw puzzle? The factory supposedly abandoned several hundred years ago—what about that? Where does the factory fit in?"

There was silence.

"The Doctor's right," said the Captain. "We still know too little. The only advantage we seem to have is that they know nothing of us, since none of their roads— grooves—run near here. But we can hardly count on that ignorance continuing. Whatever we decide must take that into account."

"At present we are virtually defenseless in this wreck," said the Engineer. "All one would have to do is block up the tunnel to suffocate us like mice. We must act quickly, because at any moment we could be discovered, and although the hypothesis of doubler aggression may be only my 'human association,' I am incapable of reasoning in any other way. I propose we begin repairing all the units and engines—immediately."

"And how long will that repair take?" asked the Doctor.

The Engineer hesitated. "You see?" the Doctor said wearily. "Why should we delude ourselves? They'll discover us before we finish. I'm no expert, but I know it will take weeks and weeks. . . ."

"Unfortunately that's true," the Captain agreed. "And we'll have to replenish our water supply. And get rid of the contaminated water that's flooded the lower level. Nor do we know if all the damage is repairable."

"Another expedition will be necessary," said the Engineer. "And more than one. They can be made at night. However, some of us—two or three—should stay near the ship. But why are we the only ones talking?" he asked, turning to the three other men, who had been silent so far.

"We ought to work as hard as possible on the ship, but study the doubler civilization, too," the Physicist said slowly. "The two activities will interfere with each other. The number of unknowns is so great that no strategy will be of much help. One thing alone is certain: whatever course of action we choose, we face tremendous risk."

"I think I see what you're all saying," said the Doctor in the same low, weary voice. "You want to make further expeditions, inasmuch as we now have the ability to deliver powerful blows—atomic blows. In self-defense, of course. Since this will mean taking on the whole planet, count me out, gentlemen. I have no desire to participate in what will be a Pyrrhic victory, Pyrrhic even if they don't have atomic energy . . . which I wouldn't bet on. What kind of engine runs the disks?"

"I don't know," said the Engineer, "but it isn't atomic. I'm almost certain."

"That 'almost' might cost us dearly." The Doctor leaned back, closed his eyes, and rested his head on a fallen bookcase, as if he had no further intention of speaking.

"Squaring the circle," muttered the Cyberneticist.

"And if we try to . . . communicate?" the Chemist asked.

The Doctor sat up straight, looked at him, and said, "Thank you. I was beginning to think nobody would say that!"

"But to attempt communication means to put ourselves at their mercy!" exclaimed the Cyberneticist, getting to his feet.

"Why?" the Doctor asked coldly. "We can arm ourselves first, even with atomic throwers. But we don't sneak up on their towns and factories at night."

"All right . . . So how do you envisage an attempt at communication?"

"Yes, tell us," said the Captain.

"I admit we shouldn't try it just now," replied the Doctor. "The more equipment we're able to repair on the ship, the better, naturally. We should arm ourselves, too, though it doesn't have to be with atomic throwers. . . . Then some of us will stay by the ship, and some—three, let's say—will approach the city. Two, approaching, will stop short and watch, while the third attempts to communicate with the inhabitants. . . ."

"You have it all figured out. You even know who will be the one to enter the city," the Engineer said grimly.

"Yes, I do."

"Well, I'm not going to stand by while you try to commit suicide!" The Engineer jumped to his feet and towered over the Doctor, who did not even look up. They had never seen the Engineer so agitated. "If we all survived the crash and emerged from the grave that this ship became—if after taking the incalculable risk of exploring this planet as if it were a place for walking tours—it wasn't so that now, with this damned, stupid drivel . . ." He became choked with anger. "I know that song. Mankind's mission! Peace and good will to the stars! You're a fool!

93

Don't tell me that no one tried to kill us today! That we didn't see a mass grave!"

The Doctor lifted his head. "Yes, they tried to kill us. And yes, it's very likely that those dead were murdered." Everyone could see the effort it took him to remain calm. "But we must go to the city."

"After what we did?" asked the Captain.

The Doctor winced. "True," he said. "The corpse we burned . . . yes. Do what you think is best. You decide. I'll go along." And he got up and left, stepping over the horizontal door frame. The others waited, as though expecting him to change his mind and come back.

"You shouldn't have lost your temper," the Captain said quietly to the Engineer.

"You know perfectly well . . ." began the Engineer, but after looking him in the eyes he said, "I shouldn't have."

"The Doctor's right about one thing," said the Captain, adjusting his bandage, which had been slipping down. "What we found to the north of us doesn't fit with what we saw to the east. We're about as far from the city as from the factory—I'd say fifteen or twenty miles as the crow flies."

"More," said the Physicist.

"Maybe. Now, I would doubt that within that radius there are any such structures to the south or west. Because that would mean we had landed in the center of a kind of island 'desert' some forty miles in diameter within an urban area. Which would be too much of a coincidence, too improbable. Do you agree?"

"Yes," said the Engineer, looking at the floor.

The Chemist, nodding, said, "We should have talked like this at the beginning."

"I share the Doctor's misgivings," the Captain went on. "But his proposal is naïve, unsuitable, under the circumstances. The rules for contact with an alien civilization do not cover the situation in which we now find ourselves: of defenseless castaways living in a wreck buried in the ground. Obviously we must repair the damage to the ship, but at the same time there is an information race—between them and us. So far, we are ahead. We destroyed the being that attacked us. Why it attacked us, we don't know. Maybe we do resemble one of their enemies. We'll have to ascertain that, too, if we can. Since the ship will not be operable in the near future, we must be ready for anything. The civilization around us is clearly developed. What I did, therefore—what we did—will only slightly delay their discovery of us. So our main effort now must be to arm ourselves."

"May I say something?" said the Physicist.

"Go ahead."

"I'd like to return to the Doctor's point of view. Emotional though it is, there is an argument in its favor. This situation of a first contact is by no means neutral. When they find us, it will be because they have been looking for us. And it will be hard then to 'reach an understanding.' There will undoubtedly be an attack, and we'll have to fight for our lives. But if, on the other hand, we go out to meet them, though the chances of reaching an understanding may not be great, they will at least exist. So, for purely tactical reasons, morality aside, it would be better for us to take the initiative."

"All right, but what does that mean in practice?" asked the Engineer.

"In practice, nothing is altered for the time being. We must have weapons, and as quickly as possible. However, as soon as we have them, we should try to make contact—though not on the terrain that we've explored so far."

"Why not?" asked the Captain.

"Because it's extremely likely that we'll be attacked before we reach the city. By the beings that drive the disks."

"And how do you know we'll find more peaceable beings elsewhere?"

"I don't. But there's nothing for us to the north or east. At least not now. I'm sure of that."

"And what else?" said the Captain.

"We must activate Defender," said the Chemist.

"How long will that take?" the Captain asked the Engineer.

"I can't say. Without the robots we can't even get to Defender. The thing weighs fourteen tons. Ask the Cyberneticist."

"It will take two days to check it. At least," said the Cyberneticist. "But first I have to have working robots."

"How long, to get the robots running?" asked the Captain.

"Let's see. . . . I'll need a repair robot first, then a lifter, and they have to be checked, too, of course, which will take a couple of days, assuming there isn't too much damage. . . ."

"Can't we take the heart out of Defender and armor it up here, beside the hull?" the Captain asked, looking at the Physicist.

The Physicist shook his head. "No. The pivot alone weighs more than a ton. Besides, the heart won't fit in the tunnel."

"The tunnel can be widened."

"It won't go through the hatch. And the freight hatch, as you know, is filled with water from the broken stern reservoir."

"Did you check the water contamination?" asked the Engineer.

"Yes. Strontium, calcium, cerium, all the barium isotopes. The works. We can't let it out—it would contaminate the soil within a radius of a thousand feet—and we can't purify it until the antirads have working filters."

"And I can't clean the filters without a robot," added the Engineer.

The Captain, looking from man to man as each spoke, observed, "We have a fair-sized list of can'ts. But it's important to take stock. What about the atomic throwers?"

"They're not throwers," said the Engineer with a grimace of disgust. "Let's not deceive ourselves. The Doctor made so much noise about them, you'd think we were planning to start a nuclear war here. Their range is less than two thousand feet. They're hand sprinklers, nothing more, and, besides, they're inconvenient. A man firing has to wear a shield that weighs two hundred pounds."

"We have a lot of heavy things on board," the Captain muttered, and nobody knew whether he meant that as a joke.

The Physicist said, "But if two throwers are placed three hundred feet apart and shoot in such a way that the beams intersect at the target, you get a supercritical concentration and can produce a chain reaction."

"That's fine on the firing range," remarked the Chemist, "but I can't see such precision under field conditions."

"In other words, we really don't have atomic throwers?" the Cyberneticist said, amazed and angry. "Then what is the sense of this whole discussion—this argument—about whether we should arm ourselves to the teeth or not? We're not thinking!"

"That's right. We haven't done a great deal of thinking," said the Captain calmly. "Not until now. But we can't allow ourselves that luxury any longer. With the throwers," he went on, "there is another tactic: one fires half the charge, and the chain reaction takes place at the target. Except that the firing must be done from the best possible cover, and at maximum distance."

"That means we have to go three feet underground before shooting?"

"Five, at least—and behind a six-foot embankment," the Physicist put in.

"For stationary warfare that's fine. For expeditions it's useless," the Chemist snorted.

"If the need arises," said the Captain, "one man with a thrower can cover our retreat."

"Without digging any embankments?"

"Without digging any embankments."

There was silence.

"How much usable water do we have left?" asked the Cyberneticist.

"Less than three hundred gallons."

"That's not much."

"True."

"Now let's have some concrete proposals," said the Captain. A red spot appeared on his white bandage. "Our goal is to save ourselves and . . . the inhabitants of this planet."

Suddenly all heads turned in the same direction. Through the wall came muffled music, a melody they all recognized.

"The player's survived?" the Cyberneticist whispered in surprise. Nobody said anything.

"I'm waiting," said the Captain. "No one? Then I'll decide: the expeditions will continue. If we make contact in favorable circumstances, we'll do everything in our power to communicate. Our water supply is too low. With no means of transport, we cannot increase it. Therefore, we must divide up. Half the crew will work in the ship, half will go exploring. Tomorrow morning we start repairing the jeep and assembling the throwers. If we're successful, we make a motorized excursion in the evening. Does anyone have anything to say?"

"I do," said the Engineer, his face in his hands, looking through his fingers at the floor. "The Doctor should remain in the ship."

"Why?" asked the Cyberneticist. But everyone else understood.

"He won't . . . do anything against us, if that's what you're thinking," the Captain said, choosing his words carefully. The red spot on his bandage was a little larger.

"You know what he did at that . . . factory, at the wall," said the Engineer. "He might have been killed."

"On the other hand, he was the only one to help me . . . trample . . ." the Captain said, but did not continue.

"True," the Engineer admitted. "That's why I was reluctant to speak."

"Anyone else?" The Captain straightened up, put his hand to his head, touched the bandage, and looked at his fingers. The music was still coming through the wall.

"Here or out there in the open—we don't know where we'll meet them first," the Physicist said quietly.

"Do we draw lots?" asked the Chemist.

"No point. The ones who stay are those who have work to do on the ship," said the Captain. He got up slowly, unsteadily, then lost his balance. The Engineer jumped up and caught him, and the Physicist held the Captain from the other side. The others spread cushions on the floor.

"No, I don't need to lie down," the Captain said, his eyes shut. "Thank you. It's nothing. The stitches seem to have opened."

"I'll turn off the music," said the Chemist, making for the door.

"No," said the Captain, "let it play. . . ."

They called the Doctor. He changed the dressing, put a clamp on the wound, and gave the Captain some medicine. Then everyone lay down. It was almost two when they finally turned off the lights and the ship fell silent.

VI

The next morning the Physicist and the Engineer drew off a gallon of enriched uranium solution from the pile reserve and transferred the thick fluid to the laboratory, to a lead tank. Wearing large plastic protective suits and oxygen masks under hoods, they used long-handled graspers and a burette to measure out, carefully, the concentrate and feed it into the specially made lead-glass capillary tubes of the throwers, which were held in place by frames on the table. When they were done, they tested the seals of the tank with a Geiger counter, then turned each thrower over and shook it.

"Good, no leaks," the Physicist said, his voice distorted by his mask.

The armored door of the radioactive storeroom, a block of lead on a shaft, slowly moved aside. They wheeled the tank back inside and, when the bolts snapped to, removed the masks and hoods from their sweaty faces with relief.

The rest of the day they worked on the jeep. Since the freight hatch couldn't be used, they dismantled the jeep first and carried the parts outside through the tunnel, which had to be widened in two places. The jeep required practically no repairs. They had not been able to use it before, because, with the reactor immobilized, there had been no fuel available—it ran on a mixture of radioisotopes, converting that to current. The vehicle had room for four persons, and at the rear there was a cage carrier able to hold up to four hundred pounds. The cleverest feature was the wheels, whose diameter was variable, regulated by air pump according to need. They could be expanded to four and a half feet.

Preparing the fuel mixture took six hours, but required only one person, who checked the pile from time to time. Meanwhile the Engineer and the Captain crawled on all fours through the passageways below the deck, checking and replacing the cables that ran between the control room and the distributor units in the engine room. The Chemist had built himself a kind of stove outside, close to the ship, and was heating up a greasy substance that bubbled like a muddy volcano. He was melting and stirring bits of plastic, the plastic that had been brought out of the ship in buckets. Nearby lay molds, with which he intended to make new instrument panels for the control room. He was in a vile temper and wouldn't speak to anyone, because his first molds had failed dismally.

The Captain, the Chemist, and the Doctor were supposed to head south at five, which was three hours before nightfall. As usual, no one kept to schedule, and it was almost six by the time everything was ready and packed. A thrower was placed on the fourth seat. And on the carrier in the back they strapped a twenty-five-gallon canister, for water.

After dinner the Engineer, equipped with large binoculars, clambered up the ship's hull. The ship had penetrated the ground at not much of an angle, but because of its length the end of the hull, the exhaust funnels, rose a good three stories above the plain. After finding a place to sit between the conical mounting of the upper funnel and the hollow of the main body, the Engineer first looked down along the huge sunlit cylinder to where the men were standing, no larger than beetles, beside the black dot that was the tunnel entrance. Then he brought the binoculars to his face with both hands and carefully pressed the eyepiece to his eyes. The magnification was considerable, but the view quivered. He had to steady his arms by propping his elbows on his knees, which was not easy. It wouldn't take much to fall off, he thought. The scratch-proof ceramite surface was smooth, almost slippery. Pressing the contoured rubber sole of his left boot against the funnel, he began to sweep the horizon systematically with his binoculars.

The air shimmered from the heat. He could feel the pressure of the sun on his face when he turned south. He was glad that the Doctor had agreed to the Captain's plan, which everyone else had accepted. The Doctor did not even want to hear of apologies—he made a joke of their argument. But what really surprised the Engineer was the end of their conversation. He had been alone with the Doctor, and it had seemed that they had nothing more to say to each other, when suddenly the Doctor tapped him on the chest.

"I wanted to ask you something. . . . Do you know how to set the ship upright when it's repaired?"

"First we get the freight robot and the digger to . . ." the Engineer began.

"No," the Doctor interrupted him. "The technical details, as you know, mean nothing to me. Just tell me if you—you personally—know how to do it."

"What, are you frightened by the figure of sixteen thousand tons? Archimedes said he could move the Earth, given the right fulcrum. We'll dig it out and . . ."

"I'm sorry, that's still not what I mean. I'm not questioning your theoretical knowledge, the textbook methods. Can you actually do it and—wait!—if you say yes, can you give me your word that you are thinking yes?"

That had made the Engineer hesitate. There were still a couple of points he was not clear on, but he had always told himself that, when it came down to it, somehow or other it would all work out. Before he could reply, the Doctor squeezed his hand.

"Henry," he said, "do you know why you shouted at me? It's because you're as big a numskull as I am and don't want to admit it."

And, smiling in a way that recalled the photograph of him as a student, which the Engineer had seen in his drawer, the Doctor added, *"Credo quia absurdum*—did they teach you any Latin?"

"Yes, but I've forgotten it all," said the Engineer.

The Doctor winked, released his hand, and walked away, leaving the Engineer alone. Still feeling the Doctor's fingers on his hand, the Engineer had the impression that the man had wanted to say something quite different, and that, if he thought hard, he might guess what the Doctor had left unsaid. . . . But he couldn't concentrate, feeling—for no clear reason—fear, despair. The Captain called him to the engine room, where fortunately there was so much work to do that there was no time for reflection.

He now recalled that scene and that feeling. He had gained no insight into it. In his binoculars was a plain with gentle hummocks separated by strips of shadow. What he had expected the evening before and had kept to himself—the conviction that they would be discovered, and that there would be a battle at daybreak—had not materialized. How many times had he resolved not to take his forebodings so seriously! He squinted to see better. The binoculars showed clumps of willowy gray calyxes obscured at times by clouds of dust. The wind must be strong there, though he could not feel it where he sat. Near the horizon the terrain gradually rose, and still farther away—though that might not be land but low clouds ten miles away—was a formation of a darker hue. Now and then something ascended and either dissolved or disappeared. It was too indistinct to tell him anything, though the phenomenon was strangely regular. Having no idea what he was watching, he measured the frequency with which the change occurred, consulting his watch: eighty-six seconds.

He put the binoculars back in their case and, planting his feet carefully on the ceramite surface, made his way down. After he had taken about ten steps, he heard something following him. He turned around—and lost his balance. Arms flailing, he fell onto the hull and heard the sound of his fall repeated.

Hunched, he got to his knees.

About twenty feet away, on the very edge of the upper funnel, sat something small, the size of a cat, watching him intently. The animal—it was definitely an animal—had a protruding pale-gray belly and sat bolt upright, like a squirrel, its paws folded across its belly, all four of them, meeting comically in the middle. The creature was clasping the rim of the ceramite funnel with something yellowish that shook like gelatin, and which issued from the end of its torso. The small, round, gray head had neither eyes nor mouth, but was covered with shiny black beads, like a pincushion with pins, stuck into it, one beside another. The Engineer took three steps toward the animal, so dumbfounded that he almost forgot where he was, and then heard a triple reverberation, the echo of his own footsteps. The creature imitated sounds. He moved slowly closer, and was wondering whether he ought to remove his shirt and use it as a net, when suddenly the animal changed.

The paws on the belly began to tremble, the abdomen spread and unfolded like a great fan, the pincushion head rose stiffly on a long hairless neck, and the creature took to the air, surrounded by a faintly flickering aureole. For a moment it hung motionless above him, then moved off, spiraling, gathering speed, circling one more time, and disappearing.

The Engineer climbed down and told the crew, as accurately as possible, what had happened.

"Good. I was beginning to wonder why there were no flying animals here," said the Doctor.

The Chemist reminded him of the white flowers by the brook.

"They looked more like insects," said the Doctor, "like, well, butterflies. But the air here is, on the whole, not highly populated. When living organisms evolve on a planet, a biological pressure develops, thanks to which every possible environment, every niche, must be filled. There's a surprising lack of birds here."

"It was more like a . . . bat," said the Engineer. "It had hair."

"That's possible," said the Doctor, who never paraded his biological knowledge before the crew. And he added, as though more out of politeness than because it interested him, "You say it imitated the sound of your footsteps? That's curious. Well, the imitation must serve some survival function."

"We should try to cover more ground this time. I don't think anything will break down," said the Captain, crawling out from under the jeep, which was now ready. The Engineer was a little put off by the indifference with which his discovery had been received, but he told himself that perhaps he had been impressed more by the unexpectedness of the encounter than by the flying creature itself.

Everyone was uncomfortable at the moment of parting. Those who remained behind stood beneath the ship and watched as the odd-looking vehicle described larger and larger circles around it under the confident control of the Captain, who sat in front, with only the narrow-barreled thrower as traveling companion by his side, while the Doctor and the Chemist sat behind him. Passing close to the ship, he called out, "We'll try to be back by midnight. Good-bye!" He increased the speed, and a moment later all that could be seen was a high and distant golden wall of dust blowing slowly westward.

The jeep was a bare metal skeleton covered only from below, by a base that was transparent so the driver could see every obstacle. It had an electric motor in each wheel, and two spare tires and a can of fuel fastened to the back. It could go forty miles an hour if the ground was smooth. Looking back, the Doctor soon lost all sight of the ship. The motors hummed, and dust rose from the parched ground, billowed, and dispersed, falling back onto the steppelike land.

Nobody spoke. The windshield protected only the driver, so the two men sitting behind him got the wind full in the face and could talk only by shouting. The land became more undulating; the gray calyxes disappeared.

They passed individual clumps of spidery scrub, scattered and distant. Lung-trees, withered, stood here and there, their leaf clusters dangling, trembling only occasionally, as if gasping. Up ahead they caught sight of long grooves, but saw no disks. The tires bounced gently when they crossed the grooves. Sharp-edged limestone, as white as dried bone, jutted from the ground; long tongues of scree snaked down the long slope they were climbing; the sharp gravel grated noisily under their tires. The slope increased, which slowed down the jeep, and though its engine had reserve power, the Captain did not use it on this rough terrain.

Higher up, between two buff-brown ridges, they saw a long thin band that seemed to block their path. The Captain reduced speed still further. Athwart the slope, where it leveled off to a plateau from which vague shapes rose in the far distance, they saw a mirrorlike strip embedded in the ground and running off in both directions. The jeep stopped, touching the edge of the strip with its front tires. The Captain got out, touched the smooth surface with his jector butt, hit it a little harder, then finally stood on it and jumped on it. The strip did not move.

"How many miles have we gone?" asked the Chemist when the Captain got back in.

"Thirty-eight," the Captain said and carefully started up. They rode over the strip, which looked like a ribbon of hardened mercury, and with increasing speed passed, to the left and to the right, masts with columns of air churning above them. Then the masts curved eastward, but the men went straight, keeping their compass needle on the letter "S."

The plateau presented a cheerless sight. The vegetation was slowly losing its struggle against the sand blown by the hot east wind. Blackened scrub, pale carmine at ground level, grew out of low dunes; leathery pods dropped from it. Once in a while something gray would move through the dry brush, or something would leap away from beneath the wheels of the jeep, but the men did not get a good look at the creature; it scurried too fast into the scrub.

The Captain picked his way carefully, avoiding the thick clumps of thorns. Once he even had to backtrack, when the glade they entered came to a dead end in a mound of sand. The terrain resembled a maze and more and more had the character of a desert: the plants rustled like paper in the wind. The jeep went between walls of overhanging branches. From burst pods yellowish dust blew into the windshield and covered the men's suits and faces. Heat poured from the thicket, and it was difficult to breathe. Then the jeep stopped.

The tableland ended a few dozen feet ahead, and the thicket ended, too, like a black brush shining amber in the sun. Beyond were distant hills rising high above a valley that the men could not see from their position. The Captain stepped out and walked to the last bush, its long withes swaying gently against the sky.

"We're going down," he said when he came back.

The jeep proceeded slowly; its rear lifted, and lifted more. The canister rattled in the carrier, and the brakes gave a warning squeal. The Captain turned on the pump, and the tires grew, compensating for the steepness of the slope. The men saw a layer of fleecy clouds, through which rose a column of brown smoke, cylindrical at the bottom and bulbous at the top. The column hung in the air undispersed, high above the hilltops, like the smoke from a volcano. It lasted a minute or two, then descended at an unusual speed and was concealed in the white clouds, as if whatever had belched it forth now sucked it back in.

The valley had two levels, one in the sun and one, lower, screened by the clouds toward which the jeep now drove, rocking and bouncing. As the sun set, its rays hit the distant hills facing the men, where squat structures amid gray and violent brushwood blazed with mirrors. It was difficult to look at them, they were so bright. The layer of cloud was closer. Behind the men, outlined high against the azure sky, stood the jagged bushes. They went slower, then were enveloped in rolling vapor, humid and stifling; everything became dim. The Captain inched the jeep forward, switched on the headlights, but turned them off immediately, since the glare in the fog made visibility worse.

Suddenly the fog cleared. It was cooler. They found themselves on much less of an incline and just beneath the clouds, which stretched into the distance toward indistinct gray and black patches deep in the valley. Ahead, something glimmered, like a light through an oily liquid, and they felt their eyes blur. The Doctor and the Chemist tried rubbing their eyes—it didn't help. A dark object came toward them out of the glimmering. The ground now was flat, and smooth enough to have been artificially leveled and hardened. The object grew larger; they could see that it was a vehicle on tires—it was their jeep, a reflection in some surface. Then they could almost see their own faces, but the image broke up and vanished at the place where they expected to find a mirror. They drove through, encountering nothing, though they were brushed by a sudden warmth, as if that marked the crossing of an unseen barrier. At the same time whatever had blurred their eyes the moment before went away.

The tires splashed: the jeep was going through puddles. Patches of turbid water gave off a faintly bitter smell, as if there were ashes in them. Mounds of lighter, upturned clay lay here and there between the puddles. Rubble appeared on the right—not fragments of wall, but pieces of crumpled, soiled fabric heaped one on top of another, rising as high as twenty feet in some places, and at ground level there were black irregular openings in them. The men drove through this area—what lurked in the holes, they could not see. The Captain stopped near one mound, so close that one of the front tires came to rest against it. He alighted, walked to the top of it, and peered into a rectangular well. Seeing the expression on his face, the others ran up to him. The Doctor slipped on the clay, but the Chemist gave him a hand.

In the hole, whose vertical walls looked as though they had been excavated by a machine, a naked corpse lay floating on its back. Only the very top of its powerful chest, from which a childlike torso protruded, was above the dark water.

The three men looked at one another, then walked down the mound of clay. Water trickled and gathered in their footprints.

"Is there nothing but graves on this planet?" asked the Chemist.

They stood by the jeep, undecided. The Captain turned away, pale, and looked around. There were mounds everywhere, in uneven rows. To the right lay more gray rubble-heaps, with a low white line snaking through them. To the left, beyond some more upturned clay, was an inclined plane, broad at the bottom and narrowing at the top, made of pitted metal. Beyond that, through wisps of vapor, they could see—barely—something vertical and black, like the sides of a huge caldron.

The Captain was climbing back into the jeep when a deep sigh, as if from underground, reached their ears. The white clouds that before had concealed everything were dispersed, on the left, by a powerful gust that a moment later enveloped the men in a bitter, penetrating odor. They then saw a monstrous chimney reaching to the sky and, spewing from it, a brown column perhaps three hundred feet across, a waterfall in reverse that forced apart the clouds and disappeared upward. This lasted a minute, then silence followed, then came another muffled groan, and a gust in the opposite direction tugged at their hair, and the clouds returned in long curls and covered the black chimney completely.

The Captain motioned to the others, they got in, and the jeep went clumsily over the uneven clay to the next mound. They looked inside. It was empty, apart from some black water. Again they heard a muffled sound, the clouds parted, a brown geyser poured from the chimney, and again the column was sucked back in. They paid less and less attention to this alternation of cloud and smoke as they rode from mound to mound, jumping onto soft clay, climbing slopes of slippery mud, and peering into the wells on top. Sometimes there would be a splash at the bottom, if a clod of clay was dislodged by their feet. Then they would return to the jeep and ride on.

Out of the eighteen wells they examined, they found corpses in seven. Oddly, their horror and repugnance diminished, the more corpses they found. They noticed, becoming more objective, more observant, that there was less water in the holes nearer the huge chimney. And in one of the holes, the entire bottom of which was covered by a body bent double, they noticed that the body was not quite like the others. It seemed paler, differently formed. They drove on, unable to verify this impression; the next two holes were empty, but in the third, which was completely dry and situated only a few hundred feet from the metal ramp, they saw a body on its side, and one of the arms belonging to its smaller torso was divided at the end into two appendages.

"What's that?" said the Chemist in a strange voice, gripping the Doctor's shoulder. "Do you see it?"

"I see it."

"A fork—instead of fingers?"

"Maybe it was maimed," muttered the Captain without conviction.

They stopped again, at the last mound before the ramp. The well looked recent—bits of clay were still dropping from the walls, as though the shoveling machine had emerged from the rectangular pit only moments before.

"Good God . . ." exclaimed the Chemist, jumping back and off the mound, and nearly falling in the process.

The Doctor faced the Captain. "If I go in there, will you give me a hand to get out?" he asked.

"Yes. What do you intend to do?"

The Doctor knelt, clutched the edge of the hole, and carefully lowered himself, trying to keep his feet clear of the large body at the bottom. He bent over it, instinctively holding his breath. From above, it had looked as though a metal bar had been thrust into the carcass, under the chest, in the place where, among coils of folded flesh, the large torso had produced another. But up close, he saw that this was not so.

Something like a protruding navel, thin-skinned, bluish, came from the body, from beneath a fold of skin, and the metal tube fit into it. The Doctor touched it delicately, then tugged at it more firmly. Bending closer, he discovered that the metal tube, visible through the stretched skin, was joined to it by a row of minute pearls, like a continuous seam. For a moment he considered severing this connection of metal and skin, and was reaching into his pocket for a knife, still undecided, when he happened to look at the face of the little head that was propped against the wall of the well—and froze.

Where the creature they had dissected in the ship had had nostrils, this creature had one wide-open blue eye, which seemed to be watching him with silent intensity. The Doctor looked up. "What is it?" He heard the Captain's voice and saw his head, dark against the clouds, and understood why they had not noticed this from above: to see the face, one had to stand where he was standing now.

"Help me out," he said, and the Captain reached down,

grasped his outstretched hand, and pulled him up. The Chemist helped, catching him by the collar of his suit, and he emerged from the well, covered with clay.

The Doctor blinked. "We understand nothing," he said. "Nothing!" And added, as if to himself, "Incredible, that a reasoning man should be in a situation in which he comprehends nothing whatsoever!"

"What did you find?" asked the Chemist.

"They vary," said the Doctor as they went back to the jeep. "Some have fingers, some don't. Some have noses but no eyes, while some have an eye but no nose. Some are larger and darker, and some paler, with a shorter trunk."

"So what?" said the Chemist, impatient. "There are different races of people, too. People have different features, come in different colors. Why does variation bother you so much? The real question here is, who committed this horrible slaughter, and why?"

"I'm not so sure there was a slaughter," the Doctor answered softly, his head bowed.

The Chemist looked at him with amazement. "What are you suggesting?"

"I don't know . . ." the Doctor said with effort. Mechanically, not consciously, he was wiping the clay from his hands with a handkerchief. "But one thing I do know," he added, straightening. "These differences are not the differences between races of the same species. The eyes and the nose, the senses of sight and smell, are too important."

"On Earth there are ants even more specialized. Some have eyes, some do not. Some can fly, some cannot. Some are food-gatherers and some are warriors. Do I have to teach you biology?"

The Doctor shook his head. "For everything that happens you import a concept, ready-made, from Earth. If a detail or fact doesn't fit that concept, you simply ignore it. I can't prove it to you now, but I know—I simply know—that this has nothing to do with races or with specialization. You remember that needle I found during the dissection?

"Just now everyone assumed, as I assumed, that this creature was murdered. But it has an appendage there— a kind of sucker or sleeve—and the metal tube was inserted into it. As one would insert a tube into a man's windpipe during a tracheotomy. Of course, this has nothing to do with a tracheotomy; the creature has no windpipe there. I don't know what it's for, but at least I'm aware of my ignorance!"

He got into the jeep and asked the Captain, "And what do you think?"

"That we should be moving on," said the Captain, his hands on the steering wheel.

VII

It was growing dark. They went around the ramp, which was not a ramp at all, and not metal, they now saw, but the flattened, farthest-reaching arm of a river of lava, whose size only now did they appreciate. The river had flowed from the upper level of the valley and hardened into dozens of fissured pools and cascades. It covered the lower part of the slope with humps of slag, but at the top, where the angle became precipitous, bare ribs of rock protruded through this inert flood. On the opposite slope a pass half a mile wide, with a dried-up, cracked clay bottom, went through a high ridge of mountain that appeared to be covered with vegetation.

The valley was much bigger than one would have guessed, looking at it from above. It branched into flat plains among loaflike outcroppings of magma. To the right the ground rose in terraces, almost bare, to gray clouds. Still higher they could hear the geyser, now blocked by a shelf of rock, and with each eruption a long hollow hiss filled the valley.

The scene slowly lost color, and shapes blurred, as though submerged in water. Ahead of the jeep, in the distance, they saw either walls or hillsides, reddish, whose complex pattern was bathed in what seemed the rays of the setting sun, though the sun was covered by clouds.

Closer, on both sides of the pass, stood rows of dark, vertical, club-shaped, giant structures resembling elongated balloons. The men rode between them, and the twilight was made darker by the shadows that these massive pillars cast. The Captain turned on the headlights, and outside their triple beam it suddenly became night.

The wheels rolled across layers of slag, cracking it like glass into fragments. The pillars glittered with a mercury sheen when the headlights touched them. The clay disappeared; the ground now was a bulging surface of hardened lava, with puddles in its hollows, which splashed beneath the wheels of the jeep. Against the clouds the men could see black, gossamer-thin lines connecting two pillars roughly three hundred feet apart. Then the headlights revealed several machines overturned, their undersides full of ragged openings from which decayed wisps of something dangled. The men pulled over. The machines had been abandoned long ago; they were rusted through.

The air was growing more and more humid, and gusts of a sickly odor and the stench of burning came from the pillars. The Captain steered toward the nearest pillar, driving over a smooth slab that crumbled at the edges and was flanked on either side by slanting surfaces that bore a series of notches. At the base of the structure, pitch-black, was an entrance. Above this the cylindrical wall rose, bulged, and blocked out the sky with a mushroom-shaped hood that was wrinkled, amorphous, as though the builder had left it unfinished.

Reaching the immense hood, the Captain took his foot off the accelerator. The entrance gaped; the headlights were lost in it. Two broad, shallow troughs ran to the left and right and spiraled upward. The jeep came to a stop, then slowly began to drive up the right trough.

They were plunged in darkness. In the beam of the headlights, telescopically half-open masts appeared and disappeared along the rims of the trough. Then something began to flash above these, and when they looked up, they saw rows of pale ghosts. The Captain directed one of the lights there and widened its beam. The beam climbed from one white cellular creature to another. Plucked from the darkness, each shone, then disappeared. At the same time thousands of tiny reflections dazzled the men.

"That's no help." The Captain's voice was distorted by echoes. "But wait, we have flares!"

He got out, and in the light in front of the jeep leaned over the edge of the trough. Something clanged; he called out, "Don't look here, look up!"—and jumped back into the jeep. Almost simultaneously the magnesium caught fire with an ear-piercing hiss, and a great glare rolled aside the darkness.

The trough in which they were standing ended, a little higher up, in a transparent corridor or shaft that climbed steeply and penetrated, like a tube of silver, a glowing jungle of bubbles that hung overhead, a dome filled with a multitude of cells, a glass hive. The flare was multiplied in the cells, and inside them the men could see skeletons, bones snowy white, almost sparkling, spatulate limbs, a fan of ribs radiating from a long oval disk of bone, and each thorax in the front, open, contained a small, slender, half-recumbent skeleton, a thing that was like a cross between a bird and a monkey, with a toothless, spherical skull. There were countless rows of such glass eggs, and they circled and spiraled higher and higher. But the cells mirrored and remirrored the light, so that it was impossible to tell real shapes from reflections.

The men sat glued to their seats for six seconds; then the flare went out, and in the darkness the bones continued to glow yellow. After a few minutes they saw that the headlights were still on, throwing dim light on the undersides of the glassy spheres.

The Captain drove to the shaft, the place where the trough became a funnel, and parked the jeep sideways, so it wouldn't roll back down if the brakes failed, and they all got out.

The transparent tube went sharply upward, but they could ascend by foot. They detached one of the headlights from its mounting and entered the shaft, trailing a cable behind them.

The shaft spiraled up through the interior of the dome, and the cells were located on either side of it, slightly above the concave floor on which they climbed. It was tiring, but the shaft soon became less steep. Each cell was flattened on the sides, where it abutted other cells, and into the shaft from each stuck a snoutlike piece that was capped tightly by a round, cloudy lens. The men walked on, and the grotesque gallery of skeletons filed past them. The skeletons varied. The men did not realize this at first, because the ones adjacent were virtually identical. Differences became apparent only if one compared examples from distant sections on the long spiral.

As the men climbed higher, the thorax openings grew smaller, and the limbs, too, as though they were being absorbed by the oval disk of bone, but the heads of the little chest monstrosities grew large, their skulls strangely distended on the sides.

Advancing single-file, the men made their way up one and a half loops of the spiral, then were stopped by a sudden jerk: the cable that connected the light to the jeep had reached the end of its reel. The Doctor wanted to go on, using the flashlight, but the Captain shook his head. From the main shaft other tunnels branched off every dozen feet or so, and it would be easy to get lost in this labyrinth of glass. They turned back. On the way they attempted to open one, then a second, then a third cap, but the lenses were all fused to the rims of the transparent containers.

The bottoms of the cells were covered with a layer of fine white dust that had thin dark marks in places, but the marks—or numbers—were unintelligible. The Doctor, who was in the rear, paused at every cell: he still had no idea how the skeletons were suspended, or what supported them. Also, he wanted to inspect one of the "clusters" in a side corridor. The Captain hurried him on, so with a sigh he followed, particularly since the Chemist, who was carrying the headlight, was now some distance away, leaving them in darkness.

They descended quickly and at last were back at the jeep, taking deep breaths of air: the air in the glass tunnel had been stale and hot.

"To the ship now?" asked the Chemist.

"Not yet," replied the Captain as he turned the jeep around, the trough being wide enough to allow this. The headlights made a sweeping arc through the darkness as they rode down the steep incline toward the entrance, which held the last light of day like a long, low screen.

Outside, the Captain decided to drive around the base of the pillar, which was a cone-shaped flange of cast metal. They were less than halfway around when their path was barred by oblong blocks with razor-sharp edges, all wedged together. The Captain raised a headlight.

A brown-black mass of lava rose behind the pillar. Descending from a height invisible in the darkness, the magma overhung the area in a crescent-shaped wall whose progress had been checked by a thick forest of masts and buttresses barring any closer approach. The intricate tangle of these constructions had pressed a network of interlocking shields into the inert flood of rock. Here and there huge dull blocks with broken pieces shining like black glass had split off above the barrier and fallen, covering the metal palisade with rubble. And the front of the magma, swelling, had pulled apart the shields in places and bent the masts, or uprooted both them and the wedge-shaped blocks that anchored them.

This picture of struggle, doomed to failure but heroic, against the natural forces of the planet was so familiar and so comprehensible to the men that they left the place heartened. The jeep backed into an open space between two giant pillars and proceeded down the straight, bizarre avenue into the valley.

They came upon calyxes growing in long rectangular patches, like cornfields, calyxes identical to the ones growing on the plain near the ship. Hit by the glare, the snakelike plants, showing pink beneath the gray of their skin, tried to contract, as though wakened, but their movement was too torpid to be converted into decisive action; it was only a wave of helpless twitches thirty feet ahead of them, in the headlights.

The men stopped again, this time at the next-to-last pillar. The entrance was cluttered by a pile of fragments. They tried to see the interior with their flashlights, but the flashlights were too weak, so they removed a headlight from the jeep again and went inside.

The darkness was filled with an acrid stench, like that of organic matter eaten by chemicals. They were up to their knees in broken glass. The Chemist got caught in a snarl of wire. As he pulled himself loose, yellow fragments appeared from beneath the debris. The headlight, directed upward, revealed a yawning gap in the dome, with clusters of cells dangling from it, some of which were cracked open and empty. Bits of bone lay everywhere. Picking their way through the rubble, the men returned to the jeep; they rode on.

They passed a group of gray ruins in a hollow, where the headlights swept over another mass of rock resisted by angular props broadening to shields at the top and anchored to the ground by hooks. The jeep stopped rocking and bouncing as the surface beneath it became smooth, like concrete. Up ahead the men saw something blocking the way. It turned out to be a row of columns, and another row behind that. There was a whole forest of them, all supporting arches, making a curious building open on all sides. Below the spot where each arch left its column, they could see what appeared to be the embryos, or buds, of future arches, coiled up leaflike, unhatched.

The jeep went up a flight of steps as small as teeth and entered between the columns. There was a remarkable quality to their shape; it was botanical rather than geometrical, for although the columns were similar, no two were exactly alike; there were small variations in proportion, differences in the location of the nodes or swellings where the winged arches nestled.

The jeep rolled noiselessly over the stone surface, and left the columns behind, with their forest of moving shadows. When the last row disappeared, there was a wide-open space before them, and a low, faint glow. They advanced more slowly across solid rock, braking, coming to a stop at last three feet from an unexpected ravine.

Below them were dark ramparts reminiscent of old forts on Earth. The tops of the ramparts were level with where the men were standing, and they could see into the interiors, into narrow, crooked streets. The walls along the streets contained rows of rectangular openings that had rounded corners and were tilted back, as though aimed at the sky. Farther, behind the next series of walls, something they couldn't see gave off a faint light that bathed the stones in a golden haze.

The Captain pointed a headlight down into the nearest passageway. The beam revealed, a hundred feet away, a solitary spindle-shaped column standing among arched walls. Water flowed silently down its sides, sparkling. Around the column, on triangular tiles, was river sand, and at the edge of the light a container lay overturned and open on one side. They could feel the night breeze and heard, in the streets below, the sound of dead leaves drifting over stone.

"A settlement . . ." the Captain said slowly, moving the headlight farther. From the small square with the well, small streets radiated, gorges framed by vertical walls that curved outward at the top like the prows of ships. One wall, curved back to the horizontal, had openings from which ran black streaks, like marks from a past fire. The beam wandered over pointed corners, passed a gaping black cellar entrance, followed turning alleys.

"Turn it off!" the Doctor said.

The Captain did so, and only now noticed, in the darkness, the change taking place in the scene before them.

The spectral light that had touched the tops of the more distant walls, outlining the silhouettes of pipes or vents of some kind, was growing fainter, breaking up into separate islands of light, which in turn were extinguished as a wave of darkness advanced from the center outward, engulfing one sector after another, until the night was without a single spark or glimmer.

"They know we're here . . ." said the Chemist.

"Maybe," said the Doctor. "But, then, why were the

lights only over there? And . . . did you notice how they went out? From the center."

The Captain took his seat in the jeep and turned off the other two lights. The darkness covered them like a black lid. "We can't drive down there. And if we go on foot, someone will have to stay here with the jeep."

They could not see one another's faces, and all they could hear was the wind. Then, behind them, from the direction of the columns, came a faint sound, as though someone were stepping carefully. The Captain barely caught it; he turned the headlight around slowly, aimed it, and turned it on.

There was nothing there.

"Who will it be?" he asked.

Nobody spoke.

"It'll have to be me, then," he decided. He started the jeep and drove along the edge of the wall. After a few hundred feet they saw, in the rock, stairs leading down. Each step was small and shallow.

"I'll be here," he said.

"How much time do we have?" asked the Chemist.

"It's nine. Be back in an hour. You may have trouble getting your bearings, so forty minutes from now I'll light a flare, and ten minutes after that, another, and five minutes after that, a third. Try to get to some sort of elevation by then, though you should see the light from below. Now let's set our watches."

They did so in silence, listening to the wind. The air was growing colder.

"Don't take the thrower—there's too little space to use it here anyway," said the Captain, unconsciously lowering his voice. "The jectors ought to be enough. Besides, we want to make contact—but not at any price. Agreed?" This to the Doctor, who nodded. The Captain went on: "Night is not the best time. Perhaps you should only reconnoiter. That would be the most sensible thing. After all, we can come here again. Make sure you keep together. Guard your rear, and avoid dead ends."

"How long will you wait?" asked the Chemist.

The Captain's face, in the reflection of the headlights, looked ashen. He smiled.

"As long as I have to. And now on your way."

The Chemist slung the jector strap over his shoulder, to have both hands free. He turned on his flashlight and made for the stairs. The Doctor was already on his way down. Suddenly a bright light came from above—the Captain was lighting the way for them—and they followed the beam along the wall until they came to a large entrance flanked on either side by columns that emerged halfway up, as though growing from the wall. The lintel was covered with stone buds in high relief. The jeep's headlights here produced only a semicircular glow against the black of the doorway, the threshold of which was worn, as if by an endless procession of feet. They entered slowly. The doorway was enormous, built for giants, and on the inside walls and ceiling there were no signs of joints, as if the entire structure had been carved out of solid rock. The hall terminated in a blind, concave wall. On either side was a row of niches, each containing a depression at the bottom, like a place to kneel, and above that a triangular, glazed vent in the wall.

They went back outside. Several dozen feet farther on was a passageway in the wall surrounded by regular but mysterious multifaceted shapes. As they turned and entered it, the half-light behind them went out. The Chemist looked around—they were in total darkness. The Captain had turned off the headlights.

The Chemist looked up. He could not see the sky, but thought he could feel its distant, cold presence.

Their footsteps reverberated. The stone walls echoed.

Without saying a word, both men put out their left hands and touched the wall near them. It was almost as smooth as glass.

The Doctor turned on his flashlight, and they found themselves in a small open space like the bottom of a well. The walls, parting narrowly for street entrances, had double rows of windows all tilted skyward and therefore difficult to see from below. In the narrowest street were steps going steeply up and, before them, a horizontal stone beam flush between the walls. A dark cask shaped like an hourglass hung from it. The men chose the widest street. Soon the air around them seemed to change. Their flashlights showed, above them, vaulting riddled like a sieve, as if someone had punched a thousand triangular holes in the stone.

They walked on, past roofed side streets like high galleries. They walked beneath domes hung with misshapen bells or casks, and gossamer strips blew in the wind from lintels covered with ornamentation in the shape of plants. They peered into spacious but empty halls that had barrel-vaulted ceilings with large round openings at the top, which were plugged with boulders. Strange corrugated gutters angled upward from the streets like dough-covered ladders. A warm gust of air sometimes hit them in the face.

Several hundred feet from the square, the street divided; they went right and began to descend. Massive buttresses filled the street, and at each was a niche containing dead leaves. The dust they raised, walking, swirled in the beams of their flashlights. Crypts gaped on either side, exuding stale air, and inside them were meaningless shapes, seemingly abandoned. The street bottomed, then rose, and the air grew fresher.

The men passed more side streets, galleries, squares. As their flashlights moved, shadows appeared to take wing or scurry away in dark packs, or crouch at entrances guarded by columns that grew out of the wall and leaned toward one another. Everywhere, the men were accompanied by the barking echo of their footsteps.

At times they sensed the presence of someone else. Then they would stop by a wall, their flashlights turned off, their hearts pounding, and hear rustling, shuffling noise, a clumsy echo, a murmur like an underground stream. Or, from a well opening in an alcove, a moan might come, accompanied by a musty smell, but it was impossible to say whether it was a creature's voice or only the sound of the air in a hollow place. They had the impression that shapes were moving around them. Then they saw a small face peering out of an alley. It was pale and furrowed. But when they went to the place, all they found was a shred of paper-thin gold foil.

The Doctor said nothing. He knew that this excursion—dangerous, mad under such conditions, at night—was being undertaken because of him, that the Captain was risking it because, though time was pressing, the Doctor, alone of the crew, had insisted that an attempt at communication be made. He told himself that as soon as they reached the next corner, the next street, they would turn back—but they went on. In a high gallery framed by circular plates of opaque glass, which also formed the ceiling, with curious underslung, gondolalike balconies, a plant pod dropped in front of them. They picked it up: it was warm, as though a hand had held it.

What most perplexed them was the darkness. Surely the inhabitants of the planet had eyes and had observed their arrival. One would have expected to encounter guards, activity of some sort, not this emptiness. The lights that the men had observed from above were evidence that the area was inhabited. . . .

This reconnaissance became more and more like a bad

dream. They longed for light—their flashlights only seemed to intensify the surrounding gloom, and all they saw were fragments, incomprehensible parts of things.

There was a shuffling, so distinct that they rushed toward it. The rhythm of flight and pursuit filled the narrow street, the echoes broken between the close walls. As they ran, their flashlights in front of them, gray reflections moved along the vaulting overhead, which lowered until it was quite near. The shuffling noise stopped—then started again. The ceiling went up and down in waves as dark side-street entrances flew past. The men came to a halt, exhausted.

"Listen . . . do you think they . . . are drawing us into a trap?" the Chemist panted.

"Don't be silly!" the Doctor said, angry.

They were standing near a well whose walls were perforated with black openings. A pale, flattened face showed in one of them, but when they pointed their flashlights there, the opening was empty.

They went on. The presence of others was no longer a matter of conjecture, they could feel it everywhere, and the Doctor found himself thinking that even an attack or a struggle in the dark would be preferable to this pointless search that led nowhere. He looked at his watch. Almost half an hour had passed; they would have to head back soon.

Several feet ahead, at a bend in the wall, was a doorway crowned by a sharply pointed arch, with bulbous stone trunks rising on either side of the threshold. The Chemist swept the dark interior with his flashlight. The beam moved across a row of niches and fell upon a cluster of naked bodies crouching and motionless.

"They're there!" he gasped, shrinking back. The Doctor entered, while the Chemist shone his light from behind. The naked group clung to the wall, huddled, frozen in place. At first he thought they were dead. Drops of water glistened, trickling down their backs.

"Hey!" the Doctor called weakly, feeling the absurdity of the situation. From outside and above came a long, penetrating whistle; then a groan of many voices resounded in the stone room. None of the creatures moved, they only groaned. But there was movement in the street; the men could hear steps, the sound of running, and several dark forms went past in great bounds. When the echoes died, the Doctor peered out—there was nothing in the street. His bewilderment turned to anger. Standing in the doorway, he switched off his flashlight and listened.

More steps in the darkness.

"They're coming!"

The Doctor felt rather than saw the Chemist clutch his weapon. "Don't shoot!" he cried.

The street was suddenly filled, humps leaped up and sideways in the beam of the Chemist's flashlight, there were soft thuds of bodies hitting bodies, and huge shadows shot out and flapped like wings. A rattling cough broke into a wail of several hoarse voices, and something heavy fell at the Chemist's feet, knocking him down. For a second he glimpsed a small face with white eyes staring at him; his flashlight hit the ground, and the darkness was total. He groped for the flashlight desperately, like a blind man running his hands over the stone of the street.

He called to the Doctor, but his voice didn't carry. Dozens of bodies passed, bumping into one another.

The Chemist grabbed the metal cylinder of his flashlight and jumped to his feet, but a powerful blow threw him against a wall. A whistle sounded from high up, and the bodies stopped. He felt the heat coming from them.

He was shoved, he staggered and cried out, feeling slippery flesh and breaths on him from all sides. He pressed the contact, and there was light again.

A row of enormous humps, and dazed eyes in miniature faces. Then, from behind, naked creatures pushing toward him. Wedged between hot, wet bodies, he made no attempt to defend himself, but let himself be pushed and pulled along. The stink of flesh was asphyxiating. The creatures near him looked at him with apprehension and tried to back away, but there was no room. The hoarse howling went on and on. Small torsos drenched in a liquid like sweat nestled in bulges of pectoral muscle.

Suddenly the group surrounding him was pushed toward the doorway. Through a jungle of intertwined limbs he could make out, for a second, a glimmer of light and the Doctor's face, the mouth wide open in a shout. The Chemist's flashlight bobbed up and down, clutched to his chest, and it showed tiny faces, eyeless, noseless, mouthless, all drooping and drenched. For a moment the pressure slackened; then another push, and his shoulders were slammed against the wall, against a column, which he caught hold of and tried to cling to, resisting with all his might the wave of shoving creatures. He had to stay on his feet; if he fell, he would be trampled to death. He felt, in the stone, a step—no, a ledge. He climbed up on it and shone his flashlight outward.

It was a terrifying sight: a river of heads surging from wall to wall. They stared at him wide-eyed as he stood in a niche and watched their desperate, convulsive efforts to avoid him. But they could not move away, helpless in the crowd that pushed down the street, that squeezed the outermost creatures into the walls. The Chemist saw the Doctor—he was caught in the crowd, like a floating chip, surrounded by huge bodies. The Chemist's flashlight fell again, went out. In the darkness, the noise continued, the thuds and groaning. He propped his back against the cold stone and tried to catch his breath. But now he could hear individual footsteps, individual leaps, which meant that the hellish crowd was thinning. Weak in the knees, he wanted to call to the Doctor but was unable to utter a sound. Suddenly a burst of white revealed the top of the opposite wall, and the Chemist realized, after a few moments, that it must be the Captain showing them the way back with a magnesium flare.

He bent down and began feeling around for his flashlight, but the air along the ground smelled so bad it made him sick, so he quickly got back to his feet. Then he heard a distant shout, a man's voice.

"Doctor! Over here!" the Chemist called. Another shout, closer now, and a tongue of light appeared between the black walls. The Doctor was heading toward him, but not in a straight line; it was as though he were drunk. . . .

"Ah," he said, "you're here. Good . . ." And he grabbed the Chemist by the arm. "They had me for a while, but I managed to move aside. . . . Did you lose your flashlight?"

"Yes."

The Doctor still held his arm. "Dizziness," he explained, trying to catch his breath. "It's nothing. . . . It'll pass. . . ."

"What was that?" the Chemist asked in a whisper.

The Doctor said nothing.

Together they listened to the darkness, to distant footsteps, to an occasional moan. The sky lit up a second time above them, showing horizontal ledges, and the glow drifted downward, yellowing, like a brief sunrise and sunset.

"Let's go," they said together.

Without the flares they probably would not have made it back before daybreak. The summoning bursts of light, which twice more filled the ravines of the streets, kept them in the right direction. Along the way they encountered several creatures, who fled in panic, and once they came across a body lying at the bottom of a steep flight of steps, already cold. They passed it without a word. A few minutes before eleven, they found themselves back in the open square with the column and the well. No sooner did the beam of the Doctor's flashlight hit it than the triple headlights of the jeep began shining from above.

The Captain was standing at the top of the steps as the Doctor and the Chemist ran up. At the jeep, when they sat, panting, on one of the running boards, he turned off the lights and paced in the darkness, waiting for them to speak.

When they had told him everything, he said, "Interesting. A good thing it ended like that. There's one of them here, by the way. . . ."

They did not understand, but when he put a light back on and aimed it at the rear, they jumped to their feet. About thirty feet from the jeep lay a doubler.

The Doctor went to look at it. The thing was naked, half reclining, the upper part of its huge torso not on the ground. A pale-blue eye gazed at them from between heaving pectoral muscles. The men could see only the edge of a flattened little face, as though they were looking at someone through a door open just a crack.

"How did it get here?" the Doctor asked softly.

"It came from below, not long before you. When I lit the last flare, it ran away, but then it came back."

"It came back?!"

"Yes."

They stood over it, not knowing what to do. The creature was breathing heavily, as if after a long race. The Doctor bent down to stroke the hulk, but it started quivering, and large drops of liquid appeared on its pale flesh.

"He's . . . afraid of us," the Doctor murmured.

"Let's leave him, let's go. It's late," the Chemist said.

The Doctor hesitated. "No, wait, listen. . . . Let's sit down."

The doubler did not move.

The Captain and the Chemist followed the Doctor's example and sat down on the flat, stony ground near the creature. In the distance they heard the sound of the geyser, and then the wind moving in unseen thickets. The settlement was invisible in the night. Threads of mist floated by. Sharply outlined in the glare of the headlight, the jeep stood motionless, like a flat on an abandoned stage. After more than ten minutes of this sitting, they began to grow impatient, but suddenly the little head looked out at them. A clumsy movement on the Chemist's part made it retreat back into its pouch of muscle.

Finally, after almost half an hour of waiting, the huge creature got up. It was six feet tall, but would have been taller if it weren't bent forward. When it moved, the lower half of its body seemed to extend or retract legs at will from a shapeless base, but this was only muscle swelling and contracting around its limbs as it walked.

No one knew how the Doctor did it—and he himself admitted later that he had no idea—but, after a variety of gentle gestures and coaxing pats, the doubler, which by now had emerged completely from its nest of flesh, allowed the Doctor to lead it by its tiny hand to the jeep. The head drooped forward and stared at them as though incredulous as they assembled in front of the headlight.

"What now?" asked the Chemist. "You're not going to start a dialogue here."

"We'll take him with us," said the Doctor.

"Are you in your right mind?"

"A good idea," said the Captain. "But he must weigh half a ton!"

133

"So? The jeep can handle more than that."

"Add the three of us, and the torsion bars might break."

"Really?" said the Doctor. "Then we should let him go." And he pushed the doubler in the direction of the steps.

At that point the big creature curled up, its skin covered with opalescent drops.

"What? I . . . No, I was only joking," the Doctor stammered. They were amazed by the thing's reaction. The Doctor managed to calm the creature.

Finding room for the new passenger was not going to be easy. The Captain let almost all the air out of the tires, so that the jeep was practically touching the rocks. He removed the two back seats and strapped them to the luggage rack, and the thrower was tied to the top of the pile. But the doubler was reluctant to get into the vehicle. The Doctor patted it on the back, talked to it, got in himself, and sat down. This would have made an amusing scene if it hadn't been so late, way past eleven, and if they hadn't had more than sixty miles to cover—in the darkness, over difficult terrain, and most of it uphill—to get back to the ship. Finally the Doctor lost patience. He grabbed one of the arms dangling from the small torso and cried, "Push him from behind!"

The Chemist hesitated, but the Captain shoved hard against the doubler's bulging back. The doubler made a whimpering sound and, losing its balance, found itself in the jeep. Everything moved quickly now. The Captain inflated the tires, and the jeep had no problem moving, though it listed a bit. The Doctor occupied the seat in front of the new passenger, while the Chemist, not comfortable in its proximity, chose to stand behind the Captain instead.

They drove past rows of columns, then entered the avenue of the club-shaped structures. The jeep gathered speed on the flat terrain, but slowed when they climbed the slope of magma at the pass. About ten minutes later they reached the clay mounds and the square wells with their terrible contents.

They drove through thick, loose mud for a long time, then came to the tracks that their own tires had made going the other way, and followed them back to the valley.

Throwing up fountains of mud from beneath its wheels, the jeep picked its way between the clay mounds. A blurred light flared up in the darkness and came toward them, growing larger, until they could distinguish three separate lights. But the Captain maintained speed, knowing it was a reflection. The doubler began to show signs of uneasiness; it moved, it grunted, it even shifted its weight dangerously, making the jeep tilt more to the left. The Doctor tried to calm the creature with his voice, though without much success. Glancing back, he saw that it now resembled a rounded sugarloaf on top—the doubler had pulled in its small torso and appeared to be holding its breath. It was only when the momentary ripple of heat and the disappearance of their reflection announced that they had crossed the mysterious line that the huge passenger relaxed, stopped fidgeting, and even seemed to enjoy the night ride.

The jeep was now climbing a steep slope. It pitched and reeled as its bulging tires lumbered over large rocks. The engine, straining, whined. Once or twice they began rolling backward, the wheels spinning in a spray of loose soil. The Captain turned the steering wheel sharply, and they stopped. Cautiously, he turned the jeep around, and they went back down the slope along a diagonal, into the valley.

"Where are we going?" asked the Chemist nervously. Gusts of night air carried tiny droplets of water, almost like rain.

"We'll try somewhere else," said the Captain.

They halted and looked uphill, using one of the headlights, but there was not much to see, so they tried again at random. The slope soon became as steep as it had been before, but here the ground was dry, and the jeep could proceed. Every time the Captain steered to keep to compass north, however, the jeep fell back on its rear tires, forcing him westward, which meant that they would run into the thicket. As far as he could remember, the thicket covered most of the edge of the plateau toward which they were climbing. But there was nothing to be done. The headlights struck a row of white figures swaying in the gloom—no, it was only mist. Drops of condensation formed and ran down the windshield and the metal tubing of the seat frames. The cold mist thickened, then thinned, and they had no idea where they were going. The Captain tried only to go uphill.

Suddenly the mist dispersed, and the headlights, now bright, revealed the top of the slope. The black sky above was filled with stars. Everyone began to feel better.

"How's our passenger?" asked the Captain, not turning around.

"All right. He appears to be sleeping," said the Doctor.

The slope became steeper, and the jeep's center of gravity, shifting to the rear, made it impossible to steer with the front wheels. They skidded several feet to the side. Then the Doctor suggested, "Maybe I should sit up front, between the headlights, on the bumper."

"Not yet," the Captain said. He released air from the tires, and the jeep, sinking, held the ground better.

They crossed a large loamy area, and the ragged line of scrub above them came closer and closer, like an overhanging black brush. Going through it was out of the question, but they couldn't turn to look for a better place to enter, so they continued upward—and came to an abrupt halt about forty feet from a wall six feet high. The headlights showed yellow clay filled with threadlike roots.

The Chemist cursed.

The Captain got out, took a shovel, and dug at the clay, which he then put under the jeep's rear tires. Digging, he moved higher. The Chemist hurried after him. The Doctor could hear them working their way into the thicket, could hear the snap and crackle of dry branches. The Captain's flashlight flickered, went out, went on again in another place.

"What awful stuff!" growled the Chemist. "This is risky."

"We are hardly strangers to risk," responded the Captain. Raising his voice, he called to the Doctor, "We're going to start a little landslide. It should clear a path for us. Try to keep our passenger from getting frightened!"

"All right!" the Doctor shouted back. He turned around in his seat to face the doubler, who was curled up and still.

Then came the sound of moving clay, and a stream of clods rolled down the slope. Lumps thudded against the jeep. The landslide stopped, though bits of soil kept trickling from the wall. The Doctor checked the creature; it showed no reaction. In front of the jeep there was now a wide, funnel-shaped breach in the overhanging lip of clay. The Captain was standing in it, working energetically with his shovel.

It was past twelve by the time they took the towline, the reel, and the grappling hook from the luggage carrier, fastened one end of the line to the jeep, and pulled the other through the breach and up into the thicket, where it was anchored. The Doctor and the Chemist got out, and the Captain turned on all the wheel motors and the front winch, which drew the vehicle forward bit by bit. Further widening of the passage was required, but half an hour later the jeep was on the plateau, plowing noisily through the dry and brittle thicket. For another hour their progress was very slow; only when the vegetation came to an end were they able to pick up speed.

"Halfway!" the Chemist shouted to the Doctor after looking over the Captain's shoulder at the odometer. The Captain didn't think that they were halfway, considering the detour they had been forced to take on the slope. He was bent forward, his face close to the windshield, his eyes on the terrain. He was trying to avoid the larger boulders and ruts and take the smaller ones between the wheels. The jeep shook and lunged until the fuel can clattered, and sometimes the jeep even bounced into the air and fell, making the shock absorbers hiss. But the visibility was not bad, and so far there were no surprises. Where the headlight beams ended in a gray haze, something flashed by—a mast, then another, then another, and the men passed through the line of them. Craning his neck, the Doctor tried to see if there were columns of vibrating air at the tops of the masts, but it was too dark. The stars twinkled peacefully. Behind him, the huge creature was still. Only once did it shift slightly, as if, tired of sitting in the same position, it was making itself more comfortable, and this very human movement strangely touched the Doctor.

They were going downhill now, crossing grooves on a plateau with a lengthwise ridge. The Captain slowed when more grooves showed in the headlights, beyond a tongue-like projection of limestone; he heard a whizzing noise to the left that rose terribly to a hollow roar. A mass crossed their path, flashed in their headlights, a glittering colossus, and disappeared. The brakes squealed, and as the men pitched forward, they felt a blast of hot, bitter air on their faces. Another whizzing approached, and the Captain turned off the headlights. In the darkness, several feet ahead of them, phosphorescent gondolas flew by, one after another, enveloped by the blur of its gyrating disk. Each turned, performing the same banking maneuver, and the men began to count them: eight, nine, ten . . . The fifteenth seemed to be the last, so the men started moving again.

"Well, *that* we haven't seen before," the Doctor said.

But then came a different noise, much slower and closer to the ground, and the Captain quickly put the jeep in reverse and backed away, the tires crunching the limestone debris, and they waited. A shape passed before them in the darkness, making a deep rumble, and the stars above the trees were blotted out. The ground shook. Another phantom went by like a heavy top, and another. There was no gondola visible, only the silhouette of a thing radial, jagged, glowing red and rotating slowly in the direction opposite to its motion.

Again there was silence, although in the distance they could hear a soft hum.

"Those were huge—did you see them?!" said the Chemist.

The Captain waited a good while longer before he finally turned on the headlights and released the brakes. Going downhill, the jeep picked up speed. It would have been easier to travel along the grooves, since the ground there was more level, but the Captain preferred not to risk it—one of those blurry monsters might overtake them from behind. Steering carefully, he went in the same direction as the disks they had encountered, eastward, though the disks might well have turned again and changed course. He said nothing, but he was uneasy.

It was after two when a shiny band flashed up ahead. The doubler, who had not moved a muscle during the passage of the disks, had been peering out and examining its surroundings for some time now. But when the jeep reached the mirrorlike strip, the huge creature suddenly started wheezing and groaning, and it worked its way to one side, as though preparing to jump out.

"Stop! Stop!" cried the Doctor. The Captain stopped three feet from the strip.

"What's wrong?"

"He wants to escape!"

"Why?"

"I don't know. Maybe because of that strip. Turn off the headlights!"

The Captain did so. The moment it was dark, the doubler sank back heavily into its seat. They crossed the strip with the lights off, and for a moment the reflection of the stars sparkled in the blackness on both sides of the jeep.

Then they were on the plain, the headlights beating against the night as the jeep sped along, its whole frame vibrating. Small stones and sand kicked up behind them, and the cold wind buffeted their faces, which made the Chemist lower his head behind the windshield. They went faster and faster, expecting the ship to come into view at any moment.

The arrangement was that a blinker would be hung from one of the fins of the ship, so they looked for a blinking light. Minutes passed and there was no light, so they turned and headed northeast, but all around them was darkness. They drove now with only their sidelights on, then the Captain turned off even those, despite the risk of hitting something. At one point they saw a flickering and went toward it as fast as possible, but soon realized that it was just a star.

"Maybe the blinker is broken," ventured the Chemist.

Nobody replied. They covered another three miles and

turned again. The Doctor stood up and strained to see into the darkness. The jeep bounced, first in the front, then in the rear: they had crossed a ditch.

"Bear left," said the Doctor.

They crossed a second ditch one and a half feet deep. A faint light appeared and, rising up through it, a long, slanting shadow, the top of which was momentarily surrounded by an aureole. The light disappeared, but the jeep accelerated straight ahead, and when the light came on again, it revealed the ship's stern and three figures. The Captain turned on the headlights, and the figures ran toward them with their arms raised.

The ship was near now. They had approached it at such an angle that the stern had concealed the blinker.

"Is that you?! All of you?!" cried the Engineer. He rushed over to the jeep, but stopped short at the sight of the fourth, headless figure.

The Captain embraced the Engineer with one arm and the Physicist with the other, and stood there for a moment, as if requiring their support. The five men formed a group near one of the sidelights, while the Doctor, not joining them, spoke quietly to the doubler, which had become restless.

"We're all right," said the Chemist. "And you?"

"In one piece," the Cyberneticist replied.

The men looked at one another for quite a while in silence.

"Do we discuss what happened, or do we go to sleep?" asked the Chemist.

"You can sleep? That's great," exclaimed the Physicist. "Sleep! Good God! They were here, did you know that?"

"I thought as much," said the Captain. "Was . . . was there a fight?"

"No. And for you . . . ?"

"No, we didn't have one, either. I . . . think the fact

that they've discovered the ship may prove to be more important than anything we found."

"Did you capture that?" asked the Engineer.

"Actually . . . he captured us. That is, he came voluntarily. But it's a long story, and complicated, and one we don't really understand."

"It's the same with us!" said the Cyberneticist. "They showed up about an hour after you left! I thought . . . well, I thought it was the end."

"You must be starving," said the Engineer.

"I completely forgot about food. Doctor!" called the Captain. "Come here!"

"Are we having a meeting?" The Doctor stepped from the jeep and came over, but he kept his eyes on the doubler, who unexpectedly jumped to the ground with a surprisingly light movement and shuffled over to the crew. At the edge of the ring of light the huge creature became motionless. As they watched silently, its muscles moved and made a gap; in the diffused glow of the lights the men saw part of a head and a blue eye regarding them.

"So they were here?" asked the Doctor, who at that moment was the only one not looking at the doubler.

"Yes. Twenty-five disks, of the kind we rode, and four much larger machines, like blurred tops."

"We saw them too!" said the Chemist.

"When? Where?"

"Maybe an hour ago, on our way back. We very nearly ran into them. What did they do here?"

"Not much," replied the Engineer. "The disks appeared in a row, we don't know from which direction, because when we came up to the surface—we had been in the ship for no more than five minutes—they were already flying around, circling us. They didn't approach. We figured this was a scouting party, a reconnaissance patrol, so we set up the thrower near the ship and waited.

But they just kept circling, always at the same distance, not moving away, not coming closer. That went on for about an hour and a half. Then the larger things appeared, the tops—one of them a hundred feet high! They're a lot slower. It seems the tops can travel only along the grooves that the other ones dig. The disks, anyway, made room for them in their circle, so that the larger and smaller machines alternated. While they were whirling around, one or two of them almost collided; their rims touched with an awful crash, but nothing happened, and they went on whirling."

"And what did you do?"

"We were sweating it out by the thrower. It wasn't pleasant."

"I'm sure it wasn't," the Doctor said seriously. "And then what?"

"Well, at first I thought that at any second they would attack. Then that they were only observing us. But their formation was odd, and the fact that they never stopped; we know that the disks can spin in place. . . . Anyway, after seven o'clock I asked the Physicist to get the blinker, because we had to hang it outside for you, except that it wouldn't have been possible for you to get through that flying wall—and then it dawned on me that this was intentional, a blockade! So I thought we had better try to communicate—while we could. Still sitting behind the thrower, we began to flash a signal, two flashes, then three, then four."

"A series?" asked the Doctor, and the Engineer was unable to tell whether he was making fun of him.

"A normal arithmetic progression," he said at last.

"And what did they do?" asked the Chemist, who had been listening carefully.

"Basically, nothing . . ."

"What do you mean, *basically?*"

"They did different things the whole time, before, during, and after the flashing, but nothing that resembled an attempt to respond or establish contact."

"What did they do?"

"They spun faster, slower, approached one another, and there was movement in the gondolas."

"Do the tops—the big machines—also have gondolas?"

"Didn't you say you saw them?"

"It was dark."

"They have no gondolas. In their center there's nothing at all. An empty space. But there is a large container of some kind that moves—floats—around the circumference. Convex on the outside, concave on the inside, and it assumes various positions and has a row of horns, conical swellings, which serve no purpose that I can see. The tops also left the circle sometimes and changed places with the disks."

"How often?"

"It varied. In any case, we couldn't make out a pattern in it. Not that we didn't try. I took note of everything, looking for some sort of response from them. They performed complex maneuvers. For example, during the second hour the tops slowed down, and in front of each one a disk positioned itself, then moved slowly toward us, though no closer than fifty feet, with the top behind it. Then they formed circles again, but now two: an inner circle with four tops and four disks, and an outer circle with the rest of the disks. I was beginning to think that I had better do something, so you could get through, when lo and behold they lined up in single file and left, in a spiral first, then straight south."

"When was this?"

"A few minutes past eleven."

"That means we probably encountered other ones," the Chemist said to the Captain.

"Not necessarily. They might have stopped on the way."

"Now tell us what happened to you," said the Physicist.

"Let's hear from the Doctor," said the Captain.

The Doctor summarized the whole expedition in a few minutes. "It's curious that everything we find here is reminiscent of things we know on Earth," he concluded, "but only partly. There are always pieces that don't fit. These vehicles of theirs, for example, showed up here like war machines. Was it reconnaissance, was it a blockade? But ultimately nothing happened, and we are left in the dark. Those wells in the clay—they were terrible, of course, but what in fact were they? Graves? We don't know. Then that settlement, or whatever it was. An incredible place, like a nightmare. And the skeletons inside the 'clubs'? Were they museums? Slaughterhouses? Chapels? Factories turning out biological specimens? Prisons? Anything is possible, even a concentration camp!

"And no one stopped us or tried to establish contact with us. That's surely the most incomprehensible thing of all. Without question, the planet's civilization is highly developed. The architecture, the construction of domes like the ones we've seen—and yet, nearby, the stone settlement, like a medieval stronghold—an astonishing mixture of levels of civilization! Their signaling system must be sophisticated, since they extinguished the lights of the stronghold less than a minute after our arrival, and we were traveling fast and saw no one along the way. They are undoubtedly intelligent, but the crowd that descended on us behaved like a panic-stricken herd of sheep. It was chaos, totally senseless, mad! And that's how it's been throughout.

"The individual we killed was covered with a kind of

foil, while these others were naked. The corpse in the well had a tube in its umbilicus, and it had an eye, an eye like the one you're looking at now, while the other corpses had no eyes. . . . I'm beginning to think that even this doubler we brought with us won't help us much. We'll try to communicate with it, of course, but I doubt that we'll have much success. . . ."

The Cyberneticist said: "All the information we've collected so far should be written down, classified, or we'll get confused. The Doctor's probably right, but . . . Those skeletons, were they definitely skeletons? And the crowd of doublers that surrounded you and then fled . . ."

"I saw the skeletons as clearly as I see you. As for the crowd . . ." And he spread his arms.

"That was absolute madness," the Chemist put in.

"Maybe you woke up the settlement, and they were surprised. Imagine a hotel on Earth, and one of these gyrating disks suddenly appearing. Of course people will panic!"

The Chemist shook his head, and the Doctor smiled.

"You weren't there, so it's difficult to explain it to you. Panic, you say . . . And when all the people have hidden themselves or fled, one of them, naked as a jaybird, runs after the disk and asks for a ride."

"But it didn't ask you. . . ."

"He didn't? And what happened when I pushed him away to make him go back?"

"Gentlemen, it's a quarter to four," said the Captain, "and tomorrow—I should say today—they could pay us a new visit, at any time. Nothing would surprise me! What did you do in the ship?" he asked the Engineer.

"Very little, since we were sitting by the thrower for four hours! One microbrain has been checked, and the remote is almost working—the Cyberneticist can give you the details. There's quite a mess, unfortunately."

"I need sixteen niobium-tantalum diodes," said the Cyberneticist. "The cryotrons are intact, but I can't do anything with the brain without the diodes."

"Can't you cannibalize?"

"I did, I took over seven hundred."

"There aren't any more?"

"Maybe in Defender—I couldn't reach it. It's lying at the very bottom."

"Listen, do we have to stand out here all night?"

"You're right, let's go. But wait—what about the doubler?"

"And what about the jeep?"

"You're not going to like this, gentlemen, but from now on we'll have to stand watch around the clock," said the Captain. "It was crazy of us not to have done that before. Who will volunteer for the first two hours, until dawn . . . ?"

"I will," said the Doctor.

"You? Don't be ridiculous. It has to be one of us," said the Engineer. "After all, we were just sitting here."

"And I was sitting in the jeep. I'm no more tired than you are."

"Enough. First the Engineer, then the Doctor," the Captain decided. He stretched, rubbed his numb hands, went over to the jeep, turned off the lights, and wheeled it around slowly, pushing it under the hull of the ship.

"And the doubler?" The Cyberneticist was standing over the recumbent creature.

"He'll stay here. He's sleeping. If he were going to run away, he wouldn't have come here in the first place," observed the Physicist.

"We can't just leave him like this. We have to secure him somehow," said the Chemist.

But the others were entering the tunnel one by one. He looked around, shrugged, and followed them. The

Engineer meanwhile put an air cushion beside the thrower and sat down. But, afraid of falling asleep, he got up and began to pace back and forth.

The sand crunched softly under his boots. The first gray light appeared in the east, and the stars gradually went out. The air, cold and fresh, filled his lungs. He tried to pick out the strange odor that he recalled from the first time they had set foot on the planet, but he could no longer detect it. The side of the creature lying nearby rose and fell rhythmically. Long thin tentacles emerged from its chest and grabbed the Engineer by the leg. He struggled, stumbled, almost fell over—and opened his eyes. He had been asleep on his feet. It was brighter now. In the east, cirrus clouds had formed into a long, slanting line, the end of which was beginning to glow as the gray of the sky turned azure. The last star disappeared.

The Engineer faced the horizon. The clouds turned from dark gray to golden bronze; fire blazed at their edges; a streak of rose now lay on the horizon. This could have been Earth.

He was pierced with despair.

"My turn!" a strong voice rang out behind him. The Engineer gave a start. The Doctor was smiling at him. The Engineer suddenly wanted to thank him, to say something, he didn't know what—something very important—but he had no words for it, so he shook his head, answered the smile with a smile, and went into the dark tunnel.

VIII

At noon five half-naked men with tanned faces and necks were lying near the ship. Around them were utensils, pieces of equipment, and a square of canvas covered with suits, boots, and towels. The smell of freshly brewed coffee came from an open thermos. Shadows of clouds moved silently across the plain. Had it not been for the creature sitting motionless several feet farther beneath the hull, the scene might have resembled a picnic on Earth.

"Where's the Engineer?" asked the Physicist. He propped himself up lazily on his elbows.

"Writing his book."

"You mean, on how to repair one's spaceship?"

"Yes, it should make for interesting reading. A thick volume!"

The Physicist looked at the speaker. "You're in a good mood. That's important. And your wound is almost healed. I don't think the cut would have closed so fast on Earth."

The Captain touched the scab on his forehead and raised

his brows. "That's possible. The ship was sterile, and the bacteria here are harmless to us. And there don't seem to be any insects. I haven't seen any, have you?"

"The Doctor's white butterflies," the Physicist said quietly, reluctant to talk in the heat.

"Well, that's only a hypothesis."

"And what isn't a hypothesis here?" asked the Doctor.

"Our presence," the Chemist said, turning over on his back. "You know, I wouldn't mind a change of scenery. . . ."

"Nor would I," agreed the Doctor.

"Did you notice how red the doubler's skin became after only a few minutes in the sun?" the Captain said.

The Doctor nodded. "Yes. That means either that he has never been in the sun before, or that normally he wears some sort of clothing. Unless . . ."

"Unless what?"

"I don't know what. . . ."

"Things aren't too bad," said the Cyberneticist, looking up from a sheet of paper covered with writing. "Henry tells me he can get the diodes from Defender. If everything checks out tomorrow, by evening we'll have the first robot working. I'll put it in charge of the rest, and if it can patch together three units, our troubles are over. We'll get the hoists going, the shovel, and in a week the ship will be up, and . . ."

"And what?" asked the Chemist. "We climb in and take off?"

The Doctor grinned. "Space travel is the purest expression of man's curiosity," he said. "Did you hear? The Chemist doesn't want to leave now!"

"No, but seriously, Doctor, what about the doubler? You've been with him all day!"

"That's true."

"Well? Don't get mysterious! We've had enough mystery!"

"I wish I had something to be mysterious about! He's behaving . . . like a child. A retarded child. He recognizes me. When I call him, he comes. When I push him away, he sits."

"You took him to the engine room. How did he react?"

"Like a baby. It didn't interest him at all. When I went behind the generator and he couldn't see me, he began to sweat with fear. If it is sweat, and if the sweat does signify fear . . ."

"Can he speak? I could hear him gurgling to you."

"He doesn't produce articulate sounds. I made tape recordings and analyzed the frequencies. Yet he can hear speech. . . . He's timid, fearful, as docile as a cow, but the whole community seems to be like that. . . ."

"Maybe he's young; maybe their young are large."

"He's not young. You can tell by the skin, its wrinkles and folds. And the soles of his feet are callused, hard, hornlike. In any case, he isn't a child in our sense of the word. On our return that night, he noticed certain things before we did, and reacted strangely, for example, to that mirage in the air, as I told you. He was afraid. Afraid, also, of that settlement. Otherwise why would he have fled it?"

"But they have built factories, the disks—they must be intelligent," said the Physicist.

"This one isn't."

"Wait," said the Chemist, sitting up and brushing the sand off his elbows. "Suppose he's . . . handicapped, or . . ."

"You're suggesting that was an insane asylum back there?" asked the Doctor. "Or an isolated place where they keep their sick?"

"And perform experiments on them," suggested the Chemist.

"What you saw you call experiments?" asked the Captain, who had been silent until now.

"I'm not judging it morally. How can I? We understand nothing, really," the Chemist replied. "The Doctor found a tube in one of them, a tube not unlike the one that was in the body we dissected . . ."

"Aha. In other words, the doubler that got into the ship at night also came from there, escaped from there?"

"Why not? Is it impossible?"

"And the skeletons?" said the Physicist, obviously not convinced by the Chemist's argument.

"Well, I don't know, maybe they're exhibits. Or perhaps they show them as . . . as a kind of shock treatment."

"Sure, and they have their own Freud, too," said the Doctor. "No, you'd better drop your asylum theory, my friend. And don't tell us that those skeletons are some sort of house of horrors in an amusement park. It's an enormous installation, and a lot of technology was needed to get the skeletons into those glass cells. Could it be a factory? But manufacturing what?"

"The fact that you can't get information out of this doubler doesn't prove anything," the Physicist said. "You might just as well try to learn about Earth's civilization from a janitor at my university."

Everyone laughed. Suddenly the laughter stopped. The doubler was standing over them, waving his little knotted fingers in the air, and his small flat face was dangling, twitching.

"What's he doing?!" exclaimed the Chemist.

"Laughing," said the Captain.

And, indeed, the torso appeared to be hiccuping in mirth, and the big clumsy feet were stamping. But, seeing five pairs of human eyes fixed on him, the creature froze, then drew itself in, retracting the small hands and head, which peered out once more from its slit of muscle. The creature hobbled back to its place and sank to the ground with a soft wheeze.

"If that *was* laughter," whispered the Physicist.

"Laughter doesn't prove anything, either. Apes laugh."

"Wait," said the Captain. His eyes sparkled in his lean, sunburned face. "Suppose they have a much wider genetic range of ability than we do. That there exist classes—castes—of creative workers and builders, and on the other hand a great number of individuals who are basically fit for no work—for nothing at all. And that these useless ones . . ."

"Are killed. Or experimented on. Or eaten. Don't be afraid, say whatever comes to mind," the Doctor replied. "No one will laugh at you, because anything is possible. Unfortunately not everything that is possible makes sense to us."

"And what about the skeletons?" the Chemist asked.

"They serve as teaching aids after lunch," the Cyberneticist said with a grimace.

"If I were to tell you all the theories that have occurred to me since yesterday," said the Doctor, "it would make a book five times larger than the one Henry is writing, though certainly not so edifying. As a boy I knew an old astronaut. The man had seen more planets than he had hairs on his head, and he was still far from bald. . . . He wanted to describe to me the landscape of a particular moon—I don't remember which. 'There are these . . . large . . . you know,' he said, spreading his arms. 'And they have these . . . It's sort of like . . . But the sky is different . . . although . . .' Finally he laughed and gave up. You can't tell someone who has never been in space what it's like to hang in the void with the stars at your feet. And we're only talking about differences in physical environments! Here we have a civilization that is at least five thousand years old. At least! And we're trying to understand it after a few days!"

"But try we must, because if we fail, the price we have to pay may be . . . too high," said the Captain. After a pause, he added, "What, then, do you think we should do?"

"What we've been doing up to now," said the Doctor, "though I think our chances of success are about one in five thousand, or however long Eden's civilization has been around. . . ."

The Engineer emerged from the tunnel and, seeing his comrades lying in the shade as though they were on the beach, got out of his suit and joined them. The Chemist greeted him with a nod.

"How is it going?" asked the Captain.

"Well, I'm three-quarters done. . . . But I haven't been working on it the whole time, because I was thinking about that first factory, the one to the north, which we theorized was abandoned and out of control. . . . What's funny? Why are you laughing?"

"I'll tell you something," said the Doctor, who was the only one to remain serious. "When the ship is ready to take off, there will be a mutiny. No one will want to leave until we find out. . . . Because if, even now, instead of sweating over your nuts and bolts . . ."

"Ah, you're theorizing, too?" said the Engineer. "And what have you come up with?"

"Nothing. And you?"

"Also nothing, but . . . I was trying to find common elements, a more general pattern to what we encountered there, and it struck me that at the factory—the automated factory—even though it worked in cycles, seemingly repeating the process, its 'finished products' varied. . . . Remember?"

There was a murmur of assent.

"And yesterday the Doctor noted that the doublers varied—that some had no eyes, some no nose, or the number of fingers was different, or the color of the skin. Everything here differs within certain limits, and the variation seems to be the result of flaws in the process, both the biological and the technological. . . ."

"Now, that's interesting!" said the Physicist, who had been listening with increasing attention.

"Yes, you have something there. Go on," the Doctor said, turning to the Engineer, who was shaking his head doubtfully.

"No, really, it's a silly idea. When a man sits and thinks on his own, all sorts of things . . ."

"Tell us the idea!" the Chemist shouted, almost indignant.

"Now that you've started," said the Cyberneticist.

"Well, I thought: In the factory we were looking at a circular process of production and destruction, and then yesterday you discovered something that resembled a factory. If it was a factory, it had to produce something."

"But there was nothing there," said the Chemist, "except for the skeletons. Of course we didn't look everywhere . . ." he added hesitantly.

"And what if that factory produces . . . doublers?" the Engineer asked softly. In the general silence, he went on: "The system is analogous: mass production, an assembly line, except that the variation is caused not so much by a lack of supervision as by the very nature of the process, because of its complexity. The skeletons did vary."

"And you think . . . they kill the ones that don't 'pass inspection'?" the Chemist asked in a changed voice.

"Not at all! My thought was that those bodies you found . . . never lived at all! That the system creates organisms equipped with all the muscles and every internal organ, but whose deviation from the norm is so great that they are unable to function . . . so they are never animated, they are removed from the production line. . . ."

"And that ditch with the bodies, what was that? More 'defective merchandise'?" asked the Cyberneticist.

"I don't know, but the possibility can't be ruled out. . . ."

"No, it can't," said the Doctor, looking toward the bluish haze on the horizon. "In what you're saying . . . that broken tube . . ."

"Maybe they introduced nutrients through it during the synthesis."

"That would also explain why the doubler you brought back appears to be retarded," the Cyberneticist observed. "If he was produced full-grown, he has no experience. . . ."

"No," the Chemist disagreed. "That doubler of ours does know things. He was afraid to return to his stone asylum—for which he might have good reason—and he was afraid, too, of that strip of mirror. And he knew something about the curious border we crossed, with the mirage. . . ."

"I don't know. The picture we get, from Henry's hypothesis, doesn't make sense," said the Captain, contemplating the sand at his feet. "The first factory produces parts that aren't used. And the second factory living beings? Why? And are you suggesting that they, too, are thrown back into the hopper?"

"What an awful thought!" said the Cyberneticist with a shudder.

"But if living beings are put back into the hopper," said the Chemist, "then disposal of individuals too defective for animation would be unnecessary. Besides, we saw no evidence of such recycling. . . ."

In the ensuing silence, the Doctor got up and swept his eyes over the group.

"We've taken the Engineer's idea," he said, "and now we're all trying to fit the facts to it, to his 'biological factory' hypothesis. Which proves only one thing, that we are very noble-minded and very naïve. . . ."

As they looked at him with surprise, he continued: "A moment ago you were attempting to imagine the most horrible possibility—and you came up with a picture a child might have drawn: a factory producing people in order to grind them up again. . . . The reality, my friends, may be much worse."

"Really!" the Cyberneticist sputtered.

"Wait, let him speak," the Engineer said.

"The more I think about what happened in that settlement, the more I am convinced that we were seeing something totally different from what we thought we were seeing."

"What, then, according to you, happened?" asked the Physicist.

"What happened I don't know, but I know what didn't happen."

"Talk clearly! No riddles!"

"After wandering through that stone labyrinth, we were suddenly charged by a crowd that then dispersed and fled. Having seen the lights go out as we approached the settlement, we concluded that the inhabitants were hiding from us, and that we had been trampled by a mob rushing for cover—or something like that. Now, in my mind I've gone over the whole sequence of events as thoroughly as I can, and I'll tell you this: one resists the truth as one fights madness."

"Get to the point!"

"The point is this. We have the following situation. Strangers from space land on a planet inhabited by intelligent beings. In what possible ways do the inhabitants react?"

Nobody replied, so the Doctor went on: "Even if the beings of this planet were created in test tubes or made in some stranger manner, I see only three possible types of behavior: to attempt to communicate with the strangers, to attack them, or to flee. It turns out, however, that a fourth type is possible—total indifference!"

"You told us that they nearly broke your ribs. That's indifference?!" the Cyberneticist sneered. But the Chemist nodded; there was a light in his eyes.

The Doctor replied: "If you were to find yourself in the path of a herd of cattle running from a fire, you might fare worse than we did. But that wouldn't mean that the herd had noticed you. I tell you, the crowd of doublers didn't see us at all. They took no interest in us. There was fear, yes, but not of us. We were merely in the way."

Then the Chemist spoke. "Yes," he said slowly. "All this time, it's been bothering me, like reading a text where the sentences are out of order. Now it falls into place. Yes, he's right. They didn't see me. Except for the closest ones, but they were the only ones who weren't in panic— almost as if seeing me had a sobering effect on them. While they were looking at me, they were simply inhabitants of a planet amazed to see an alien creature. They had no wish to harm me. In fact, if I recall correctly, they even helped me extricate myself from the herd. . . ."

"And what if someone set that herd on you, to drive you into the open?" asked the Engineer.

The Chemist shook his head. "There was no one there like that, no flying disks, no guards, no organization— there was chaos, confusion. Yes," he added, "it's odd that I see that only now! That those who noticed me appeared to regain their senses, while all the others were berserk with fear!"

"But in that case," said the Captain, "why were the lights extinguished at precisely the moment of our arrival?"

"What puzzles me," said the Doctor, "is the panic itself."

"Yes, what could have caused it?"

"Perhaps a decline in the planet's civilization," suggested the Cyberneticist after a moment's silence. "A period of regression, disintegration, or a kind of cancer of society."

"Unconvincing," said the Captain. "On our Earth, which is an average planet, there have been periods of regression, and many civilizations have risen and fallen, but, taking our history as a whole, you get a picture of ever-increasing complexity, and of life's growing value. We call this 'progress.' Progress is a normal phenomenon. Yet, by the law of large numbers, there will be statistical deviations from the norm, in both positive and negative directions. We may have landed on a world at the far negative end of that distributional curve. . . ."

"Mathematical mysticism," muttered the Engineer.

"But that factory exists," the Physicist said.

"The first factory, yes. The existence of the second is a hypothesis only."

"In other words, we need another expedition," said the Chemist.

The Engineer looked around. The sun was sinking in the west; the shadows on the sand were growing longer. A light wind blew.

"Today . . . ?" he asked, looking at the Captain.

"Today we should go for water—nothing more." The Captain stood up. "An interesting discussion," he said, though obviously thinking about something else. He picked up his suit.

"This evening," he continued, "we'll drive to the stream, for water. We shouldn't be diverted from that by anything short of a direct threat." He turned to the men sitting on the sand, considered them for a while, then said, "I don't like this."

"What don't you like?"

"Their leaving us in peace after that visit two days ago. No community acts like that when an alien spaceship drops out of the sky."

"Such indifference would support what I said," said the Cyberneticist.

"About a 'cancer' affecting Eden? Well, from our point of view that wouldn't be the worst thing that could happen. Except . . ."

"Except what?"

"Nothing. Listen, let's have a look at Defender. Let's dig it out. Its diodes ought to be intact."

IX

For two hours they cleared the lower bay of robot pieces, of almost impossibly interlocked parts that covered Defender's casing like rubble from an avalanche. The heavier objects they lifted with a small hoist, and the Engineer and the Captain took apart whatever wouldn't fit through the door. Two metal plates, which were wedged between Defender's turret and a case of lead weights, finally had to be cut up with an electric arc, for which cables were lowered from the instrument panel in the engine room. The Cyberneticist and the Physicist sorted out the pieces pulled from the heap. What couldn't be repaired was scrapped. The Chemist, in turn, divided up the scrap into metal and plastic. Sometimes they had to drop what they were doing to help move some particularly massive piece. By six o'clock they had gained sufficient access to Defender's flattened head to open its upper hatch.

The Cyberneticist was the first to jump into the dark

interior. A light was lowered to him on a wire. They could hear his shout, muffled as if coming from a well.

"They're all here!" he cried triumphantly. "Everything's working! You could get in and drive off!"

"Well, Defender was built to take punishment," said the Engineer, beaming. He had bleeding scratches on his forearms.

"Gentlemen, it's six. If we're going to get water, we'd better do it now," said the Captain. "The Cyberneticist and the Engineer have their hands full, so I think we should use the same crew as yesterday."

"I don't agree!"

"Look . . ." the Captain began, but the Engineer said, "You can manage here as well as I can. I'm going this time."

They argued for a while, but finally the Captain gave in. The expedition would consist of the Engineer, the Physicist, and the Doctor. The Doctor insisted on going again.

"The canisters are ready," said the Captain. "It's about twelve miles to the brook."

"If we can, we'll make two trips," said the Engineer. "That would give us a hundred gallons."

"We'll see."

The Chemist and the Cyberneticist wanted to accompany them out, but the Engineer put up his hand. "We don't need an escort. That's silly."

"I have to be outside anyway," said the Chemist.

They went up the steel ladder.

The sun was low in the sky. After checking the suspension, the steering, and the fuel supply, the Engineer took the driver's seat. But the moment the Doctor got in, the doubler, who had been lying in the shade of the ship, stood up, straightened to its full height, and shuffled toward him. When the jeep began moving, the huge creature whined and set off after it at a speed that amazed the Chemist. The Doctor shouted to the Engineer, and the jeep came to a halt.

"Now what?" grumbled the Engineer. "We're certainly not taking him with us!"

The Doctor, not knowing what to do, looked with embarrassment at the head and shoulders towering above him as the doubler, shifting its weight from one foot to the other and making wheezing sounds, stared down into his face.

"Lock him up in the ship. He'll follow you otherwise," advised the Engineer.

"Or put him to sleep," said the Chemist. "If he runs after us, he might attract something else."

That was enough to persuade the Doctor. The jeep turned back to the ship, and the doubler rushed after them, making its peculiar leaps. Then the Doctor coaxed the giant into the tunnel, which was no easy task. He returned a quarter of an hour later, angry and upset.

"I put him in the first-aid room," he said, "where there's no glass or anything sharp. But he might panic."

"You sound like a mother hen," said the Engineer.

The Doctor bit his lip, but said nothing in reply.

They set off again, circling the ship in a wide arc. The Chemist went on waving even when all that was visible was a high, thinning cloud of dust. Then he paced back and forth near the shallow trench that contained the thrower.

Two hours later he was still pacing there when a cloud of dust reappeared among the slender calyxes and their long shadows. The red, swollen, egg-shaped solar orb had just touched the horizon, and now there was a bank of bluish clouds in the north. But the coolness that usually came at that time of day was missing; it was still stifling.

The jeep approached, bouncing over disk-grooves. It

was lower to the ground, and the tires were flatter. The Chemist could hear water splashing in all the canisters. There was even a full can on the empty seat. "How was it?" he asked.

The Engineer removed his dark glasses and wiped the sweat and dust from his face with a handkerchief.

"Very pleasant."

"You didn't meet anyone?"

"There were disks, as usual, but we passed them at a distance. We came out on the other side of that copse with the hollow in it—you know the one. The only problem was filling the canisters. A pump would have come in handy."

"We're going back," the Physicist said.

"But first you'll have to put the water into—"

"Oh, there's no point," said the Physicist. "We have so many empty canisters, we'll take some of them. Afterward we can carry the whole lot down at once."

He and the Engineer exchanged a look, as though they shared some secret thought. The Chemist failed to notice this, though he was surprised at the haste with which they unloaded the canisters and threw the new ones on the rack. A moment later they were off in a cloud of dust, which, in the light of the setting sun, made a long crimson wall across the plain.

The Captain stepped out of the tunnel. "Still not here," he said.

"They were here, exchanged their canisters for empty ones, and left."

The Captain was more puzzled by this than angry. "That quickly?" He told the Chemist that he would replace him on watch in a moment, then went down to report to the Cyberneticist, who was working on the master robot.

The Cyberneticist nodded abstractedly, having some twenty transistors in his mouth, which he spat into his hand like pits. Wrapped around his neck and smoothed out over his chest were hundreds of wires of different colors, which had spilled from the robot's entrails. These he was now connecting at such speed that his fingers seemed to be flying. Sometimes he would stop suddenly and, for a full minute or longer, stare in amazement at the diagram spread out before him.

The Captain returned to the surface, replaced the Chemist (who went off to prepare supper for the crew), and sat down beside the thrower. To kill time, he made notes in the margins of the assembly manual that the Engineer had prepared.

For two days now they had been racking their brains over what to do with the twenty-five thousand gallons of radioactively contaminated water in the loading bay. In order to purify the water, they needed to get the filters working, but the cable that supplied the filters with power and had to be repaired lay in the flooded area. The ship was equipped with diving gear, though not the type that was radiation-shielded. Nor was there much point in jury-rigging a shield with lead; it would be easier now to wait for the robots to be repaired and have them do the job.

The Captain sat in the night under the ship's stern, under the blinking light. He made his notes as quickly as possible, because the light, each time, lasted no more than three seconds. Later he would laugh, seeing the scrawl this had made of his handwriting. He glanced at his watch: almost ten.

He stood up, paced, looked for the jeep's headlights, but could see nothing. He began to walk in the direction from which the jeep would be returning.

As usual when he was alone, he looked up at the stars. The Milky Way was climbing steeply through the blackness. From Scorpio the Captain moved his eyes left, and suddenly held his breath. Capricorn's brightest stars were barely visible, lost in a pale glow, as though the Milky Way had expanded and absorbed them. Then he understood: it was a reflection in the sky directly above the eastern horizon. His heart began to pound, and he could feel a pressure in his throat. He clenched his teeth. The reflection was whitish, dim, but later brightened, flaring several times in succession: The Captain closed his eyes, listened with the utmost concentration, but all he could hear was the pulsing of his own blood. The constellations were now almost invisible. He stood stock-still, staring at the horizon, which was filling with misty light.

His first thought was to return to the ship and tell the others. They could bring the thrower to the battle. But on foot that would take at least three hours. Besides the jeep, they had a small helicopter, but it was sitting in radioactive water, wedged between cases. All they had been able to see of it was its broken blade, and the cabin was probably in worse condition. That left Defender. They might simply climb inside Defender, open the loading hatch by remote—there was a transmitter in the engine room— and ride down through the water, which in any case would pour out as soon as the hatch was open. In Defender they would be shielded. But could the hatch be opened? And what would they do later with all the radioactive soil around the ship? It would cover an enormous area. . . .

He decided to wait ten minutes. If he didn't see the headlights by then, they would go. He looked at his watch: thirteen minutes after ten. The reflection—no, he was not mistaken—was spreading slowly along the horizon, approaching Alpha Phoenix, a strip of pink on top and dull white below. He looked at his watch again. Four minutes to go. He saw the headlights.

At first they were like a twinkling star; then they divided in two, jumped up and down, and finally grew dazzling. The Captain could now hear the sound of tires. The men were traveling fast, but not at breakneck speed, and the fact that they were in no great hurry set his mind completely at rest. As usual in such circumstances, he now felt anger.

Without realizing it, he had walked a good three hundred feet from the ship. The jeep braked sharply, and the Doctor shouted, "Get in!"

The Captain jumped into an empty seat, pushing a canister aside, which he found to be empty. He looked at the men—they appeared to be unhurt—and then leaned over and touched the barrel of the thrower. It was cold.

A questioning look at the Physicist yielded no response, so the Captain waited, saying nothing. At the ship the Engineer veered sharply, which pushed the Captain back into his seat and made the empty canisters clatter. The jeep came to a halt in front of the tunnel entrance.

"The water all evaporated?" the Captain asked with irony.

"We couldn't get the water," said the Engineer. He swung around on his swivel seat. "We couldn't get to the brook."

No one stepped out of the jeep. The Captain searched the Engineer's face, then the Physicist's.

"On our first trip we saw something different," said the Physicist, "but we didn't know what it meant. We wanted to check it again."

"And if you didn't return, what good to us would your circumspection have been?" asked the Captain, no longer able to hide his anger. "I want to hear everything. Now!"

"They're doing something there, by the brook, on this side of it and beyond it, and in the hills and all the hollows, along the grooves. In a radius of several miles," said the Doctor. The Engineer nodded.

"The first time, when it was still daylight, we saw a group

of those huge tops. They were in a V formation, throwing up earth as if doing some kind of excavation. We only noticed them from the top of the hill on our way back. But I didn't like what I saw."

"What didn't you like?" the Captain asked.

"That the vertex of their wedge pointed in our direction."

"And you went back there without saying a word about this?"

"All right, it was foolish," said the Engineer. "But we thought that, well, there would be arguments about who should go, who should risk his life, et cetera, so we decided it would be simpler and quicker to go ourselves. I figured that when night fell, the tops would have to light up their workplace."

"They didn't see you?"

"No. At least, there was no indication that they did. We weren't attacked."

"How did you go?"

"Along the ridges of the hills, not on the ridges themselves but a little lower, so we wouldn't be seen against the sky. Our headlights off, of course. That's why it took so long."

"So you had no intention of getting water? You took the canisters only to deceive the Chemist?"

"It wasn't like that," said the Doctor. They sat in the jeep, in the light of the blinker going on, going off. "We wanted to approach the brook farther up, from the other direction. But we couldn't."

"Why?"

"They were doing the same thing there. And now, since nightfall, they've been pouring some kind of luminescent liquid into the trenches. It gives off enough light for us to see perfectly."

"What is it?" the Captain asked the Engineer.

The Engineer shrugged. "Maybe the trenches are molds. Though the liquid appears too thin to be metallic."

"How do they carry it?"

"They don't. They laid something along the grooves— a pipeline, maybe, but I can't say for sure."

"They run molten metal through pipes?!"

"I'm telling you what I saw in the darkness, through binoculars. The lighting was poor—the middle of each excavation glowed like a mercury lamp, there was a lot of glare—and we were at least half a mile away."

The blinker went off; for a moment they sat unable to see one another; then it came on again. "We ought to disconnect that damn thing," said the Captain.

They saw the Chemist emerging from the tunnel. "Now what?" said the Captain. The Chemist came over to the jeep, and there was a hurried exchange of questions and answers. Meanwhile the Engineer went below and switched off the current to the blinker. In the ensuing darkness, the glow on the horizon was much brighter. It had moved more to the south.

"There were hundreds of them," said the Engineer, who had come back up and was now standing beside the ship and looking toward the glow, his face gray in the light.

"Those huge tops?"

"No, doublers. You could see their silhouettes against the liquid. They were working quickly—evidently the stuff thickens—and were shoring it up with gratings of some sort, on the sides, in the back. But the front, the part facing us, was left open."

"What do we do? Sit and wait, twiddling our thumbs?" the Chemist asked, his voice shrill.

"No," said the Captain. "Let's check Defender's systems."

For a moment they watched the glow in silence. At times it seemed to intensify.

"Do you want to release the water?" the Engineer asked doubtfully.

"For the time being, no. I've been thinking about that. We'll try the hatch. If the lock mechanism is working and the hatch opens, we'll shut it immediately. At worst, a few dozen gallons will spill out, but that won't present a problem—we can clear that up. And we'll know that in an emergency we can use Defender."

"What good will Defender be if there's a nuclear attack?" asked the Chemist.

"Ceramite can withstand a blast at a thousand feet from ground zero."

"And at three hundred feet?"

"Defender can withstand a blast at three hundred feet."

"Only in earthwork," the Physicist corrected him.

"If we have to, we'll dig ourselves in."

"But even at fifteen hundred feet the hatch will melt shut, we won't be able to get out. We'll cook like lobsters!"

"This is silly. At the moment there are no bombs falling. Besides, let's admit it, we can't abandon ship. If the ship is destroyed, what do we make another one out of?" The Engineer's question was greeted by silence.

A thought came to the Physicist. "But wait—Defender isn't complete. The Cyberneticist removed its diodes."

"Only from the sighting system. We can aim without them. Anyway, if antiprotons are used, you don't need a direct hit. . . ."

"I'd like to ask something," the Doctor said. Everyone turned to him. "It's not important. I just wanted to know how the doubler's doing. . . ."

There was silence, then laughter, as if suddenly all danger had disappeared.

"He's sleeping," said the Captain. "Or at least he was sleeping at eight, when I looked in on him. Almost all he seems to do is sleep. Does he ever eat?" he asked the Doctor.

"Not anything here. He hasn't touched a thing I offered him."

"Yes, we all have our problems," mock-sighed the Engineer, grinning in the darkness.

"Hello!" The voice came from below. "Attention, please!"

They turned around quickly as a large dark form crawled from the tunnel and with a slight grating sound stood erect. The Cyberneticist appeared behind it with a glowing light on his chest.

"Our first universal!" he said proudly. But then he looked at his colleagues' faces. "Something's happened?"

"Not yet," replied the Chemist. "But more might happen than we've bargained for."

"Well . . . we have this robot," said the Cyberneticist, somewhat lamely.

"Wonderful. You can tell it to get to work right away."

"Doing what?"

"Digging our graves!" And the Chemist pushed his colleagues aside and walked off. The Captain stood watching him, then went in the same direction.

"What's wrong with him?" asked the Cyberneticist, stupefied.

The Engineer explained. "They're making preparations against us in the valleys east of here. We discovered this on our excursion to the brook. They'll probably attack, but we don't know what form it will take."

"Attack?"

The Cyberneticist had been so absorbed in his work that he seemed not to understand what the Engineer was saying. He stared at the men, then turned toward the plain. Two figures silhouetted against the glow were slowly making their way back. The Cyberneticist looked up at his robot, which was motionless, as though hewn from stone.

"We must do something . . ." he whispered.

"We're activating Defender," said the Physicist. "Whether that helps or not, at least it gives us something to do. Tell the Captain to send the Chemist down. We'll be repairing the filters. The robot can do the electrical work. Let's go, gentlemen."

The Physicist and the Cyberneticist entered the tunnel, and the universal robot turned and followed them.

The Engineer looked with admiration at the machine and said to the Doctor, "You know, Blackie will come in handy. It can work underwater."

"But how will you give it orders? Sound won't carry," the Doctor asked abstractedly, speaking only to keep the conversation going. He was watching the two men in the night. They were turning away again. It looked like a pleasant stroll beneath the stars.

"With a microtransmitter. You know that," said the Engineer, following the Doctor's gaze. Then he continued in a different tone: "It's because he knew we'd succeed. . . ."

"Yes," the Doctor said, nodding. "That's why he didn't want to leave Eden too soon. . . ."

"It doesn't matter." The Engineer was already making for the tunnel. "I know him. It'll pass when the action starts."

"Yes," agreed the Doctor, following him.

After about a quarter of an hour, the Captain and the Chemist returned to the ship. Before the work began, Blackie was sent up to erect a six-foot embankment around the tunnel entrance, packing down the earth, and then to bring everything below—except for the entrenched thrower and the jeep. Dismantling the jeep would have taken too much time; anyway, they needed the robot.

At midnight they got down to work in earnest. The Cyberneticist inspected all Defender's circuits, the Physicist and the Engineer repaired and adjusted the radiation filters, and the Captain, in protective clothing, monitored the well in the lower level of the engine room. The robot was at the bottom, six feet underwater, working on the cables.

It turned out that the filters, even after they were repaired, did not work at full capacity, because several of the units were not functioning; the men solved this problem by accelerating the pumps. The purification proceeded under fairly primitive conditions: every ten minutes the Chemist took samples from the tank for analysis, because the automatic radiation gauge was broken, and its repair would have required time they did not have.

At three in the morning the water was almost completely clean. They didn't bother to weld the tank from which it had burst when the front plate struck one of the main ribs. Instead, they simply pumped the water into an empty reserve tank on the side. In normal circumstances, such an unbalanced load would have been unthinkable, but for the moment the ship was not going anywhere. After pumping the water out, they blew compressed air through the lower chamber. A little radiation remained on the walls, but no one had any reason to go in there for the time being. Next they worked on the hatch. According to the indicators, the mechanism was in perfect order, but on the first try the hatch refused to open. After they debated whether or not to use the hydraulics, the Engineer decided finally that it would be safer to inspect the hatch from outside, so they went out to the surface.

It was not easy to reach the hatch, which, located near the bottom of the hull, was now more than twelve feet in the air. Hurriedly they threw up a scaffold and a platform, using scrap metal (this was no problem now, with the robot doing the welding), and brought their lights to bear on the place.

The sky in the east had become gray; the glow was no longer visible. Above, the stars were slowly going out. Large drops of dew trickled down the ceramite plates of the hull.

"Curious," said the Physicist. "The mechanism is working. Nothing wrong with the hatch, except that it won't open."

"I don't like things that are curious," remarked the Cyberneticist.

"Well," said the Captain, "what about applying an age-old method?" And he raised a twenty-pound hammer.

"You can tap the rim, but not too hard," agreed the Engineer reluctantly. He disliked that "method."

The Captain, with a look at the black robot, which stood like a square statue in the gray dawn as it steadied the scaffold with its chest, hefted the hammer in his hands, swung it a little—not too much—and struck. He struck again, steadily, and again, each time a few inches higher, which was awkward at the angle he stood, but the physical activity felt good. The rhythm of the tapping was broken by a different sound, a groaning that seemed to come from the very ground beneath them. Then they heard a piercing, rising whistle, and the scaffold began to shake.

"Down!" cried the Physicist. They leaped off the platform one by one; only the robot didn't move. Dawn was already breaking; both the plain and the sky were the color of ash. The groaning increased, and so did the whistle, and the men instinctively crouched and covered their heads with their arms as they took cover under the ship. A quarter of a mile away, soil shot up like a geyser. The sound that accompanied it was strangely faint and muffled.

They ran for the tunnel, and the robot followed. The

Captain and the Engineer stopped behind the protection of the embankment and looked east, where the thunder was. The whole plain shook. The whistling intensified, and the sky filled with organlike squeals, as though squadrons of invisible aircraft were diving straight at them. In the foreground, jets of sand and earth rose black against the lead sky.

"A normal civilization, wouldn't you say?" said the Physicist from below, in the tunnel.

"They're flying overhead, but I don't see them," muttered the Engineer. The Captain couldn't hear him: the squealing continued and the ground went on spouting, though the spouting came no nearer the ship. The two men watched: nothing changed. The thunder on the horizon merged into a single, protracted, unvarying bass rumble, and now the missiles fell without explosion, almost silently. The earth thrown up by the impacts lay in low mounds, like molehills, surrounding the strikes.

"The binoculars," the Captain shouted into the tunnel.

A moment later he had them in his hand. As he looked, his astonishment grew. At first he thought that the attacking artillery was finding the range, but no, the invisible missiles kept falling in the same way. Sweeping the landscape with his binoculars, he saw spurts in all directions. Some were nearer, some farther, but none closer to the ship than six hundred feet.

"What is it?! They're not atomic, are they?!" came the muffled cries from the tunnel.

"No! Not atomic!" he shouted back, straining his voice. The Engineer put his mouth to the Captain's ear.

"Did you see? They keep missing!"

"I can see!"

"We're surrounded on all sides!"

He nodded yes. The Engineer took the binoculars and looked.

Any minute now it would be sunrise. The pale sky, looking washed, filled with a diluted blue. On the plain nothing moved, except for the spouts of earth, which, like a bizarre, flickering hedge that kept vanishing and then rising from the ground anew, surrounded the small hill where the ship was embedded.

Suddenly the Captain made a decision. He crawled out from behind the embankment and in three leaps reached the crest of the hill. There he dropped flat on the ground and looked in the opposite direction, which he had been unable to do at the tunnel entrance. The scene was the same: a wide crescent of strikes, a quivering, smoking hedge of explosions.

Someone hit the parched ground beside him: it was the Engineer. They lay shoulder to shoulder, watching, now almost unaware of the thunder at the horizon, which came in waves and at times seemed to recede—that was the effect of the morning wind, the air heated by the first rays of the sun.

"Those aren't misses!" shouted the Engineer.

"Then what are they?"

"I don't know. Let's wait. . . ."

"No, let's go!"

They ran down the slope—although the missiles were not falling nearby, the howling and whistling were not pleasant—and jumped into the tunnel, one after the other. They left the robot in the passage and entered the ship, pulling the others in with them. They headed for the library, where it was quiet. Here even the ground tremors were almost imperceptible.

"Now what? Do they want to hold us here? To starve us?" asked the Physicist, when they told what they had seen.

"Who knows? I'd like to have a closer look at one of

those missiles," said the Engineer. "If the barrage lets up, it might be a good idea to go out and . . ."

"The robot can go," the Captain said.

"The robot?" asked the Cyberneticist, almost in a groan.

"Nothing will happen to it, don't worry."

They felt a thud, faint but unmistakable. They looked at one another.

"We've been hit!" cried the Chemist, jumping up.

The Captain ran to the tunnel. Up on the surface, nothing appeared to have changed. The sky still thundered—but on the sunlit sand beneath the stern of the ship lay something black and speckled, like a burst bag of shot. He tried to find the place where the strange missile had hit the hull, but the ceramite bore no marks. Before the men behind him could stop him, the Captain began picking up the fragments and putting them into his empty binoculars case. They were still warm.

The Chemist shouted at him. "You're crazy! That could be radioactive!"

They ran back inside. The fragments were not radioactive; the counter, brought near them, was silent. Curiously, they were not cased in any kind of metal. In the hand they crumbled into glistening grains.

The Physicist examined the grains with a magnifying glass, then quickly took them to a microscope. Peering, he whistled.

"Well? Well?" They literally had to pull him from the eyepiece.

"They're sending us watches . . ." the Chemist said softly, looking up from the microscope after his turn.

There in the field of vision lay hundreds of tiny cogs, wheels, springs, and spindles. The men put a different sample under the lens and saw the same thing.

"What in the hell is it?" said the Engineer.

The Physicist paced—they were in the library—from one wall to another, his hair ruffled. He stopped and stared at them with a wild look, then continued pacing.

"An extremely complicated mechanism of some kind," mused the Engineer, holding a pile of grains in his hand. "There must be millions, if not billions, of these little gears and wheels here! Let's go up," he said, "and see what's happening."

The attack was still going on. The robot, standing guard in the tunnel, had counted 1,109 hits.

"Let's try the hatch now," said the Chemist when they returned to the ship.

The Cyberneticist was hunched over the microscope, looking at the grains. He did not answer when they spoke to him.

In the engine room, the indicator light for the lock was still on. When the Engineer flicked the switch, the light obediently blinked: the hatch was opening. He closed it immediately and announced, "We can ride Defender out anytime."

"Even with the hatch twelve feet off the ground?" asked the Physicist.

"For Defender that's no problem."

At the moment, however, there was no urgent need to leave, so they returned to the library. The Cyberneticist was still at the microscope.

"Let him be. Maybe he'll come up with something," said the Doctor. "And now . . . we shouldn't just sit here. I suggest we get back to repairing the ship."

With a sigh they rose from their seats. Indeed, what else was there to do? The five descended to the engine room, where the damage was the greatest. The distributor required hours of painstaking work: each circuit had to be tested twice, first with the current off, then on. Every so often the Captain would go out on top and return, saying nothing. In the control room, which was buried forty-five feet underground, they could feel a slight vibration. Noon passed. Their work would have gone much faster with the help of the robot, but they needed it in the tunnel. By one o'clock it had counted more than eight thousand hits.

Although no one was hungry, they ate lunch, to keep up their strength, as the Doctor said. At twelve past two the vibration stopped. Everyone immediately made for the tunnel. On the surface, a small cloud covered the sun, and the whole plain lay shimmering in the heat. There was still dust in the air, from the explosions, but silence reigned.

"Is it over?" the Physicist asked in a voice that sounded strangely loud: over the last few hours they had grown accustomed to the barrage.

Total hits, according to the robot: 10,604.

About eight hundred feet from the ship, all around it, there was a strip of pulverized soil. In places individual craters ran together to form a ditch.

The Doctor began climbing over the embankment at the mouth of the tunnel.

"Not yet," said the Engineer, holding him back. "Let's wait."

"How long?"

"Half an hour or, better, an hour."

"Delayed charges? But there are no explosives there!"

"We don't know that."

The cloud moved away from the sun. It grew brighter.

The Captain heard the rustling first. "What's that?" he whispered.

The others listened. Yes, they could hear it, too. The sound was like the wind moving through leaves or bushes.

But there were no leaves or bushes in sight, only the furrowed ring in the sand. The air was still. But the rustling continued.

"Where is it coming from?"

"There?"

They spoke in whispers. The sound seemed to come from all sides now. Could it be the sand shifting?

"But there's no wind . . ." the Chemist said.

"It's coming from where the missiles hit. . . ."

"I'll have a look."

"Are you crazy? What if those are timed devices?"

The Chemist paled, drew back. And yet the day was so bright, and everything so quiet. . . . He clenched his fists. This was a hundred times worse than the barrage!

The sun was at its zenith. Shadows of cumulus clouds slowly swept across the plain. The clouds, layered and with flat bases, resembled white islands. There was no movement on the horizon; the land everywhere was empty. Even the gray calyxes, whose indistinct silhouettes before had stood above the distant dunes, were gone! It was only now that the men noticed this.

"Look!" cried the Physicist, pointing. But it didn't matter in which direction they looked. The same thing was happening everywhere.

The cratered ground began to tremble. Something shiny was emerging from it. Each place a missile had fallen, there were sprouts. They rose in even rows, almost like the teeth of a comb.

Someone rushed out from the tunnel and ran toward the curved line of glimmering sprouts. It was the Cyberneticist. Everyone shouted and chased after him.

"I know what they are!" he cried, dropping to his knees before the glassy rows of sprouts.

They were finger-length now, and at the base thick as

a fist. The sand swirled gently around each one; something was at work below.

"Mechanical seeds!" the Cyberneticist said. With his hands he tried digging up the nearest sprout, but the sand was too hot.

Someone ran and brought shovels, and then the sand and soil flew, revealing long, segmented, tangled strands of a lustrous material. The material was so hard, it rang like metal against the shovels. When the hole was more than three feet deep, the men tried to pull the strange growth out, but couldn't—it was too tightly connected to its neighbors.

"Blackie!" cried a chorus of voices. The robot approached. "Pull it out!"

Steel pincers closed on a shiny shoot as thick as a man's arm. The robot's torso stiffened, and the men watched as its feet began sinking slowly into the ground. There was a high hum, as of a string stretched to its limit.

"Let go!" commanded the Engineer. Blackie stepped awkwardly out of the ground and stood unmoving.

The sprouts, a hedge now, were almost a foot and a half high. At their base they began filling slowly with a darker, milky blue color.

"So," said the Captain calmly. "It seems they want to fence us in."

No one spoke for a while.

"But isn't this rather primitive? I mean, we can still leave," said the Chemist.

The Captain said, "That scouting party of theirs must have done their job well. Look, it's an almost perfect circle around us."

"Mechanical seeds," said the Cyberneticist. He was calmer now, brushing the sand from his hands. "Inorganic spores sown by artillery."

"But the stuff is not metal," observed the Chemist. "Blackie would have bent it. It must be something like supranite."

"No, it's sand, only sand!" said the Cyberneticist. "Don't you see? This is the product of an inorganic metabolism! Sand is converted catalytically into some macromolecule based on silicon. Those shoots are made of that—just as plants extract salts from the soil."

The Chemist knelt and touched the shiny substance. He looked up. "And what if they had landed on a different kind of soil?" he asked.

"They would have adapted. Of that I'm certain! That's why they're so hellishly complex: designed and programmed to produce the most resistant material possible from what they have at their disposal."

"If it's just silicon, Defender should have no problem getting through it," said the Engineer with a smile.

"I wonder if this was really an attack," the Doctor said thoughtfully. The others looked at him in surprise.

"How would you describe it?"

"Perhaps . . . an attempt at defense. To isolate us."

"And then? Are we supposed to sit here and wait like worms under a bell jar?"

"Why do you need Defender?"

The question made them hesitate. The Doctor went on: "We're no longer short of water. The ship will be repaired—in all likelihood—in a week, in ten days. The nuclear synthesizers should be functioning in a few hours. I don't see this as a bell jar. A high wall, rather. An impassable barrier for them, and therefore they assume for us as well. With the synthesizers, we'll have food. We require nothing from them, and they could hardly have been clearer in telling us that we're not welcome here. . . ."

They listened, frowning. The Engineer looked and saw that the tips were almost knee-level, and that they were joining, fusing. The rustling was now so loud that it sounded like a hundred beehives. The bluish roots at the base of the wall had swollen almost as thick as tree trunks.

"Could you bring the doubler here?" the Captain asked unexpectedly.

The Doctor looked at him strangely. "Now? Here? For what reason?"

"I don't know. Just bring him. Please."

The Doctor nodded and left. The others stood silent in the sun until he reappeared. With difficulty the naked giant crawled out of the tunnel behind him. It seemed animated, almost satisfied, following the Doctor and gurgling softly. Then its flat little face tensed, its blue eye widened, it wheezed. It turned around and began to wail. It ran toward the shiny wall with great leaps, as though intending to hurl itself at it, but instead, hopping grotesquely, the creature ran along the entire circle, whining and coughing. Then it ran to the Doctor and began plucking at the chest of his suit with its stubby fingers and peering into his eyes. Sweat poured off it. It pushed at the Doctor, jumped back, looked around again, and, drawing its small torso into its trunk with an unpleasant noise, fled into the dark tunnel. They could see the flat, twitching soles of its feet as it crawled inside.

"Were you expecting that?" the Doctor finally asked the Captain.

"No . . . not really. I just thought that the wall wouldn't be strange to him. I expected a reaction. Some kind of recognition. But nothing like this . . ."

"It was recognition, all right," the Physicist muttered.

"Yes," said the Doctor. "He's seen this before. Something similar, in any case. And he's petrified by it."

"Execution, Eden-style?" the Chemist murmured.

"I don't know. In any case, this indicates that they use the 'living wall' not only against invaders from space."

"Maybe he's simply afraid of anything that shines," suggested the Physicist. "That would also explain the incident with the mirror strip."

"No. I showed him a mirror in the ship, and he was not interested," said the Doctor.

"Then he's not that stupid," said the Physicist. He was standing by the glassy hedge, which was now up to his waist.

"Once bitten, twice shy."

"Listen," said the Captain. "This is getting us nowhere. What do we do now? Repairs? Yes, of course, but I was thinking . . ."

"Of another expedition?" said the Doctor.

The Engineer smiled ruefully. "I'm always game. Where? To the city?"

"That will mean war," the Doctor said. "Because the only way you'll get there is with Defender. And with its antiproton launcher, before you know it, you won't be gathering information, you'll be blasting away."

"I wasn't thinking of an encounter," the Captain replied. "Everything we've seen indicates that the population of Eden is highly stratified. So far we have not been able to establish contact with the stratum responsible for intelligent activity. Yes, I can see that they would regard an advance toward the city as an attack. However, the west is still unexplored. With Defender, two men will be enough crew. The rest can work on the ship."

"You and the Engineer?"

"Not necessarily."

"It would be better with three," said the Engineer.

"Who wants to go?"

They all did.

The Captain smiled. "Hardly have the guns ceased to roar than curiosity begins to consume them."

"Let it be the Chemist and me," the Engineer said. "And the Doctor can accompany us as a representative of reason and virtue. You stay," he said to the Captain. "You know the procedures. Set Blackie to work immediately on the lifters, but don't start digging under the ship until we return. I'll want to check the statics."

"As a representative of reason and virtue, I want to know the purpose of this expedition," said the Doctor. "The moment we open the hatch, we're entering the stage of confrontation, like it or not."

"Make a counterproposal," the Engineer said.

Behind them hummed, almost melodiously, the hedge, rising over their heads. The sunlight was broken into rainbows by its tangle of glassy veins.

"I don't have one," the Doctor admitted. "Events are happening too fast, and so far all our plans have led to surprises. The most rational thing, I think, would be not to make any more expeditions. In a week or two the ship will be ready for flight, and we can circle the planet at low altitude and possibly learn more than we can now, and more easily, too."

"You can't believe that," the Engineer said. "If we learn nothing here at close quarters, what will a flight above the atmosphere tell us? And as for 'rational' . . . if people were rational, we wouldn't be here in the first place. What's rational about flying to the stars?"

"I didn't think I'd convince you," muttered the Doctor. He turned and walked along the wall of glass.

The others went back to the ship.

The Captain said to the Engineer, "Don't count on making any sensational discovery. The terrain to the west will probably be similar to what we have here."

"What makes you think that?"

"It's unlikely that we landed in the center of a small barren area. To the north there's a factory, to the east a city, to the south a 'settlement.' Chances are, we're sitting on the edge of a desert that's to our west."

"We'll see."

X

A few minutes past four, the loading-bay hatch slowly opened downward, like the jaw of a shark. It came to a stop, making a platform more than four feet off the ground.

The men who were assembled near the ship stood on both sides of the hatch, looking up. First appeared two tractor tracks, wide apart, sliding forward with a roar, as though the huge machine were going to dive wildly into the air. They could see its grayish-yellow underside. Then it rocked and lurched forward, hitting the platform flat, and so hard that there was a great clang. Moving on its tracks, it drove-fell across the gap to the ground, catching the ground at a sharp angle and biting into it. In the next second, Defender's flattened head was level, and after about forty feet it came to a halt with a pleasant rumble.

"Well, now, friends"—the Engineer stuck his head out the small rear door—"go in the ship, because it's going to get hot, and stay there for at least half an hour.

Better yet, send Blackie out first and let him check for radioactivity."

The door closed. The three men entered the tunnel, taking the robot with them. Shortly afterward a metal piece appeared in the tunnel mouth, filling the opening entirely. Inside Defender, the Engineer wiped the screens, checked the dials, and said, "Let's get started."

Defender's nose—short and slender, and encircled by little cylinders—turned westward.

The Engineer, centering the hedge in his cross hairs, glanced to the side at the dials and stepped on the pedal.

For a second the screen went dark, and Defender was rocked by a blast of air and a noise as if a giant had pressed his mouth to the ground and said, "Oof!" The screen cleared.

A fiery cloud rose, and the air blurred around it like a liquid. A thirty-foot section of hedge had disappeared, and steam billowed from a depression with an incandescent red rim. Farther on, molten glass glittered in the sun.

"Too much power," thought the Engineer, but all he said was, "All right, let's go." The hulk moved toward the crater with a strange lightness; the crew hardly shook at all as they rode through it. At the bottom, some of the glowing glass had begun to solidify. "We're barbarians," the Doctor thought. "What am I doing here?"

The Engineer made a slight correction for direction and accelerated. Defender rode as though on a highway, the tracks turning smoothly and softly. They were doing almost forty miles an hour without even noticing it.

"Can we open the top?" asked the Doctor, who was sitting in a low seat. Over his shoulder there was a small convex screen, like a porthole.

"Of course," the Engineer said and pushed a button.

From the rim of the turret a fluid squirted in needle-sharp streams, washing the bits of radioactive ash off the armor plates. Then everything became bright—the head opened, the top slid back, and the sides collapsed into the body—and they rode on, now protected only by a thick windshield that curved around them. The air ruffled their hair.

"I'm afraid the Captain was right," the Chemist muttered some time later. The landscape was unchanging. They sailed over a sea of sand, the heavy vehicle swaying gently as it crossed fin-shaped dunes in the same uninterrupted rhythm. The Engineer increased speed, the ride became much rougher, and the tracks threw up clouds of sand, some of which got inside.

At thirty miles the excessive rocking stopped. They traveled in this fashion for more than two hours.

"Yes, I guess he was," said the Engineer, changing course from west to southwest.

The next hour brought no change, and they turned again, heading in a more southerly direction. By now they had gone ninety miles.

The sand changed. From white and very fine, trailing behind them like a long sweeping tail, it became reddish, coarser, and didn't rise in clouds when the tracks churned it up. The dunes became fewer and lower. From time to time they passed the protruding stalks of buried bushes. Blurry patches appeared in the distance, slightly off course. The Engineer steered toward them. They grew quickly in size, and a few minutes later the men saw vertical slabs rising from the sand, resembling fragments of walls.

Entering a narrow passage, on either side of which stood slanting quoins eaten by erosion, they slowed down. A huge stone blocked their way. Defender raised its head and rode over that obstacle easily; they found themselves in a long alley. Through the gaps between the slabs they could see other ruins, all worn and pitted. Then they drove out into an open space, dunes appeared again, but small, packed, producing no dust, and the terrain began to slope downward. In the distance, below, they could see truncated club-shaped rocks and more ruins.

The bottom was littered with speckled stones. They crossed it and went up another slope. The ground grew harder; the tracks no longer sank into it. The first clumps of scrub appeared. They were almost black, but appeared deep red in the low sun, as though their podlike leaves were filled with blood. Farther on, the scrub rose higher, blocking their way in places. Defender pushed through it, not slowing down. This produced an unpleasant hollow crackling, the sound of thousands of small blisters bursting, squirting a dark sticky substance that stained the ceramite plates. Soon the whole vehicle, up to the turret, was reddish brown.

They had gone 120 miles. The sun now touched the western horizon, and the shadow of the vehicle lengthened more and more. Suddenly there was a terrible grating under them, a crunching. The Engineer braked, but it took Defender about forty feet to come to a stop. In the wide trail that they had beaten down behind them lay, among the mangled bushes, pieces of a rusted metal frame. They rode on—and again hit metal, twisted grillwork, sheets riddled with holes, curved ribs. Smashed beneath Defender's tracks, this scrap was covered with the substance that oozed from the broken plants.

The wall of scrub grew still higher before them, but the awful grating and squealing of rusted metal stopped. Unexpectedly, the black stalks that had been battering them parted, and the crew entered a glade fifty to sixty feet wide and hemmed in, at the other end, by the same dark thicket. The Engineer turned, and they went down a long sloping clearing that resembled a forest path. The surface was clayey, covered with loamy patches, which indicated that water occasionally flowed there.

The clearing did not run straight. Sometimes the red sun, half sunk in the horizon and enormous, appeared in front of the machine, dazzling them. Sometimes the sun was hidden and sent blood-red flashes through the dense thicket that now was nine feet high. Then they saw the whole sunset, and a vast multicolored expanse before it. The land was about two thousand feet below them.

A sheet of water sparkled in the distance, reflecting the sun. On the shore of this lake, which was uneven and covered with patches of dark scrub, stood buildings, machines on splayed legs, and nearer the cliff where Defender had halted was a mosaic of structures, rows of vertical masts, bright avenues. There was considerable animation below: gray, brown, and white dots crept along the avenues, intermingling, forming clusters, spreading out in long strings. This entire scene of habitation was filled with tiny flashes, as though the people were continually opening and closing the windows of their houses and the sunlight played in the panes.

The Doctor gave a cry of delight. "Henry, you've done it! At last, something normal. Everyday life, and what a great observation post!" And he began to climb out of the open turret.

The Engineer stopped him. "Hold on. Don't you see the sun? In five minutes it'll be down, and we won't be able to see a thing. We ought to put this entire panorama on film, and quickly, too."

The Chemist had already pulled the cameras out from under the seat, and together they set up the largest, which looked like a blunderbuss. The tripod they threw to the ground. The Engineer took a coil of nylon line, tied one end of it to the turret, tossed the rest of it over Defender's front end, and jumped down. The other two had already raised the tripod and were running to the cliff edge. He caught up with them and fastened the line to a snap-hook on each man's belt.

"In case you fall," he said.

The sun was sinking into the fiery waters of the lake. There was a hasty murmur of machinery, and the enormous lens tilted downward. The Doctor knelt to support the front legs of the tripod, and the Chemist put his eye to the finder and grimaced.

"Too much glare," he said. "I need the diaphragm!"

The Engineer ran back and returned a moment later with the attachment, and the shooting began. Holding the bar with both hands, the Engineer slowly moved the camera from left to right. Now and then the Chemist stopped it, increasing the resolution on places where the finder showed a greater concentration of detail. The Doctor went on kneeling as the camera purred. The film flew, and the spools were changed almost without a pause. Barely a sliver of the solar disk remained above the water as the lens pointed at the movement directly below. The Doctor had to lean over the edge now with the camera, hanging on to the taut line, and beneath him he saw the folds of the clay wall bathed in a crimson that grew dimmer and dimmer. Near the end of the second spool, the red disk disappeared. The sky still glowed, but a gray-blue shadow fell over the plain and the lake, and apart from the flashes there was nothing more to be seen.

The three men carried the camera back carefully, as though it were a treasure.

"Do you think the pictures will turn out?" the Chemist asked the Engineer.

"We'll find out in the ship. We can always come back."

They put the camera and the spools in Defender and returned to the cliff. Only now did they notice that on the eastern shore of the lake was a steep wall that merged into the landscape. Its summit caught the final pink gleam of the sunset, and above it, far in the distance, a russet column of smoke poured into the sky with the first stars.

"Ah, that must be the valley, the geyser," the Chemist exclaimed to the Doctor.

They looked down again. White and green sparks slowly spread in a line along the edge of the lake, the line sometimes forking, like a river. As it grew darker, the number of lights increased. The tall thicket, now completely black, rustled peacefully overhead. They turned away reluctantly, so beautiful was the view, and took with them the image of the lake reflecting milky stars.

As they walked back, the Doctor asked the Chemist, "What did you see?"

The Chemist smiled, embarrassed. "Nothing. I wasn't really looking, I was concentrating on making the adjustments, on the focusing, and Henry moved so quickly. . . ."

"It doesn't matter," said the Engineer, leaning against Defender's cold hull. "We took two hundred frames a second, and we'll see everything when the film is developed."

"An idyllic excursion," said the Doctor.

The Engineer switched the rear telescreen and put Defender into reverse. They went uphill for a while, but when they came to a wider place, they turned and headed due north.

"We're not taking the same route back," said the Engineer. "That would add something like sixty miles. I'll follow the clearing as long as I can. We should be there within two hours."

XI

The road was winding, the thicket walls pressed in on Defender, stalks struck the windshield, and now and then a pod-leaf would drop in the Chemist's or the Doctor's lap. The Doctor raised one to his nose and sniffed.

"A nice smell," he said, surprised.

They were in a wonderful mood. In the crystal-clear sky the serpentine Milky Way sparkled like a mass of diamonds. A gentle breeze combed the thicket with a sigh. Defender, rolling along, hummed softly.

"Curious that there are no tentacles on Eden," the Doctor said. "In all the science fiction I ever read, other planets are full of tentacles out to strangle you."

"And their inhabitants have six fingers," added the Chemist. "Almost always six."

"Six is a mystical number," said the Doctor. "Half of six is three, and success only comes on the third try."

"Stop that jabbering, or I'll lose the way," said the Engineer, who was sitting higher up. He still hadn't turned on the headlights, although now one could not see much without them—but the night was unusually fine, and he would ruin it if he switched them on. And traveling by radar meant closing the turret. Inside, all he could see were his own hands at the controls, and the dials glowing pale green and rose on the panel in front of him, and the atomic indicator arrows twinkling like orange stars.

"Can you call the ship?" asked the Doctor.

"No," said the Engineer. "There's no ionosphere here. There is one, actually, but it's riddled with holes. And for shortwave we haven't had the time to adjust the transmitter. You know that."

The tracks started rattling; the machine began to sway. The Engineer switched on the lights and saw that they were traveling over round white rocks, while high overhead limestone crags assumed fantastic shapes. They were in a canyon.

This bothered him, because he had no idea where, other than the general direction, the road was taking them, and not even Defender could negotiate such walls. They rode on. There were more and more rocks, and the thicket was replaced by separate clumps that shone black in the headlights. The road twisted, went uphill, went level. The cliffs became lower on one side, then disappeared altogether, and the men found themselves in a meadow rimmed by limestone ridges from which ran small scree-filled gullies. At ground level, green-gray stalks stood among rocks.

They had been going in too northeasterly a direction for about a quarter of an hour now, and it was time to get on course again, but the limestone wall to their right would not permit this.

"Still, we were lucky," the Chemist said unexpectedly. "We could have gone off that cliff. . . ."

The way was blocked by something like netting with

long hairy fringes. Defender approached the barrier slowly, and the netting adhered to it. The Engineer accelerated a little, and the bizarre netting tore and disappeared, some of it mashed into the ground under the tracks. The lights picked tall black shapes out of the darkness, a forest of shapes, like a petrified army. The men nearly crashed into the base of a column. The large middle spotlight came on and traveled up the tapering black object.

It was a statue, a gigantic statue, which at last they recognized as a doubler—that is, its smaller torso only, enlarged a hundredfold. Its arms were crossed, upraised, and it had a flat, almost concave face, with four symmetrical eye sockets, a face therefore different from the ones they had seen, and the doubler was leaning to the side, as though watching them.

For a long time nobody spoke. Then the spotlight left the statue, probed the darkness, hit other bases, other columns, other torsos, which were dark, spotted, though sometimes there would be a white one, as if carved from bone. Every face had four eyes, but some were deformed, swollen, with an enormous ridge across the forehead. Farther off, at a distance of perhaps six hundred feet: a wall of giant hands reaching upward, or pointing to different constellations in the sky.

"It's like a cemetery," said the Chemist in a lowered voice.

The Doctor had already climbed out onto the rear section of the vehicle, and the Chemist followed. The Engineer turned the spotlight to the limestone wall. In its place he saw a frieze filled with worn, nearly obliterated carvings, an intricate tangle of forms and figures that his eyes couldn't follow. Sometimes he thought he saw something familiar, but the sense of it escaped him.

The Chemist and the Doctor walked among the statues

while the Engineer lit their way from the turret. Then the distant, indistinct murmur that he had not paid attention to before, too absorbed by the unusual scene, became a virulent hissing close at hand. Gray clouds drifted out from the rows of statues, and a pack of doublers rushed through them, leaping, whining, coughing, wailing. They fled blindly, colliding into one another.

The Engineer jumped into his seat and grabbed the lever. His first thought was to ride over to his men. A hundred feet away, at the end of an overgrown lane, he could see the pale, astonished faces of the Doctor and the Chemist. But he couldn't move, because the fleeing creatures, totally disregarding the machine, ran right in front of it. Several of the enormous bodies had fallen. The hissing was all about him now; it seemed to come from the ground itself. And, indeed, a flexible tube had emerged, close to the ground, from the nearest base lit by Defender's headlights, and foam was pouring from it. When the foam hit the soil, it began to smoke violently, spreading a gray mist.

As the first wave of mist swept over the turret, the Engineer felt that there were hundreds of needles in his lungs. Blinded, tears pouring down his cheeks, he made a strangled cry and pressed the accelerator. Defender lurched, knocked over a statue, climbed onto it, rolled along it, screeching. The Engineer couldn't breathe, the pain was atrocious, but the turret couldn't be closed; first he had to pick up the others, so he rode on, barely able to see the statues that Defender was knocking down. The air became clearer, and the Chemist and the Doctor—he could hear them—leaped out of the thicket and climbed on. He wanted to shout to them, "Get in!" but no sound emerged from his burned throat. The other two jumped inside, coughing and choking. The Engineer groped for the lever, and the dome closed over them, but the throat-searing mist was still inside. Groaning, with the last of his strength, he grappled with a valve on a pipe, and oxygen burst out in a jet; he could feel it strike his face. The gas, at high pressure, hit him like a fist between the eyes, but he did not mind, thankful for the life-giving flow. The other two bent over his shoulders and inhaled greedily.

The filters were working, and the oxygen replaced the toxic mist. The men could see again. Panting, they felt an intense pain in their chests—each breath seemed to be made through a raw wound—but this sensation passed. The Engineer, having recovered his sight completely, switched on the screen.

A few bodies still quivered among the columns in a side lane where he had not gone; the majority were not moving at all. A jumble of small hands, torsos, and heads disappeared and reappeared through the gray mist. The Engineer turned on the sound monitor and heard feeble coughing, whimpering; something pattered in the rear, and a chorus of broken, rasping voices was raised again in the direction of the frieze. But there was nothing to be seen there, except for the flowing mist. The Engineer made certain that the turret was hermetically sealed and, clenching his teeth, began to turn Defender around. The tracks clattered over the stone fragments; the three head-light beams tried to penetrate the haze. He moved past the fallen statues, looking for the hissing tube—and guessed that it was in the foam gushing about thirty feet ahead, where a cloud was covering the upraised arms of the statue.

"No!" cried the Doctor. "Don't shoot! Some of them may be alive!"

It was too late. The screen went dark for a split second; Defender recoiled, was thrown back with a terrible grinding; and the antiproton beam, emerging from the tip of the generator concealed in its nose, crossed the distance of forty feet to the source of the foam and there annihilated an equivalent amount of matter.

When the screen cleared, there was a fiery crater surrounded by scattered, broken statues.

The Engineer strained his eyes, trying to find the source of the tube. He turned Defender ninety degrees and proceeded slowly along the row of fallen statues. The mist was thinner here. They passed three or four rag-covered bodies. The Engineer braked and steered to avoid running over the nearest ones. A large shape loomed in the thicket ahead. A long clearing opened up, and at the other end of it silvery shapes fled, taking cover. Instead of small torsos in their chests, they had narrow helmets flattened at the sides, with beaks on top.

Something thudded into Defender's front; the screen darkened, then brightened again. The left light had gone out.

The Engineer ran the middle light along the edge of the copse, picking out numerous glints of silver among the branches. Behind the silver, something began to gyrate. It went faster and faster, branches and whole bushes flew, and the huge whirling mass, churning the air in the gleam of the headlights, moved sideways. The Engineer aimed the nose at the point of the greatest activity and depressed the pedal. A muffled roar shook the turret.

It looked as if the sun had risen. They were in the middle of the clearing now, and where the copse had stood, a fifth of the horizon was a white sea of fire. Against this wall of flame and smoke, a glittering sphere rolled toward them.

The Engineer could hear nothing but the roar of the

fire. Defender was a bug on the ground compared with this colossus, which spun faster, becoming a whirlwind high as a mountain and divided in the middle by a black zigzag. He had it in his cross hairs, then saw, several hundred feet away, pale silhouettes fleeing.

"Brace yourselves!" he yelled, feeling that there were nails in his throat.

A hellish scraping, a jolt, a deafening crash, and for a moment it seemed that the turret was falling toward him. Defender groaned, its dampers overloaded; the hull rang like a bell; when Defender fired, the screen darkened and brightened, and a hundred hammers began pounding on them. The din abated; the blows became slower, fewer; a long arm continued to flail; then a clatter across the armor, and several arms, spider arms, opened and closed convulsively in front of the screen. One of them tapped rhythmically on the hull, as though stroking it, and finally stopped. The Engineer tried moving, but the tracks wouldn't turn—they were jammed—so he switched into reverse, and slowly, through twisted pieces of metal, Defender crawled crabwise. The obstructions gave way with a clang, and the vehicle, released, shot backward.

Against the flaming copse, the wreck looked like a crushed ninety-foot spider. One severed arm still thrashed, digging into the ground. Among the limbs was a horned globe; it was open now, and silvery figures were leaping from it.

Without thinking, he pressed the pedal.

There was thunder, and a new sun tore through the clearing. Fragments of the wreck flew in all directions, whistling, as a column of seething clay, sand, and soot rose in the center. The Engineer felt suddenly weak, he felt that he was going to vomit. Cold sweat trickled down his back and poured from his face. He was putting his hand to a lever when he heard the Doctor shout, "No, turn back! Do you hear? Turn back!"

Reddish smoke gushed from the crater, as though it were a volcano, and slag flowed down the slope, kindling what remained of the crushed vegetation.

"But I am," said the Engineer. "I am turning back. . . ." But he didn't move. Sweat continued to trickle down his face.

"Are you all right?" The Doctor's voice seemed to come from far off.

The Engineer saw the Doctor's face over him; he shook his head and blinked. "I'm fine," he mumbled. The Doctor returned to his seat.

Defender shuddered and swung around, but they could hear nothing over the sound of the fire, whose roar was like the ocean. They retreated by the same route they had come.

Their single headlight—they had lost the middle one in the collision—again swept over toppled statues and dead bodies, both covered now with a metallic gray deposit. The men rode between the fragments of two white statues and headed north. Like a ship cutting through waves, Defender plowed through brushwood. Several pale forms darted panic-stricken from the light.

The men picked up speed, and the ride grew bumpy. The Engineer took deep breaths, fighting his weakness. He could still see the swirling ashes, all that remained of the leaping silvery forms. Defender pushed uphill, springy branches smacking its hull, and the tracks grated against something that the men could not see. Now they moved faster, uphill, downhill, across small gullies, through winding ravines, knocking down tangled, woody scrub. The machine went like a battering ram through a copse of spider trees, and their prickly abdomens hit the hull with soft, forceless blows as mashed stalks cracked and hissed. The glow of the fire was still visible in the rear screens. Slowly it faded; then darkness covered everything.

XII

An hour later they were on the plain. The night was full of stars. The bushes were few and far between, then disappeared altogether, and there was nothing but dunes, which undulated in the single headlight. Defender took them quickly, as though impatient. The seats rocked, the tracks whistled. The lights on the control panel shone pink, orange, green. The Engineer had his face to the screen, looking for the ship.

What before had been accepted matter-of-factly—that they had gone off without radio contact—now seemed madness to him. As though the extra hour or two it would have taken to modify the transmitter was too much. When he was almost certain that he had passed the ship in the dark and was now to the north of it, he sighted it—not the ship, that is, but a strangely luminous bubble. Defender slowed down. The slanting walls gleamed like silver and fire in its headlight. When the blinker inside went on, the effect was extraordinary: a high dome, open at the top, erupted in tangled rainbows.

Reluctant to shoot, the Engineer made for the spot where the vehicle had previously carved a way for itself. But the mirrorlike wall had filled in the gap from both sides; the only sign of passage was a patch of fused sand at the base of the structure.

With the full force of its sixteen tons, Defender pushed at the wall until the hull complained. The wall did not yield.

The Engineer backed away slowly to six hundred feet, aimed the cross hairs as low as possible, and touched the pedal. Not waiting for the seething rim of the opening to cool, he moved forward. The turret grazed it, but the material, softened by the heat, gave. Defender glared one-eyed through the empty ring and with a low murmur rode up to the ship.

Only Blackie was there to greet them, and it turned immediately and left. Then there was the inevitable delay of having to clean the hull and take radiation readings before they could leave the cramped interior of the machine.

The blinker came on. The Captain, the first to emerge from the tunnel, looked at the black patches on Defender's front, the two broken headlights, and the grim faces of the returning crew, and said, "You were in a fight."

"Yes," the Doctor replied.

"Come below. It's still 0.9 roentgen per minute up here. Blackie can stay."

Without another word, they descended. In the passage to the engine room the Engineer noticed a second, smaller robot connecting leads, but he didn't even stop to have a look at it. There were lights on in the library; a small table had been set with aluminum plates and cups and a bottle of wine in the center.

The Captain said: "This was supposed to be a . . . celebration, since the gravimetric distributor was found to be intact, and the main pile is working. If we can raise the ship, we'll be able to take off. Now . . . it's your turn."

There was silence. "Well, you were right," said the Doctor, looking at the Engineer. "It's desert to the west. We did almost a hundred and twenty miles, then turned southwest." He told about the inhabited place by the lake, how they had filmed it, and how on their way back they had come upon a group of statues. Here he hesitated.

"It looked like a cemetery, or perhaps a temple. It's hard to describe what happened next, because I'm not sure what it meant—but that's nothing new here. A pack of doublers appeared, running in panic; it looked as though they had been hiding, or had perhaps been driven there as part of a roundup. That's just my impression. About a quarter of a mile farther down—this all happened on a slope—there was a small woods, and other doublers hiding there, doublers like the one in silver that we killed. Behind them, possibly camouflaged, was one of those gyrating machines, a huge top. But before we saw that, there was a tube, a flexible tube at ground level, giving off a foam that converted into a poison suspension or gas. I assume we can analyze it; it must have left a deposit in the filters, don't you think?" He turned to the Engineer, who nodded. "Anyway, the Chemist and I got out to have a look at the statues, the turret was open, and we were gassed, Henry the worst of all, because the first wave of gas made straight for Defender. When we had got back in and pumped oxygen into the turret, Henry fired at the tube—or, rather, at where we thought it was, because you couldn't see much in that mist."

"You used antimatter?" the Captain asked quietly.

"Yes," replied the Engineer.

"Couldn't you have used the small thrower?"

"I could have, but I didn't."

"We were all . . ." The Doctor searched for the right word. ". . . shaken. Those doublers were not naked. They wore rags—as if, perhaps, their clothes had been torn in a struggle. They died, were dying, right before our eyes. And, as I said, before that we had very nearly been poisoned ourselves. That was the situation. Then Henry tried to find the continuation of the tube, if I remember correctly. Is that right?"

The Engineer nodded.

"So we rode down toward the woods, and saw those silvery creatures. They were wearing masks. Maybe gas masks. They shot at us—I don't know what they were using—and we lost a headlight. At the same time, the huge top started moving. It attacked us from the side, out of the bushes. Then . . . Henry fired."

"At the woods?

"Yes."

"At the silvery creatures?"

"Yes."

"And at the top?"

"No, the top hit us and broke against Defender. There was a fire, of course. The scrub burned like paper."

"Did they try to establish contact?"

"No."

"Did they pursue you?"

"I don't know. Probably not. The disks could have caught up with us."

The Engineer disagreed. "Not in that terrain. There are a lot of ravines, gullies, a little like the Jura back on Earth."

"I see. And then you came directly here?"

"We backtracked, went east."

They sat in silence.

The Captain raised his head. "Did you kill . . . many of them?"

The Doctor glanced at the Engineer, saw that he was not going to answer, and said, "It was dark. They were in the woods. I think I saw . . . maybe twenty. But farther back something else was shining. There could have been more of them."

"The ones that shot at you, they were definitely doublers? Nothing else?"

"I saw no smaller torsos on them, only those helmets. But, judging by their shape, size, and way of moving, they were doublers."

"What did they use to fire at you?"

The Doctor was at a loss.

"Projectiles, probably nonmetallic," said the Engineer. "That's only a guess. I didn't inspect the damage—I didn't even look. Not of much force, that was my impression."

"Yes," the Physicist agreed. "The two headlights—I took a quick look at them—are dented, not punctured."

"One was smashed in the collision with the top," the Chemist said.

"And the statues, what did they look like?" asked the Captain.

The Doctor described them as best he could. When he came to the white statues, he paused and smiled. "Again, unfortunately, we can only speak in metaphors. . . ."

"Four eyes? Prominent foreheads?" the Captain prompted.

"Yes."

"Were they stone carvings? Metal? From molds?"

"I can't say. But definitely not from molds. The main thing, there was a certain . . . alteration of the proportions. A kind of, almost . . ." He hesitated.

"Yes?"

"Idealization," the Doctor said, not without embarrassment. "Though we saw them only briefly, and so much happened afterward . . . It is too easy to make analogies. A cemetery. Escaped prisoners. A police roundup. Genocide, using gas. But we know nothing. Yes, some of the planet's inhabitants killed others before our eyes. That cannot be disputed. But who killed whom—and whether the killed and the killers were really the same . . ."

"And if they were not the same, does that explain anything?" asked the Cyberneticist.

"Well . . . I've thought about one possibility. A macabre one, I admit. For mankind, as we know, cannibalism is taboo. Yet moralists find nothing terrible about eating roast monkey. My point is, what if biological evolution here has developed in such a way that the external differences between beings of human intelligence and beings that have remained at the animal level are much less than those between man and monkey? What we witnessed, then, might have been a hunt."

"And what about that ditch toward the city?" said the Engineer. "Were those trophies of the hunt, Doctor?"

"But we can't be certain . . ."

"In any case, we have the film," said the Chemist, interrupting. "I don't know why, but until now we really haven't seen any normal, everyday existence on this planet. The film shows normality—at least that's the impression I got."

"Impression?" the Physicist asked, surprised. "But didn't you see . . . ?"

"We were in too much of a hurry trying to take advantage of the remaining light. And the distance was considerable, more than twenty-five hundred feet. But we have two spools of film taken with a telescopic lens. What time is it? Not yet twelve! We can develop them now."

"Give them to Blackie," said the Captain. "Gentlemen,

I can see you're upset. It's true, we've got ourselves in a god-awful mess here, but . . ."

"Do contacts between higher civilizations inevitably come to this?" asked the Doctor.

The Captain shook his head, stood up, and took the bottle of wine from the table. "We'll put this away," he said, "for another occasion. . . ."

When the Engineer and the Physicist left to examine Defender, and the Chemist went to supervise the development of the film, the Captain took the Doctor by the arm and brought him over to the library shelves, where he asked in a lowered voice, "Listen, is it possible that it was your unexpected appearance that caused the doublers to flee, and that it was only you, and not the doublers, who were the object of attack?"

The Doctor's eyes widened. "You know, that never even occurred to me," he admitted, then was lost in thought for a while.

"I don't know," he said at last. "I would say not . . . unless it was an attack that failed and then turned against . . . some of them. But there's another explanation," he added, straightening. "Suppose we rode into an area that was off limits. The ones fleeing were trespassers, say, a group of pilgrims, who knows? The sentries guarding the place brought out their weapon—that tube—just as Defender came on the scene. An unfortunate coincidence. Yes, it might have been like that."

"You really think so?"

"Well, such an explanation is as valid as our first one. They could have put guards or sentries in the area when the news about us spread. Before, when we were in that valley, they had no knowledge of us, and that's why we encountered no weapons. . . ."

"We have yet to come across even a trace of their information network," the Cyberneticist remarked from the depths of his cabin. "Writing, radio, recordings . . . Every civilization creates a technology of some kind to pool and save its experience. This one must as well. If only we could go to their city!"

"With Defender we could," said the Captain, turning to him. "But that would precipitate a battle, whose outcome and consequences we cannot predict."

"Then, if only we could sit down with one of their scientists or engineers . . ."

"And how do we do that?" asked the Doctor. "Put an ad in the paper?"

"If I only knew! It shouldn't be that difficult. We arrive on the planet with a computer translator, we draw a couple of Pythagorean triangles in the sand, exchange gifts. . . ."

"Stop that babbling." It was the Engineer, standing in the doorway. "Come on. The film's been developed."

They went to the laboratory to see it, since that was the largest room on the ship. The Captain sat behind the projector. Everyone took a seat, and the robot switched off the light.

The first length of film was completely scorched. The lake flashed several times; then its shoreline came into view. There were ramps, and towers linked by struts, fretwork, over the water. The image blurred, came into focus again, and they could see that on the top of each tower were two five-bladed propellers turning in opposite directions. Turning very slowly. Objects slid down the ramps into the lake and submerged. It was impossible to distinguish their shapes, though they, too, moved very slowly. The Captain reran this part at a higher speed, but the only new thing they saw were the rings the objects made on the surface of the water. A doubler stood at the shore, its back to them. Only the upper part of its huge torso was visible above a barrel-shaped machine from which jutted a slender whip that terminated in windblown wisps.

The shore was replaced by flat, boxlike objects set on pylons. Moving across the screen, the objects carried various barrels like the one at the harbor containing the doubler. But they were empty.

There were flashes, blotches, blurs. The film had been overexposed. Between the blotches, small foreshortened figures, doublers, were moving about in pairs, in different directions, and their smaller torsos were covered with fluff, so that only the little heads showed, but the picture was not sharp enough for the men to see the individual faces.

Now a large mass, rhythmically rising and falling, filled the screen. It spread toward one of the bottom corners like syrup. Dozens of doublers walked across it, and it looked as if they were holding something in their tiny hands, and touching, stroking, or brushing the mass into clumps. Occasionally it gathered into a peak, from which emerged a gray calyx. The picture shifted, but the moving mass continued to fill it. The detail was very sharp. In the center was a bunch of willowy calyxes, and over each calyx stood two or three doublers, lowering their faces to it, taking turns. The Captain reran this part slowly: now the doublers appeared to be kissing the calyxes. While one kissed, the others, their smaller torsos extended halfway, watched.

The picture shifted again. Now the men could see the edge of the mass, which was marked by a dark line, and near the line moved whirling spheres, much smaller than the disks the men knew. Their gyration was slow and jerky; one could see the strutted arms swinging. But this was an effect of the film, of the speed of the frames.

Slowly the screen filled with activity, but everything, in slow motion, seemed to take place in a liquid. What the men had taken to be the "center of the town" was a dense network of grooves, along which ran curious half-barrels, rounded only on one side. From two to five doublers, usually three, sat in each one. Their small torsos seemed to be encircled by a belt connected to the outside of the "barrel," but that might have been only a reflection. The long shadows thrown by the setting sun confused the picture in places.

Above the grooves ran elegant openwork bridges. Here and there on the bridges huge tops spun, and again the gyration appeared as a series of complex movements, as though jointed limbs were pulling something invisible from the air. One top came to a stop, and doublers covered with a shiny material emerged from it. Just as the third doubler was getting out, pulling something hazy behind him, the image shifted.

Through the center ran a thick line, much closer to the lens than the rest of the picture. This line—or pipe—swayed gently; connected to it was a cigar-shaped object that spilled what looked like a cloud of leaves, though they were heavier than leaves, because they did not flutter but fell like weights. Below, on a concave surface, stood many rows of doublers, and sparks flew from their outstretched hands to the ground. But the rain of objects disappeared before it reached them.

The image shifted. Two doublers were lying motionless at the very edge. As a third approached them, they slowly got up. One of them swayed; with its small torso concealed, it looked like a sugarloaf. The Captain reran that segment. When the recumbent bodies appeared, he stopped the film, sharpened the image, then went up to the screen with a large magnifying glass. But all he saw were dots.

It went dark: the end of the first spool. The beginning

of the second showed the same picture, but at a slightly different angle and darker. The sun was setting. The two doublers slowly walked away; now the third was on the ground. Streaks shot across the screen; the camera was moving too fast. They were looking at a large grid with pentagonal openings. In each opening stood a doubler. In a few there were two doublers. Beneath the grid quivered another grid, blurry. Then they realized that the grid below was a shadow on the ground. The ground was smooth, slick, like wet concrete.

The doublers in the grid openings wore dark-colored, bulky clothing and were all performing the same movements: their smaller torsos, veiled by something semitransparent, bent to one side, then the other, as if in a peculiarly slow gymnastics. The picture flickered and tilted; for a while it was difficult to see anything. It was also growing darker. They saw the edge of the grid of lines. One line terminated in a large disk, motionless, resting at an angle. More "traffic"—bulging objects full of doublers going in different directions.

Again the grid, this time from directly above. Doublers, foreshortened, waddled along in pairs; a whole herd of them, divided in two, like two lanes in a street. A cable extending beyond the picture moved down the center, pulling on blurred wheels something that emitted sharp flashes, oblong crystal or a block covered with mirrors. It rocked from side to side, throwing licks of light on the pedestrians it passed. Suddenly it halted and grew transparent, revealing a recumbent figure inside.

The Captain reversed the spool, rewound it, and, after the oblong object again approached, rocking, and displayed its contents, stopped the film. Everyone went up to the screen. There, between the two lanes, the two rows of doublers, lay a man.

"I think I'm going mad," someone said in the darkness.

"Well, let's watch it through to the end," said the Captain.

They went back to their seats, the spool turned, the picture flickered and brightened. One by one, long objects moved through the crowd, but now they were covered with some bright fabric that hung down and trailed on the ground. The picture shifted to a desolate area bordered on one side by a slanting wall. There were clumps of scrub along the wall. A lone doubler walked in a groove that ran the whole length of the screen. The doubler leaped from the groove, as though in panic, and a gyrating top passed; there was a bright flash, then a mist. After the mist cleared, the doubler was lying motionless. Everything became darker, almost black. The doubler seemed to twitch, or perhaps began to crawl away, until stripes shot across the screen, and the screen went white. The film was finished.

When the lights were turned back on, the Chemist took the spools to the darkroom to make some enlargements of selected frames. The others remained in the laboratory.

"Well, now, what do we make of all this?" said the Doctor. "Without trying, I could give two, even three different explanations."

This angered the Engineer. "If you had done a proper study of the doubler's physiology," he said, "we'd know a great deal more than we do now!"

"And when was I supposed to do that?" inquired the Doctor.

"Gentlemen!" cried the Captain. "This is beginning to sound like a scientific convention! All right, that figure shocked us. A dummy, undoubtedly, made in some sort of modeling material. Probably, through their information network, they've sent pictures of us to every settlement on the planet, and from the pictures they fashioned human effigies."

"But why would they want to make such portraits?" asked the Doctor.

"For scientific or religious purposes, who knows? We won't solve that one, no matter how long we discuss it. Still, it's not all that strange. What we've seen is a rather small center where things are being manufactured. We may also have observed their . . . recreation, perhaps their art, a street scene—though what they were doing in the harbor, that pouring of objects, was none too clear."

"None too clear," the Doctor said. "Well put."

"And there were what looked like scenes from army life—the ones dressed in silver, as we've seen before, serve a military function. As for the episode at the end . . . it may have been the punishment of an individual who broke a law, perhaps by using a groove reserved for the tops."

"Summary execution for jaywalking seems a bit severe, don't you think?" said the Doctor.

"Does anyone else have something to say?" asked the Captain, nettled.

The Physicist spoke. "The doublers appear to travel on foot only in exceptional circumstances. That might be because of their size and weight—and the disproportion in their limbs, particularly between the hands and the trunk of the body. It would be interesting to try to draw an evolutionary tree that could produce such a shape. You've all noticed how they gesticulate—but none of them use their hands to lift loads, to pull or carry. Perhaps their hands serve another purpose."

"Such as?" the Doctor asked, interested.

"I don't know, that's your field. I just think that, instead of attempting to understand the structure of their society, we ought to study, first, the individual, the building block of that society."

"You're right," said the Doctor. "The hands, yes, that's a problem . . . the evolutionary tree. We don't even know if the doublers are mammals. That question I could answer in a few days—but it's not the thing that impressed me the most in this film."

"And what's that?" asked the Engineer.

"The fact that, among the pedestrians, I saw not one who was solitary. Did you notice that?"

"Except at the very end," said the Physicist.

"Precisely."

No one said anything for a while.

"We'll have to look at the film again," said the Captain at last. "The Doctor is right: there were no solitary doublers. They went at least in pairs. Though, at the beginning—yes!—one of them was by itself in the harbor."

"It was sitting in that cone-shaped thing," said the Doctor. "In the disks, too, they sit individually. I was talking only about pedestrians."

"There weren't many of them."

"There were several hundred. Imagine a bird's-eye view of a street in a town on Earth. The percentage of solitary pedestrians would be considerable. At some hours they would even be in the majority. But here there were none at all."

"What does that mean?" asked the Engineer.

The Doctor shook his head. "I have no idea."

"But the one that came with us . . . he was by himself."

"Consider the circumstances that led to that."

The Engineer made no reply.

"Listen," said the Captain, "this is getting us nowhere. We didn't gather information systematically, because we're not a research team. We had other worries, of the 'struggle-for-survival' variety. Now we must decide on a course of action. Tomorrow Digger will be working. We'll have a total of two robots, two semiautomata, Digger and Defender, who may also help in the unearthing of the ship. I don't know if you're familiar with the plan the Engineer and I worked out. The basic idea is to lower the ship first to the horizontal, then stand it upright by packing soil under the hull. That's the method the ancient pyramid-builders used. We'll cut our 'glass wall' into pieces we can use to build a scaffold. There's enough material, and we already know that the substance can be melted and welded at high temperatures. Using the wall that the inhabitants of Eden have so thoughtfully provided us with will shorten the task dramatically. We may be able to take off in three days." He paused, seeing the men stir. "Therefore I wanted to ask you: do we take off?"

"Yes," said the Physicist.

"No," said the Chemist, almost at the same time.

"Not just yet," the Cyberneticist said.

A silence. Neither the Engineer nor the Doctor had voted.

"I think we should leave," the Engineer said at last. Everyone looked at him with astonishment. He went on:

"I felt differently before. It's a question of the price. Just the price. Undoubtedly we could learn much more, but the cost of obtaining that knowledge . . . it might be too great. For both sides. After what has happened, the possibility of peaceful contact, of coming to an understanding, is, it seems to me, extremely remote. Each of us, whether we like it or not, has his own concept of this world. Mine was that terrible things were going on here, and that we should intervene. As long as we were Robinson Crusoes going through our wreckage and making repairs, I said nothing. I wanted to wait until I knew more, and until we could make use of our machines. But I see now that each intervention on behalf of what we hold to be good and right will end the way our last excursion did:

with the use of the annihilator. We can always justify our-selves, of course, argue self-defense, and so on—but in-stead of helping, we're destroying."

"If we only had better knowledge . . ." said the Chemist.

The Engineer shook his head.

"With better knowledge we'd see that each side was right in its own way. . . ."

"Whether the murderers are right or wrong," the Chemist objected, "someone should give thought to their victims."

"But what can we offer them besides Defender's anni-hilator? Suppose we reduce half the planet to ashes in order to stop these incomprehensible roundups and ex-terminations. What then?"

"It's not a simple matter of right and wrong," said the Captain, joining the argument. "Everything that's happen-ing here is part of an ongoing historical process. Your impulse to help is based on the assumption that the soci-ety is divided into heroes and villains."

"Into oppressors and oppressed," said the Chemist. "That's not the same thing."

"All right. Let's imagine that a highly developed race, arriving on Earth during our religious wars several hundred years ago, had decided to enter the conflict—on the side of the weak. Wielding its power, it forbids the burning of heretics, the persecution of dissenters, et cetera. Do you honestly think it would be able to make its humanitarian rationalism accepted throughout the planet? Remember: almost the whole of mankind were believers then. The aliens would have to pound us down to the last man, in which case there would be no one left to benefit from their idealism!"

"Then you think it's impossible for us to help!" said the Chemist with vehemence.

The Captain looked at him a long time before replying.
"Help, my God. What do you mean by help? What's taking place here, what we're witnessing, is the product of a specific civilization, and we would have to destroy that civilization and create a new one—and how are we supposed to do that? These are beings with a physiology, psychology, and history different from ours. You can't transplant a model of our civilization here. And you would have to construct one, too, that would continue to function after our departure. . . . I suspected, for quite some time, that you had ideas similar to those of the Engineer. And that the Doctor agreed with me, which is why he kept discouraging us from making analogies to Earth. Am I right?"

"Yes," said the Doctor. "I was afraid that through an access of noble-mindedness you would all want to establish 'order' here, which in practice would mean a reign of terror."

"Maybe the oppressed would like a different life . . . but are too weak," said the Chemist. "And if we saved some who were condemned . . ."

"We saved one," the Captain retorted. "Now perhaps you can tell us what to do with him."

The Chemist had no reply.

"The Doctor is also in favor of leaving?" said the Captain. "Good. Including me, that makes a majority."

He broke off. His eyes grew round. He had been sitting facing the door—the half-open door. In the silence they heard only a faint lapping of water, and turned to follow the Captain's stare.

In the doorway stood the doubler.

"How did he get out . . . ?" But the Physicist's words died on his lips. He saw his mistake. This was not their doubler. Theirs was locked in the first-aid room.

On the threshold was an enormous dark-skinned doubler, its smaller torso bent low and the head almost touching the lintel. The creature was dressed in a brown material that hung straight and encircled the small torso like a collar. Wound around the collar was a thick tangle of green wire. Through a slit on the side gleamed a broad metallic belt. The doubler did not move. Its flat, wrinkled face and two large blue eyes were covered by a transparent, funnel-shaped shield. From the shield ran thin gray strands that coiled around the smaller torso several times and crisscrossed in front, forming a kind of pocket, in which rested its hands, similarly bandaged. Only the knobby tips of the fingers protruded.

Everyone sat in amazement at the sight. The doubler bent over even more and with a cough moved slowly forward.

"How did it get in? . . . Blackie is in the tunnel . . ." whispered the Chemist.

Then the doubler slowly withdrew. It went out, stood in the dark corridor for a moment, and entered a second time—or, rather, only stuck its head in just beneath the lintel.

"It's asking if it can enter," the Engineer said in a whisper. Then he shouted, "Come in! Come in!"

He got up and backed away along the opposite wall, and the others followed him. The doubler regarded the empty center of the cabin blankly. It entered and slowly looked around.

The Captain went to the screen, tugged at it to make it whir upward, which uncovered the blackboard. He asked the men to step aside, took a piece of chalk, and drew a small circle, then drew an ellipse around the circle, and a larger ellipse outside that, and another, and another—four in all. On each ellipse he placed a small circle. Then he approached the giant in the center of the room and stuck the chalk in its little fingers.

The doubler accepted the chalk awkwardly, looked at it, looked at the blackboard, then slowly went toward it. It had to incline its smaller torso, which stuck out at an angle from the collar, in order to touch the board with a bandaged hand. The men watched with bated breath. Clumsily, with effort, the doubler tapped the circle on the third ellipse several times; it nearly filled the circle with crushed chalk.

The Captain nodded. Everyone breathed freely. "Eden," he said, pointing at the circle. "Eden," he repeated.

The doubler watched his mouth with interest. It coughed.

"Eden," said the Captain slowly, enunciating clearly.

The doubler coughed several times.

"It can't speak," said the Captain, turning to his colleagues. "That's for sure."

They stood, not knowing what to do. The doubler moved. It dropped the chalk. There was a sound like that of a lock being opened. The brown material parted, as though ripped from top to bottom, and they saw a broad gold belt.

The belt unwound, rustling like metal foil. The doubler's smaller torso leaned far over, as if to step from its body; bending almost in two, it grabbed the end of the foil with its fingers. The belt had uncoiled into a long sheet, which it held out, apparently offering it to them. The Captain and the Engineer reached out simultaneously, and both jumped. The Engineer gave a little cry. The doubler, apparently surprised, coughed several times, and the transparent shield wavered on its face.

"An electrical charge, but not very strong," the Captain explained to the others, then reached for the foil a second time. The doubler released it. They examined the gold surface in the light: it was completely smooth, featureless. The Captain touched it at random and once again felt a mild electric shock.

"What is it?!" growled the Physicist, and began to run his hand over the foil. Electric shocks made his fingers quiver. "Give me some powdered graphite!" he said. "It's there in the cabinet!"

He spread out the foil on the table, paying no attention to the twitching of his hand, sprinkled the foil with the graphite that the Cyberneticist had given him, and blew off the excess.

On the gold surface were tiny black dots scattered seemingly at random.

"Lacerta!" the Captain cried suddenly.

"Alpha Cygni!"

"Lyra!"

"Cepheus!"

They turned to the doubler, who was watching them calmly. Triumph gleamed in its eyes.

"A star map!" exclaimed the Engineer.

"Well, now we feel at home." The Captain grinned.

The doubler coughed.

"Is it electrical writing?"

"Apparently."

"How are the charges maintained?"

"Perhaps they have an electric sense!"

"Gentlemen, please! Let's proceed logically," said the Captain. "What now?"

"Show it where we're from."

"Right."

The Captain quickly erased the board and drew the constellation of the Centaur. He hesitated, calculating in his head how that region of the Galaxy would be seen from Eden. He made a thick dot to indicate Sirius, added a dozen lesser stars, and on top of the Great Bear drew a small cross indicating the Sun. Then he touched his own chest and that of all his men in turn, swept his arm around the room, and again tapped the cross with his chalk.

The doubler coughed, took the chalk from him, pushed its small torso over to the board, and filled in the Captain's sketch with three dots: Alpha Aquilae and the binary system of Procyon.

"An astronomer!" whispered the Physicist. "A colleague . . ."

"Very likely!" replied the Captain. "Now let's go on!" What followed was a great amount of drawing. The planet Eden, the ship's path, its entry into the gaseous tail, and the collision. Then the ship embedded in the ground—a cross-section of the hill and the ship.

The doubler looked at the drawings on the blackboard and coughed. It went to the table. From the green convolutions of its collar it extracted a thin, flexible wire, leaned over, and began moving the wire across the foil with extraordinary speed. This continued for some time. It stepped back, and the men sprinkled the foil with graphite, whereupon something strange occurred. Even as they were blowing away the excess powder, the emerging lines began to move.

First they saw a hemisphere with an oblique column inside. Then a small spot appeared and crept over the edge of the hemisphere. It grew larger and larger. They recognized the outline of Defender, though the sketch was inexact. Part of the curve of the hemisphere disappeared, and Defender entered through that gap. At that point everything disappeared, and the graphite on the foil was even. Suddenly it gathered to form the star map. Through the map emerged the figure of a doubler, sketched in long strokes. The doubler standing behind them coughed.

"That's him," said the Captain.

The map disappeared, leaving only the doubler. Then

the doubler disappeared, and the map replaced it. This was repeated four times. Spread as though by an invisible breath, the graphite once again arranged itself into an outline of the hemisphere with the broken curve. The doubler's silhouette appeared, much smaller, crawled toward the gap, and made its way in. The hemisphere disappeared. The oblique cylinder of the ship became larger. In front, beneath the hull, there was an opening. Through it the doubler entered the ship. The graphite scattered in random clumps: end of message.

"That's how it got here, through the loading hatch!" said the Engineer. "We left the damn thing open!"

"Wait—do you know what occurred to me?" the Doctor said. "Maybe they wanted, with that wall, not so much to shut us in as to prevent their—their scientists from contacting us!"

They turned to the doubler. It coughed.

"Well, enough of this," said the Captain. "It's been a very pleasant social gathering, but we have more important business before us! As for guerrilla warfare—forget it. We must go about this systematically. I suppose we ought to start with mathematics. The Physicist can handle that. Mathematics, and metamathematics, of course. The theory of matter, field theory. And then information theory, programming languages, semantics. Grammar, logic, vocabulary. All that belongs to you," he said to the Cyberneticist. "And once we've set up that bridge, there's biology, metabolism, economics, social forms, group behavior, and so on. There we won't have to be in such a hurry. Meanwhile"—he turned to the Cyberneticist and the Physicist—"you two get started. You have the films to help you, the computer, the library. Use whatever you need."

"To start with, we could take him around the ship," said the Engineer. "What do you think? That might tell him a few things. And he'll see that we're hiding nothing from him."

"Yes, that's important," the Captain agreed. "But—until we're able to communicate with him properly—don't let him into the first-aid room. That might cause some sort of misunderstanding. Now, let's make a tour of the ship. What time is it?"

It was three in the morning.

XIII

The tour of the ship took quite a while. The doubler was especially interested in the atomic pile and the robots. The Engineer drew sketch after sketch for it, filling four notebooks in the engine room alone. The guest made a detailed inspection of the microgrid, was amazed to find it entirely submerged in a tank of liquid helium—a cryotronic brain, superconductive for quick reactions—but soon grasped the purpose of the cooling. It coughed for a long time and looked with approval at the diagram the Cyberneticist drew for it. Evidently they could communicate much more easily by diagrams than by trying to represent basic words through gestures or symbols.

At five in the morning the Chemist, the Captain, and the Engineer went off to bed. Blackie, after closing the loading hatch, stood guard in the tunnel, while the other three men took the doubler to the library.

"Wait," said the Physicist as they passed the laboratory.

"Let's show it the periodic table. There are illustrations of the electron orbitals of the atoms."

They went in. The Physicist was rummaging through a pile of papers in the cabinet when they heard a ticking.

"What's that?" the Doctor asked.

The Physicist looked up, heard the ticking, too. His eyes widened. "It's the Geiger. There must be a leak. . . ."

He ran to the counter. The doubler, looking at the different instruments, now approached the table, and the counter began rattling like the roll of a drum.

"It's the doubler!" said the Physicist, aiming the metal cylinder with both hands at the huge alien. The counter whirred louder.

"He's radioactive? What does that mean?" asked the Cyberneticist.

The Doctor, pale, took the cylinder from the Physicist and swept the air with it in the direction of the doubler. The higher he raised it, the weaker the sound. Near the creature's clumsy, stout legs, the counter whirred and its red light went on.

The doubler moved its eyes from one man to another, surprised but not alarmed by what they were doing. It clearly didn't understand.

"He came through the opening Defender made in the wall," the Doctor said softly. "There's a radioactive patch there. . . ."

"Keep your distance!" the Physicist said. "He's giving off more than a milliroentgen a second! Unless we wrap him in ceramite foil; then perhaps we could risk it. . . ."

"I'm more concerned about him!" the Doctor said, raising his voice. "How long do you think he was exposed? What kind of dosage did he get?"

"I—I have no idea . . ." the Physicist said. "You should do something! An acetate bath . . . Look at him—he doesn't know!"

The Doctor rushed out of the laboratory without saying a word. He returned a moment later with the first-aid radiation kit. At first the doubler resisted their gestures for telling it to lie down, but eventually it submitted.

"Gloves!" the Physicist shouted, because the Doctor was touching the doubler's skin with his bare hands.

"Should we wake the others?" asked the Cyberneticist, standing off to the side.

"No need," muttered the Doctor, pulling on thick gloves. He leaned over the doubler. "So far, nothing . . . There'll be a rash in ten, twelve hours, assuming . . ."

"If we could only communicate," the Physicist said, half to himself.

"A transfusion . . . but how?" The Doctor closed his eyes. "The other one!" Then added, more softly, "No, I can't. First I would have to type both bloods, test for agglutination. . . ."

"Listen." The Physicist pulled him aside. "It's probably bad. He must have crossed the radioactive area the second the temperature dropped, and there would have been plenty of isotopes there, rubidium, strontium, rare earths. Are there white corpuscles in his blood?"

"Yes, but they're not like human ones."

"All rapidly multiplying cells are hit in the same way, regardless of the species. Though he probably has more resistance than man. . . ."

"What makes you say that?"

"Because background radiation here is almost twice that of Earth. To some degree they must have adapted to it. And I don't suppose your antibiotics . . . ?"

"Of no use. The bacteria here are altogether different."

"In that case . . . we should try to communicate with him on as broad a range of subjects as possible. The reaction, the apathy, if he behaves like a human being, won't begin for another several hours. . . ."

The Doctor looked quickly at the Physicist. They were standing five feet from the doubler, who did not take its blue eyes off them. "In other words, to pump as much information as we can out of him before he dies."

"I wasn't thinking of it quite like that," said the Physicist, turning red in the face. "But any one of us, in his place . . . our first thought would be to complete the mission!"

The Doctor smiled bitterly. "Perhaps, knowing the score. But we gave him no choice. He was injured by us! It was our fault."

"And now what? You want to expiate your sin? Don't be ridiculous!"

"You don't understand. That"—he pointed at the recumbent figure—"is a patient, and this"—he slapped himself on the chest—"is a doctor. And, except for a doctor, no one has any business here."

"But . . . this is our only chance. We won't be doing him any harm. It wasn't our fault that . . ."

"It was! The doubler was injured because he followed Defender! But that's enough. I have to take blood from him."

He approached the creature with a syringe, hesitated, went back to the table for a second syringe. "I'll need your help," he said, turning to the Cyberneticist.

He approached the doubler now with both syringes and bared his arm. As the doubler watched, the Cyberneticist took a syringe, extracted a little of the Doctor's blood, and stepped back. The Doctor took the second needle, touched the doubler's skin with it, found a vein, inserted it. The doubler did not move. Its light-red blood filled the plastic cylinder. The Doctor deftly removed the needle, pressed the puncture with a cotton ball, and left the room.

The Cyberneticist, still holding the syringe containing

the Doctor's blood, asked the Physicist, "And now what? Should we wake the others?"

"The Doctor will only make the same argument. No . . . the doubler must decide for himself. If he agrees, the Doctor will have to go along."

The Cyberneticist gave him a look of surprise. "But how will the doubler decide? He doesn't know—and we can't tell him!"

"Of course we can," the Physicist said, regarding the plastic cylinder containing the Doctor's blood. "We have fifteen minutes while the Doctor counts corpuscles. Bring the blackboard here!"

"The blackboard!" And the Physicist began gathering bits of chalk.

The Cyberneticist took the blackboard off the wall, and together they set it up opposite the doubler.

"Not enough chalk! Bring some from the library, colored pieces!"

As the Cyberneticist went out, the Physicist took a stick of chalk and quickly sketched a hemisphere with the ship inside it. He felt the creature's pale-blue eyes on him. When he was finished, he turned to the doubler, tapped the blackboard with his finger, wiped it with a wet sponge, and went on drawing.

The wall intact. Before the wall, Defender. Defender's nose, the nuclear beam. The Physicist went over to the creature, touched it, returned to the blackboard, and tapped the chalk on the sketched figure. Then, quickly, he erased the picture, put the wall up again, rubbed another gap in it, surrounded the gap heavily with violet, and placed the doubler there, erased everything except the doubler, replaced the doubler with a larger doubler. Standing so that the doubler could see his every move, the Physicist began rubbing crushed violet chalk onto the feet of the figure. He turned around.

The doubler's small torso, which had been resting on a rubber pillow that the Doctor had inflated, slowly rose, and the wrinkled monkey face and intelligent eyes turned from the blackboard to the Physicist, as though asking him what all this meant.

The Physicist nodded, grabbed a can and a pair of protective gloves, and dashed out of the laboratory. In the tunnel he almost ran into a robot, which, recognizing him, stepped aside. Outside, on the surface, the Physicist put the gloves on and ran to the gap in the crystal wall. At the shallow crater there he dropped to his knees and as quickly as possible took a few pieces of sand-turned-to-glass and threw them into the can. Then he ran back to the ship and through the tunnel. There was someone standing in the laboratory, waiting: the Cyberneticist.

"The Doctor?" the Physicist asked.

"He hasn't returned yet."

"Move back. Sit over there, by the wall." And he emptied the contents of the can, pale-violet pieces of vitrified sand, on the floor in front of the blackboard.

"You're crazy!" hissed the Cyberneticist, jumping to his feet. At the other end of the table, the Geiger came to life and began clicking rapidly.

"Quiet! Don't interfere!" The Physicist's voice shook with such ferocity that the Cyberneticist sat down again.

The Physicist glanced at his watch. Twelve minutes had passed. The Doctor might return at any moment. The Physicist leaned forward, pointed to the violet pieces, picked up a handful of them, held them in the palm of his hand, and brought them to the sketched figure, to its feet, smeared with violet chalk. He rubbed one of the fragments on the drawing, looked into the doubler's eyes, dropped the rest on the floor, and backed away.

Then he approached again, with a determined step, as

though he had a great distance to cover, and walked into the patch of violet pieces. He stood there for a while, closed his eyes, and slowly fell. His body thudded on the floor. He lay there for a moment, got up, went over to the table, grabbed the Geiger, and went back to the blackboard. When the cylinder was brought near the chalk-drawn feet, it burst into a loud staccato. The Physicist passed the counter by the blackboard several times, repeating the effect as the doubler watched intently, turned to the doubler and began moving the counter toward the bare soles of its feet.

The instrument began to chatter.

The doubler made a small noise, as if it were choking. For several seconds—which seemed an eternity—it looked into the Physicist's eyes. Drops of sweat trickled down the Physicist's brow. The doubler suddenly went limp, shut its eyes, and sank back on its cushion, strangely tensing the fingers of both hands. After lying still for a moment, it opened its eyes, sat up again, and gave the Physicist a long look.

The Physicist nodded, put the counter on the table, nudged the blackboard with his foot, and said quietly to the Cyberneticist, "He knows now."

"Knows what?" muttered the other, shaken by this pantomime.

"That he's going to die."

The Doctor entered, saw the blackboard and the scattered pieces of violet glass. "What's this?" he asked angrily. "What does it mean?"

"It means you have two patients now," the Physicist said. And as the Doctor watched in amazement, he calmly took up the Geiger again and pointed it at his own body. The instrument chattered. Radioactive dust had penetrated the Physicist's suit.

The Doctor paled, clutched the syringe he was holding,

almost as if it were a weapon. Then slowly he relaxed. "All right," he said. "Let's clean you up."

As soon as the two of them left, the Cyberneticist threw on a protective suit and hurriedly disposed of the radioactive fragments. Then he vacuumed the whole area carefully. The doubler lay still, watching, coughing quietly a few times. After about ten minutes the Physicist returned with the Doctor; he was now wearing a white canvas suit and had thick bandages on his neck and hands.

"Well, that's taken care of," he said almost cheerfully. "Nothing serious. A first-degree burn, maybe not even that."

The Doctor and the Cyberneticist began helping the doubler up. The doubler, understanding, got up and followed the Doctor submissively.

"And what was the point of all that?" asked the Cyberneticist. He was pacing the room nervously, poking the Geiger's black muzzle into every nook and cranny. Now and then the clicking would accelerate slightly.

"You'll see," the Physicist said.

"Why didn't you put on a protective suit? It would have taken only a minute."

"I had to keep it simple," said the Physicist. "And as natural as possible. A special suit might have confused him."

They fell silent. The hand on the wall clock slowly shifted. The Cyberneticist began to feel sleepy. The Physicist yawned.

Then the Doctor, in a smock, burst in and yelled at the Physicist. "It was you, wasn't it? What did you do to him?!"

"What's wrong?" asked the Physicist.

"He won't lie down! He barely let me examine him, then got up and headed for the door."

Behind him, the doubler entered, hobbling. The loose end of a bandage dragged along the floor behind it.

"You can't treat him against his will," the Physicist said coolly. He stood. "I suggest we take the computer from the navigation room. It has the greatest range of extrapolation." This he said to the Cyberneticist, who got to his feet with a start, blinked stupidly for a moment, and walked out, leaving the door open.

The Doctor stood in the middle of the laboratory, his fists in the pockets of his smock. At the sound of soft shuffling, he turned around and looked at the giant alien.

"You know, don't you?" he said with a sigh.

The doubler coughed.

The other three of the crew slept the entire day. When they woke, night was falling. They went straight to the library, which they found in chaos. The tables, the floor, every chair was buried under piles of books, atlases, scattered pages with sketches, hundreds of them. Mixed in with the books and paper were machine parts, photographs, cans of food, plates, lenses, calculators, and cassettes. The blackboard, propped against a wall, dripped water and chalk dust, and chalk dust covered the fingers, sleeves, and even the knees of the Physicist, Doctor, and Cyberneticist. Unshaven and with bloodshot eyes, they were sitting opposite the doubler and drinking coffee from mugs. In the middle of the room, where the table had been, stood a large computer.

"How is it going?" asked the Captain, in the doorway.

"Beautifully. We've analogized sixteen hundred concepts," said the Cyberneticist.

The Doctor got up. He was still in his smock. "This was against my advice," he said, and pointed at the doubler. "He's been seriously wounded."

"Wounded!?" The Captain entered the room.

"He walked through the radioactive area at the gap in the wall," explained the Physicist, leaving his coffee and kneeling by the computer.

"He has ten percent fewer white corpuscles than seven hours ago," said the Doctor. "And there's hyaline degeneration, exactly as you would expect in a human. I wanted to isolate him—he needs rest—but he won't let me treat him, because the Physicist told him that he is beyond help."

"Is that true?" asked the Captain, turning to the Physicist. The latter nodded without looking up from the whirring machine.

"And is he . . . beyond help?" asked the Engineer.

The Doctor shrugged. "I don't know! If he were human, I'd say he had a thirty percent chance. But he's not human. He's growing apathetic, but that could be due to exhaustion, lack of sleep. If I could isolate him . . ."

"You can still do that," said the Physicist as he fiddled with some knobs, using his bandaged hands.

"And what happened to you?" asked the Captain.

"I showed the doubler how it had exposed itself to radiation."

"And for that you had to expose yourself, too?!" exclaimed the Engineer.

"That's right."

No one spoke for a while.

"What's happened, has happened," the Captain said at last, slowly. "Whether for good or for bad. And now what? What have you learned?"

"Plenty."

It was the Cyberneticist who answered.

"He's already mastered hundreds of our symbols—the mathematical ones especially. In fact, we're well into information theory. The biggest problem is his electrical writing: we can't learn it without special equipment, and there's no time to construct that. Remember those fragments of tubing leading into the body in the pit? A writing instrument! When a doubler comes into the world, a

235

tube is immediately implanted, just as baby girls on Earth once had their ears pierced in some societies. . . . On either side of the body—the larger body, I mean—they have electrical organs. They're like plasma batteries that transmit charges directly to the 'writing tube.' In this doubler, the tube terminates in those wires on the 'collar.' It varies from individual to individual. But apparently writing is something they have to learn. The tube surgery, which has been carried out for thousands of years, is only a preliminary step."

"So he doesn't speak?" asked the Chemist.

"He does. That coughing you heard—that's actually speech. A single cough is an entire sentence, articulated at great speed. We taped it—it resolves into a whole spectrum of frequencies."

"Ah! So it's speech based on modulated sound!"

"But voiceless sound. Their voices are used solely to express states of emotion."

"And do these electrical organs also serve as defenses?"

"I don't know. Let's ask him."

He leaned over and from a pile of papers pulled out a board containing a diagram of a doubler. He pointed to two oblong segmented shapes inside the body and asked, putting his mouth to a microphone, "Defense?"

A speaker near the recumbent creature squawked. The doubler, who had raised his small torso a little when the other men entered, froze for a moment, then coughed.

"Defense. No," croaked the loudspeaker. "Many planetary revolutions. Ago. Defense."

The doubler coughed again.

"Organ. Rudimentary. Biology evolved. Secondary adaptation. By technology," the speaker said in a lifeless monotone.

"Well, well," murmured the Engineer with pleasure. The Chemist stood rapt, his eyes narrowed.

"Genetic engineering!" the Captain exclaimed. "And their physics?" he asked.

"From our point of view, peculiar," said the Physicist. He got up off his knees. "I can't eliminate that static," he said to the Cyberneticist. "In classical physics," he went on, they're very knowledgeable. Optics, electricity, mechanics, and especially molecular mechanics—a kind of chemical physics. There they've made some interesting discoveries."

"Such as?!" The Chemist pushed forward.

"Details later. We recorded everything, don't worry. They arrived at information theory by a completely different route. But the study of it is forbidden to them, outside certain special areas. In atomic science they're weakest, particularly nuclear chemistry."

"Wait—what do you mean, forbidden?" asked the Engineer.

"They're not allowed to pursue research in information theory."

"Who forbids it?"

"That's a complicated business," the Doctor said. "We're still at sea when it comes to their social dynamics."

"There's no incentive, probably, for nuclear research," said the Physicist, "because they have no shortage of energy."

"One thing at a time! What about this forbidden research?"

"Pull up a chair. We'll be asking him more questions," said the Cyberneticist.

The Captain put his face to the microphone, but the Cyberneticist stopped him. "Wait. The more complex the structure of a sentence, the more difficulty the computer has with grammar. And the sound analyzer is inadequate. So the answers don't always make sense. But you'll see for yourselves."

"There are many of you on the planet," said the Physicist into the microphone, enunciating carefully. "What is the organizational system of you on the planet?"

The speaker squawked twice, went silent. For some time the doubler made no reply. Then he coughed hoarsely.

"Our organizational system. Binary. Our relations. Binary," said the speaker. "Society. Central control. The whole planet."

"Perfect!" cried the Engineer, excited. The three new participants in the questioning were all excited, but their colleagues sat quietly, weariness—indifference, almost—in their faces.

"Who rules your society? Who is at the top, an individual or a group?" the Captain said into the microphone. The speaker crackled, there was a buzz, and a red light flashed on the instrument panel.

"You can't ask that way," the Cyberneticist explained. " 'At the top' is imprecise and figurative. Let me." He leaned forward. "How many of you make the decisions at central control? One? Several? A large number?"

The speaker squawked. "One. Several. Large number. Control. Do not know. Do not know," it repeated.

"What is that supposed to mean?" asked the Captain, surprised.

"Let's ask."

"You do not know, or no one on the planet knows?" the Cyberneticist said into the microphone.

The doubler coughed, and the computer translated:

"Binary relations. One thing. Known. Other thing. Unknown."

"I don't—" the Captain began.

"Wait," said the Cyberneticist, because the doubler slowly moved his face again to his own microphone and coughed twice.

The computer continued:

"Many planetary revolutions. Ago. Central control. Divided. Pause. One doubler. Pause. One hundred and thirteen planetary revolutions. Pause. Planetary revolution one hundred and eleven. One doubler. Death. Pause. Other doubler. Death. One. One. Death. Death. Pause. Then. One doubler. Who unknown. Central control known. Unknown who."

"And what do you make of that?" asked the Captain.

The Cyberneticist replied: "He says that up to the year one hundred and thirteen, counting back from today—this would be year zero—they had a multimember central government. Then followed reigns of individuals. In the years one hundred and twelve and one hundred and eleven there were violent palace coups. Four rules succeeded one another within two years. Their deaths obviously were not natural. Then a new ruler appeared, whose existence was known but not his identity."

"You mean, an anonymous ruler?" the Engineer asked.

"It would seem. Let's try to find out more."

He turned to the microphone. "It is known that one individual makes decisions at central control, but it is not known who that individual is?"

The doubler coughed, hesitated, coughed again, and the speaker said, "No. Pause. Sixty planetary revolutions. Known. One doubler decides. Pause. Then known that no doubler. Pause. No one at central control. Known."

"Now I'm in the dark," said the Physicist.

The Cyberneticist sat hunched toward the computer, chewing his lips.

"The general information is that there is no central government?" he asked. "But in reality there is a central government?"

The computer conferred with the doubler, exchanging noises. The men waited, their heads near the speaker.

"True. Yes. Pause. The information that there is a

central government. Who has it, is. Is not. Who has this information. Is, then is not."

They looked at one another.

"Whoever says that the government exists ceases to exist?" the Engineer asked in a half-whisper.

The Cyberneticist slowly nodded.

"But that doesn't make sense!" said the Engineer. "The government must have a headquarters, after all, must issue directives, laws, and have bodies that implement them, a hierarchy, an arm. Didn't we encounter soldiers?" The Physicist put a hand on his shoulder. The Engineer fell silent.

The doubler began coughing, and the computer's green eye flickered rapidly. The speaker said, "Information binary. Pause. One information. Who has it, is. Pause. Other information. Who has it, is, then is not."

"There is information that is secret?" the Physicist asked. "Whoever has this secret information is killed?"

Again the speaker squawked, and the doubler coughed on the other side of the computer.

"No. Who is, then is not. Not death."

The men took a deep breath.

"Ask what happens to such individuals," said the Engineer.

"I don't think I can," said the Cyberneticist. But the Captain and the Engineer insisted, so he muttered, "All right, but I'm not promising anything in the way of an answer."

"What is the future of one who spreads secret information?" he said into the microphone.

The dialogue of noises between the computer and the doubler went on for a while; then the speaker replied:

"Who. Such information. In a self-controlling group. Unknown degree of probability. Degeneration. Pause. The cumulative effect. Nonexistent term. The necessity of ad-

aptation. Conflict. And the weakening of the force poten-
tial. Nonexistent term. Pause. A small number of planetary
revolutions. Death."

"What did he say?" asked the Chemist, and they all
turned to the Cyberneticist, who shrugged.

"I have no idea. I told you. The question is too complex. We have to proceed gradually. My guess is that the
fate of such an individual is unenviable. He can expect an
untimely death—the last sentence was clear—but as to
the mechanics of the whole process, I don't know. The
self-controlling group is interesting, but we already have
plenty to speculate on."

"Ask him about that factory to the north," said the
Engineer.

"We did," said the Physicist. "That's another complex
question. We have a theory about it. . . ."

"What do you mean, a theory? Didn't he give you an
answer?" the Captain interrupted.

"After a fashion. The factory was abandoned before
it went into operation. That we know. But the reason is
not so clear. About fifty years ago a plan of biological
reconstruction was inaugurated among them. The remodeling of bodily functions—and forms. It's a confus-
ing story. Virtually the entire population of the planet
underwent a series of surgical procedures. But this apparently was not so much a matter of changing the present
generation as future ones, through the engineered muta-
tion of hereditary material. That, at least, is how we in-
terpret it. In the area of biology communication becomes
difficult."

"What kind of remodeling was it? In what direction?"
asked the Captain.

"That we haven't learned," said the Physicist.

"Well, we've learned some things," the Cyberneticist
said. "Biology—physiology in particular—has a special,

almost doctrinal significance for them, distinct from the other fields of science."

"It could be religious," said the Doctor. "Though their beliefs are more a system of prohibitions and rules than a transcendental theology."

"They've never believed in a creator?" asked the Captain.

"We don't know. Remember, such abstractions as faith, god, and the soul cannot be analogized in a computer. We have to ask a multitude of factual questions, and from the answers and half-answers attempt to construct a reasonable theory. What the Doctor calls religion I think may be simply tradition, historically stratified customs and rituals."

"But what can either religion or tradition have to do with biological research?" asked the Engineer.

"We don't know. But a connection seems to exist."

"Maybe it was a matter of their trying to make certain biological facts conform to their beliefs or prejudices."

"No, it's much more complicated than that."

"To return to the subject," said the Captain, "what were the consequences of this biological program?"

"Individuals came into the world with no eyes or a varying number of eyes, or unfit for life, deformed, noseless. And there were a significant number of mental defectives."

"Ah! Our doubler, and the others!"

"Yes. Evidently the theory on which they relied was wrong. Over a period of a dozen years, tens of thousands of deformed mutants appeared. They are still reaping today the tragic fruits of that experiment."

"The plan was abandoned?"

"We didn't even ask him that," the Cyberneticist admitted. He turned to the microphone.

"The plan of biological remodeling, does it still exist? What is its future?"

The computer seemed to be arguing with the doubler, who made feeble hawking sounds.

"Is he in a bad way?" the Captain asked the Doctor in a low voice.

"No, better than I expected. He's exhausted, but refused to leave before. And I couldn't give him a transfusion, either, because our doubler's blood appears to be incompatible. . . ."

"Shh!" hissed the Physicist. The speaker was beginning to crackle.

"The plan. Is, is not. Pause. First was, now was not. Now mutations, disease. Pause. Information correct. Plan was, now was not."

"I'm lost," confessed the Engineer.

"I think he's saying that now the existence of the plan is denied, as though there had never been such a plan, and the mutations are attributed to a disease. The disaster, in other words, was not acknowledged to the community."

"Acknowledged by whom?"

"Their allegedly nonexistent government."

"Wait," said the Engineer. "If, since the passing of the last anonymous ruler, there has been a kind of 'epoch of anarchy,' who introduced the plan?"

"But you heard. No one introduced it. There was no plan. That's what they say today."

"Yes, but what did they say fifty years ago?"

"Something else."

"That's absurd!"

"Not at all. Even on Earth there are certain things not admitted publicly, though everyone knows them. In the area of social life, for example, a certain amount of hypocrisy is indispensable. But what for us is a limited phenomenon is central, universal, here."

"I find it hard to believe," said the Engineer. "And what does it have to do with the factory to the north?"

"The factory was supposed to produce something necessary for the plan. Perhaps an object of use only to the future, 'reconstructed' generations."

"Surely there were other factories?"

"The factories connected with the biological plan—were there many of them, or few?" asked the Cyberneticist.

The doubler cleared his throat, and the computer answered almost immediately: "Unknown. Factories. The probability, many. Information. No factories."

"What a society—it's horrifying!" said the Engineer.

"Why? You never heard of military secrets, or other kinds of classified information?"

"What type of energy runs these factories?" the Engineer asked the Cyberneticist, but he spoke so close to the microphone that the computer immediately translated the question. The speaker buzzed, then said:

"Inorganic. Nonexistent term. Bio bio. Pause. Entropy. Constant. Bio. System." The red light flashed on the panel.

"The computer doesn't have the vocabulary," explained the Cyberneticist.

"Why don't we remove the semantic filters?" the Physicist suggested.

"You want it to start babbling like a schizophrenic?"

"We might understand more."

"What are you talking about?" asked the Doctor.

"He wants to reduce the computer's selectivity," explained the Cyberneticist. "When the conceptual spectrum of a word, its semantic distribution, is blurred, the computer says that no corresponding term exists. If I remove the filters, it will start contaminating linguistic fields, producing words found in no human language."

"That way we'll get nearer the doubler's language," said the Physicist.

"All right. We can try it."

The Cyberneticist threw a few switches. The Captain looked at the doubler, who now lay with his eyes closed. The Doctor went over to him, examined him for a moment, and returned to his seat without a word.

The Captain said into the microphone, "To the south of this place is a valley. There are large buildings there. The buildings contain skeletons, and in the earth, all around, are graves."

"Wait, you can't say graves." The Cyberneticist pulled the flexible arm of the microphone closer to himself. "To the south are architectural constructions, and near them, in holes in the earth, are dead bodies. The bodies of doublers. What does that mean?"

On this occasion the computer exchanged a long series of coughs and squawks with the doubler. The men noticed that for the first time the machine appeared to be asking, and repeating, a question of its own. Finally the speaker spoke in a monotone.

"Doubler. Physical work, no. Pause. Electrical organ. Organ work, yes, but acceleration involution degeneration overload. Pause. South is exemplification of self-directed procrustics. Bio- and socio-occlusion deathavoid. Pause. Social isolation not with force, not by compulsion. Voluntary. Pause. Group microadaptation autocentroattraction. Production, yes. No."

"Brilliant suggestion," the Cyberneticist said to the Physicist. "Autocentroattraction, deathavoid, bio- and socio-occlusion. I warned you."

"Just a minute," said the Physicist. "This has something to do with forced labor."

"Just the opposite. He said 'not with force, not by compulsion.' It was voluntary."

"Well, we'll ask again." The Physicist bent over the microphone. "Not clear," he said. "Tell us, very simply, what is in the valley to the south? A penal colony? A labor camp? What do they produce? And why?"

The computer had another discussion with the doubler. After almost five minutes it replied:

"Microgroup voluntary. Interadhesion by compulsion, no. Pause. Each doubler against the microgroup. Chief relationship centripetal. The binding agent is anger. Pause. Who transgresses is punished. Punishment is microgroup voluntary identification. What is the microgroup? Feedback interrelations polyindividualized. Anger is the selfaim. Anger is the selfaim. Pause. Circulation sociopsychointernal. Deathavoid."

"Wait, what does 'selfaim' mean?" asked the Cyberneticist, seeing that the others were growing impatient.

"Selfaim, selfsave," said the computer, this time not even consulting the doubler.

"The instinct of self-preservation?" asked the Physicist.

"Yes, yes, self-preservation," said the computer.

"You mean to say you understand that?" cried the Engineer, jumping up from his seat.

"Understand it, no, but I think he's talking about a prison system. You have small groups within that community, and they keep one another under control."

"Without guards? Without surveillance?"

"He said there was no compulsion."

"Impossible!"

"Not at all. Imagine two people: one has matches, the other has a matchbox. They hate each other, but can strike a light only together. Anger, he said. Cooperation results from feedback. The compulsion somehow is a product of the internal dynamics of the group."

"But what are they doing? What are they making? Who is lying in those graves? And why?"

"You heard what the computer said? 'Procrustics.' That's obviously from 'Procrustean bed.' Assuring conformity by violent means."

"Ridiculous! How would the doubler know Greek mythology?"

"It's the computer, not the doubler! It finds the nearest equivalent on the conceptual spectrum! There's a work camp there, but the work may have no purpose or meaning. He said both yes and no after 'production.' The work is their punishment."

"But how are they forced to work if there are no guards?"

"The compulsion, as I said, arises from the situation itself. On a sinking ship, for example, one has few choices. Perhaps they're on the deck of that kind of ship all their lives. . . . Since hard physical labor might be harmful to them, perhaps this 'bio-occlusion' operates through their electrical organs."

"He said 'bio- and socio-occlusion.' "

"Well, there is adhesion, interadhesion, within the group, a mutual pull that separates the group from society."

"That doesn't say much."

"I know no more than you do. We're communicating, remember, at a double remove, the computer between us, displacing the meaning in both directions! Maybe they have a special scientific discipline, maybe procrustics is the theory of the dynamics of such groups, the planning of activities, conflicts, and attractions to produce a special equilibrium based on anger, an equilibrium that unites them and at the same time cuts them off from the outside. . . ."

"Those are your personal variations on the theme of the computer's schizophrenic babble—not an explanation," growled the Chemist.

"He's exhausted," said the Doctor. "One or two more questions, no more. Who wants to ask them?"

"I pass. Maybe you'll have better luck."

There was a moment's silence.

"I have a question," said the Captain. "How did you learn of our existence?" he asked into the microphone.

"Information. Meteorite. Ship," the computer replied after a brief exchange with the doubler. "Ship from another planet. Cosmic rays. Death rays. Degeneration. Pause. Glass encapsulation to destroy. Pause. Observation from observatory. Explosions. I took bearings. Direction of sound, source. Target of rockets. Pause. I went at night. Waited. Defender opened encapsulation. I entered, am."

"They told you that a ship had landed, with monsters in it?" asked the Engineer.

"With monsters. Degenerated. From cosmic rays. And that we are protected. With this glass. I took sound bearings. The target. Calculated. Found."

"You weren't afraid of the monsters?" the Captain asked. "You weren't . . . deathavoid?"

"Yes," replied the speaker almost immediately. "But the chance. One in a million planetary revolutions."

The Physicist nodded. "Each one of us would have tried to come here for that reason."

"Do you wish to stay with us? We will cure you. There will be no death," the Doctor said.

"No," answered the speaker.

"You wish to leave? To return to your people?"

"Return, no," said the speaker.

The men looked at one another.

"We can cure you! You won't die!" said the Doctor. "Tell us, what will you do when you're cured?"

The computer squawked, and the doubler made a sound so brief that it was barely audible.

"Zero," said the speaker, and repeated, as though not sure the men had understood correctly, "zero."

"He doesn't want to stay and doesn't want to go back," muttered the Chemist. "Could he be delirious?"

They looked at the doubler. His pale-blue eyes were fixed on them. The men could hear his slow, shallow breathing.

"That's enough," said the Doctor, getting up. "Everyone out."

"And you?"

"I'll join you soon. I took two psychedrins—I can sit with him a while longer."

When the men made for the door, the doubler's smaller torso fell back and his eyes closed.

In the corridor, the Engineer said, "We asked him all those questions—why didn't he ask us any?"

"Oh, but he did, earlier," said the Cyberneticist. "About conditions on Earth, our history, the development of space travel. A half-hour before you arrived, he was much more talkative."

"He must be weak now."

"He received a heavy dose of radiation. And his trek through the desert probably tired him, too, since he is old."

"How long do they live?"

"About sixty revolutions of the planet, slightly less than sixty of our years. Eden's year is shorter."

"What do they eat?"

"That was a surprise. It appears that evolution here has taken a different path from the one on Earth. They can assimilate certain inorganic substances directly."

"Ah," said the Chemist, "the soil that first one brought in!"

"Yes, but that was thousands of years ago. Now they've modernized, using those plants, the calyxes on the plain, as food accumulators. The calyxes extract from the soil and store compounds that serve the doublers as nourishment. There are different calyxes for different compounds."

"Of course, they cultivate them," said the Chemist. "To the south we saw whole fields of them. But the doubler who got into the ship, why was he digging about in the clay?"

"The calyxes retract below ground level after dark."

"Even so, there was plenty of soil available. . . ."

"Gentlemen, to bed with you," the Captain said to the Physicist and the Cyberneticist. "We'll take over. It's almost twelve."

"Twelve midnight?"

"We've lost all sense of time."

They heard footsteps behind them. It was the Doctor coming from the library. They looked at him questioningly.

"He's sleeping," he said. "He's not well. When you went out, I had the impression, even, that . . ." He didn't finish.

"Did you say anything to him?"

"I did. I asked him—I thought, you see, it was all over—if we could do anything for them. For all of them."

"And what did he say?"

" 'Zero.' " When the Doctor said this, it was like the computer's lifeless voice.

"Go lie down, all of you," said the Captain. "But first, since we're all together, let me ask you: Do we leave?"

"Yes," said the Engineer.

"Yes," said the Physicist and the Chemist at the same time.

"Yes," said the Cyberneticist.

"And you? Why are you silent?" the Captain asked the Doctor.

"I'm thinking. You know, I was never that interested in . . ."

"Yes, you were more concerned about how we could help them. But now you know that that's impossible."

"No. I don't know," the Doctor said softly.

XIV

An hour later Defender was riding down the lowered loading hatch. The Engineer drove it the six hundred feet to the wall of glass, which was curved inward above like unfinished vaulting, and set to work. Darkness fled in gigantic leaps into the depths of the desert, as lines brighter than the sun, thundering, cut the wall. Slabs tumbled to the ground, half molten, and overhead white smoke rose, shimmering. The Engineer left the fragments to cool and went on cutting with the annihilator, hewing out windows from which dripped fiery icicles. In rows of rectangular holes now appeared wells of starry sky. Smoke coiled across the sand. The vitreous mass groaned, creaked, glowed.

Defender finally returned to the ship. From a safe distance the Engineer checked the radiation level of the chunks. The counter chattered.

"Ideally, we should wait at least four days," said the Captain. "But let's send out Blackie and the cleaning robots."

"Yes, only the surface is really hot. A jet of sand will take care of that. And the smaller pieces can be buried."

"We'll put them in the empty tank in the stern." The Captain looked thoughtfully at the cherry-red rubble.

"Why?" said the Engineer. "It's of no use to us, just unnecessary ballast."

"I'd rather not leave radioactive traces. . . . They know nothing of atomic energy, and it's better that they don't."

"Maybe you're right," murmured the Engineer. "Eden . . . You know, the picture I get, based on what the astronomer-doubler told us . . . it's terrifying."

The Captain nodded slowly. "An abuse—so total, so thorough, as to arouse one's admiration—of information theory. It shows that it can be an instrument of torture far worse than anything physical. Isolating, repressing, compelling without compelling—they've made a ghastly science of it, their 'procrustics,' as the computer called it."

"Do you think they realize . . . he realizes . . . ?"

"You mean, does he consider such a state normal? Well, I suppose he does. He knows nothing different. Though he did refer to their earlier history—tyrants of the ordinary type, and then those 'anonymous' ones. So he is able to make comparisons."

"If to him tyranny means the good old days, I shudder to think . . ."

"And yet there's a logic in it. One of a series of tyrants hits upon the idea that anonymity may be advantageous. Society, unable to focus its resentment on one person, becomes, as it were, disarmed. . . ."

"In other words, a tyrant without a face!"

"And after a certain time, when the theoretical foundation of this procrustics has been established, a successor goes one step further and does away even with his 'incognito,' abolishing himself and the whole system of government—only in words, of course, in public communications."

"But why is there no liberation movement here? That I can't understand! If they punish their 'offenders' by putting them in these isolated groups, and there are no guards, no surveillance, no external force, then individual escape, even organized resistance, should be possible."

"For organization to take place, there must first be a means of communication."

The Captain held the Geiger outside the turret hatch: the chatter was slower.

"It's not that they do not have names for things, and for the relations between things, but that the names they have are in fact false, are masks. The monstrous mutations among them are called a disease, a plague. It must be that way with everything. In order to control the world, one must first name it. Without knowledge, weapons, and organization, and in isolated groups, there is little they can do."

"Yes," said the Engineer. "But that scene at the cemetery . . . and in that ditch in the direction of the city suggest that the system may not be running as smoothly as our unknown ruler would like. And the fear the doubler showed when he saw the wall of glass—remember that?"

The Geiger, put outside again, ticked sluggishly. The rubble by the wall no longer glowed, but the ground around the ship still smoked, and the air shimmered, making the stars high above appear to weave.

"We're going," the Engineer went on. "If only we had learned their language better. And figured out how that damned government of theirs, which pretends not to exist, operates. And given them weapons . . ."

"Weapons for poor wretches like our doubler? Would you put an antimatter gun into his hands?"

"In that case we ourselves could have—"

"Destroyed the government?" the Captain said calmly. "Liberated the population by force?"

"If there was no other way."

"In the first place, these are not human beings. Remember, you spoke only with the computer, and therefore understand the doubler no better than it does. Second, no one imposed all this upon them. No one, at least, from space. They themselves . . ."

"If you use that argument, then there's nothing, nothing that should be done!" shouted the Engineer.

"How else can it be? Is the population of this planet a child that has got itself into a blind alley and can be led out by the hand? If things were only that simple! Liberating them, Henry, would have to begin with killing, and the fiercer the struggle, the less idealistic the killing becomes. In the end we would be killing merely to beat a retreat, to counterattack; then we would kill everything that stood in Defender's way. You know how easily that can happen!"

The Engineer nodded. "Anyway," he said, "they're undoubtedly observing us now, and those windows that we just opened in their wall, I doubt that they like that. There could be another attack."

"There could," the Captain agreed. "Maybe it would be worthwhile to post some remote-control sentries. Electronic eyes and ears."

"That would take time and require parts we can ill afford."

"True . . ."

"Two roentgens per second. We can send out the robots now."

"All right. Let's park Defender close to the ship, just in case."

That afternoon the sky clouded over and, for the first

time since they arrived on the planet, a light, warm rain began to fall. The wall of glass darkened, and thin, pale streams of water trickled down it. The robots worked tirelessly. The sand thrown by the pulsomotors hissed over the surface of the piled slabs. Bits of glass shot into the air. The sand and rain formed a watery mud.

Blackie hauled containers filled with radioactive fragments into the ship after the other robot checked their seals with the Geiger. Next the two robots dragged the cleaned slabs to positions designated by the Engineer. Then, throwing fountains of sparks, the welding machines went to work, and the slabs softened and fused together, forming the frame of the future platform.

It soon became evident that there would not be enough slabs, so at dusk, after a whole day of work, Defender again rolled forth and faced the wall. It was a strange sight as, through the heavy rain, rectangular suns blazed and boomed, and glowing chunks of glass plunged to the ground. Thick clouds of smoke billowed, and puddles of rainwater boiled with an earsplitting hiss. Even the rain in the air boiled. High above, motionless, rainbows in pink, green, and yellow reflected the bolts of light below. Defender, black as if hewn from coal, turned amid the lightning, pointed its nose, and spat more lightning, and again the area shook with thunder.

"This could be a good thing!" the Engineer shouted into the Captain's ear. "With these fireworks, maybe they'll leave us in peace! We need at least two more days!" His face, bathed in sweat—the turret was as hot as an oven—looked like a mercury mask.

After the men retired for the night, the robots emerged again and worked until morning, dragging sand pump hoses after them, moving the slabs of glass. The rain sparkled, a dazzling azure, around the welding machines; the loading hatch swallowed up more containers. Slowly, behind the stern of the ship, a parabolic structure rose, and meanwhile the robot diggers excavated the hill beneath the belly of the ship, gnawing fiercely.

At daybreak, when the men got up, some of the glass slabs had been used to shore up the tunnel.

"That was a good idea," said the Captain. They were sitting in the navigation room, rolls of blueprints before them on the table. "Had we removed the beams without them, the roof would probably have collapsed and crushed the diggers, or trapped them."

"Do we have enough power to take off?" asked the Cyberneticist, standing in the doorway.

"Enough for ten takeoffs. If we had to—though it won't be necessary—we could always jettison the radioactive debris we're taking with us in the stern tank. We'll introduce heat ducts into the tunnel and raise the temperature to the point at which the glass begins to melt. The props will slowly sink. If they sink too quickly, we pump liquid nitrogen into the ducts. We should be able to free the ship by evening. And then the job of standing it up . . ."

"That's chapter two," said the Engineer.

By eight the clouds had dispersed and the sun was shining. The enormous cylinder of the ship, which until now had been embedded fast in the hillside, began to move. The Engineer, using a transit, monitored the slowly diminishing angle of the stern. He stood at a distance, near the wall, which now resembled, with its square holes, the ruins of some ancient glass coliseum.

The men and the two doublers had been evacuated from the ship. The Engineer saw the small figure of the Doctor; it was approaching, going around the hull in a wide arc; but he paid no attention to it, too absorbed in his instruments. Only a thin layer of earth and, beneath that, the melting props now bore the weight of the ship. Eighteen cables ran from the funnels to anchors set in the massive chunks cut from the wall. The Engineer thanked heaven for the wall: without it, it would have taken them four times longer to right the ship.

Other cables, winding across the sand, brought current to the ducts inside the tunnel. From its mouth, visible directly below the place where the hull entered the slope, came smoke. Yellow-gray clouds marched slowly across the still-wet plain. The ship sank, inch by inch; whenever it began to fall more rapidly, the Engineer flicked a switch at hand, valves opened, and liquid nitrogen coursed into the tunnel ducts. There was a rumbling, and dirty-white clouds were belched out.

Suddenly the hull shuddered and, before the Engineer could open the valves, the ship, more than three hundred feet long, gave a groan, and the stern fell twelve feet. At the same time the nose of the ship burst free of the ground, throwing up sand and marl. The ceramite colossus came to rest. The cables and ducts lay beneath it; one of them, torn open, spewed a roaring geyser of condensed air.

"We did it! We did it!" yelled the Engineer. Then he saw, in front of him, the Doctor. The Doctor was saying something, but he couldn't understand it.

"It looks as if we're going . . . home," said the Doctor. "He'll live."

"What? What?"

"He's pulled through."

Then the Engineer understood. He looked again to reassure himself that the ship was free. "Is he going with us?" he asked, moving away, anxious to examine the hull for damage.

"No," the Doctor answered, following. But then, after several steps, he stopped.

It was cooler, because of the fountain of condensed gas that continued to pour out of the broken pipe. Small figures climbed up on the hull, one disappeared, and after a few minutes the seething column fell; for a moment it still spouted foam that froze the air; then it, too, stopped, and everything became strangely quiet. The Doctor looked around, as though wondering how he had got there, and slowly walked on.

The ship stood upright, white, whiter than the clouds, among which its sharp, distant peak already appeared to be moving. There had been three days of hard work. The loading was completed. The huge parabolic ramp built from the pieces of the wall that had been meant to imprison them lay abandoned on the hillside. Two hundred and forty feet above the ground, four men stood in the open hatchway, looking down. On the flat, dun-yellow surface they could see two tiny figures, one slightly lighter in color than the other. The men watched. The doublers, standing no more than 150 feet from the slightly flared exhaust funnels, did not move.

"Why don't they leave?" the Physicist asked, impatient. "We can't take off."

"They won't leave," said the Doctor.

"What is that supposed to mean? He doesn't want us to go?"

The Doctor said nothing.

The sun was high in the sky. Banks of clouds were drifting in out of the west. From the open hatchway, as though from the window of a soaring spire, they could see the hills in the south, the blue summits mingled with the clouds, and the great western desert that extended for hundreds of miles in strips of sunlit dunes, and the violet mantle of forest on the eastern plateau. Below them, the circle of the wall resembled a lacy skeleton. The ship's shadow moved across it like the style of a giant sundial, and now the shadow approached the two small figures.

There was thunder in the east, followed by a long-drawn-out whistle, and flame flashed in the black sphere of the explosion.

"Something new," said the Engineer.

Another clap of thunder. An unseen projectile howled nearer; an unearthly whistling, it seemed to make for the ship. The ground shook, dirt flew a few hundred feet away. They could feel the ship sway.

"Crew," said the Captain. "To your seats!"

"What about them?" the Chemist asked, peering down. The hatch closed.

In the control room they heard no thunder. But the aft screens showed bushes of flame jumping across the sand. Two figures remained motionless at the base of the rockets.

"Fasten your belts!" said the Captain. "Ready?"

"Ready," came the murmured reply.

"Twelve zero seven hours. Prepare for takeoff. All systems!"

"The pile on," said the Engineer.

"Critical mass," said the Physicist.

"Circulation normal," said the Chemist.

"The grav axis okay," said the Cyberneticist.

Suspended midway between the concave ceiling and the foam-padded floor, the Doctor was watching the screen.

"Still there?" asked the Captain, and everyone glanced at him: the question was not part of the takeoff ritual.

"Still there," said the Doctor. An explosion closer than the others made the ship rock.

"Blast off!" the Captain cried. With a hard face the Engineer engaged the drive. There was a small, muffled roar; it seemed to be taking place in another world. Gradually it intensified; then everything seemed to dissolve into it. Swaying, they fell gently into the embrace of an irresistible power.

The ship lifted.

"On the normal," said the Captain.

"Now over," said the Cyberneticist, and all the nylon cords tautened. The shock absorbers began to hum.

"Oxygen masks," the Doctor said, as though awakening, and bit down on his own plastic mouthpiece.

Twelve minutes later they left the atmosphere. Maintaining velocity, they set off into the starry void along an expanding spiral. Seven hundred and forty lights and dials pulsed soundlessly on the panels. The men unsnapped their belts and went up to the controls, fingered the buttons and switches as if in doubt—were any leads overheating, was there the faint crackle of a short circuit? They sniffed the air for the smell of burning, tapped the dials on the astrodesic computers. But everything was as it should be: the air was pure, the temperature correct; the distributor worked as if it had never been a pile of broken pieces.

In the navigation room, the Engineer and the Captain were bending over maps. The star charts, larger than the table, hung over it, torn at the edges. The men had said, a long time ago, that they needed a larger table in the navigation room, because they kept stepping on the maps. The table was still the same.

"Have you seen Eden?" asked the Engineer.

The Captain looked at him, not understanding. "What do you mean?"

"Now."

The Captain turned around. On the screen was a glowing opal sphere that made the neighboring stars pale.

"Beautiful," said the Engineer. "It drew our attention because it was so beautiful. We wanted only to fly by it."

"Yes," said the Captain, "only to fly by it . . ."

"All those colors. None of the other planets are like that. The Earth is merely a blue marble."

They watched the screen together.

"And the doubler stayed?" the Captain asked softly.

"That's what he wanted."

"You think."

"I'm sure. He preferred it to be us—and not them. That was all that we could do for him."

Neither of them spoke for a while. Eden grew smaller.

"Beautiful," said the Captain. "But, you know, going by the probability curve, there must be others even more beautiful."